Praise for the Books of Sheila Connolly

"There is a delightful charm to this small-town regional cozy. . . . Connolly provides a fascinating whodunit filled with surprises."

—*The Mystery Gazette*

"A true cozy [with] a strong and feisty heroine, a perplexing murder, a personal dilemma, and a picturesque New England setting."

—*Gumshoe Review*

"There's a depth to the characters in this book that isn't always found in crime fiction. . . . Sheila Connolly has written a winner for cozy mystery fans."

—*Lesa's Book Critiques*

"The premise and plot are solid, and Meg seems a perfect fit for her role."

—*Publishers Weekly*

"A wonderful slice of life in a small town. . . . The mystery is intelligent and has an interesting twist."

—*The Mystery Reader*

"[A] clever, charming, and sophisticated caper. . . . A real page-turner!"

—Hank Phillippi Ryan, award-winning author of
The Perfect Life

"Connolly's wonderful new series is a witty, engaging blend of history and mystery."

—Julie Hyzy, author of the White House Chef Mysteries

Books by Sheila Connolly

Orchard Mysteries

One Bad Apple
Rotten to the Core
Red Delicious Death
A Killer Crop
Bitter Harvest
Sour Apples
"Called Home"
Golden Malicious
Picked to Die
A Gala Event
Seeds of Deception
A Late Frost
Nipped in the Bud

Museum Mysteries

Fundraising the Dead
Let's Play Dead
Fire Engine Dead
"Dead Letters"
Monument to the Dead
Razing the Dead
Privy to the Dead
Dead End Street

Victorian Village Mysteries

Murder at the Mansion
Killer in the Carriage House
The Secret Staircase

More Books by Sheila Connolly

County Cork Mysteries

Buried in a Bog
Scandal in Skibbereen
An Early Wake
A Turn for the Bad
Cruel Winter
Many a Twist
Tied Up with a Bow
The Lost Traveller
Fatal Roots

Relatively Dead Mysteries

Relatively Dead
Seeing the Dead
Defending the Dead
Watch for the Dead
Search for the Dead
Revealing the Dead

Glassblowing Mysteries
(Writing as Sarah Atwell)

Through a Glass, Deadly
Pane of Death
Snake in the Glass

Also Available

Reunion with Death
Once She Knew

Relatively Dead

Sheila Connolly

BEYOND THE PAGE
PUBLISHING

Relatively Dead
Sheila Connolly
Copyright © 2013 by Sheila Connolly
Cover design and illustration by Dar Albert, Wicked Smart Designs

Beyond the Page Books
are published by
Beyond the Page Publishing
www.beyondthepagepub.com

ISBN: 978-1-954717-83-1

Chapter 1

She didn't want to be here. But Brad had told her she ought to get out more, find some interests of her own, so here she was standing in front of the last house on the walking tour of Waltham's most noteworthy mansions, relics of the town's nineteenth-century industrial heyday. Could she summon up the energy to go through one more? She'd already seen four, and her feet hurt. How could this one be any better than the others?

But she wanted to be able to tell Brad that she'd taken the house tour today. Not part of the house tour, not some of the house tour: the whole tour. That meant she had to grit her teeth and go through this one. Then she could go home, make a nice cup of tea, and take her shoes off.

The house looked nice, she had to admit. It was not too big or too posh-looking. Friendly, almost. The house sat on a rise, and when she reached the broad terrace Abby turned to contemplate the low roofs of Waltham below. Not much of a view, but at least the house nestled proudly on its land, lawns spread out like skirts around it. She turned back to the house to study the details. High Victorian, the house sprouted chimneys, dormers, porches, a porte-cochere, and a wealth of gingerbread trim. It was a full three stories, with a turret on one end. She made her way to the front door.

When she stepped into the paneled hall, a man about her own age greeted her and handed her an information sheet. A name badge in a plastic sleeve, clipped to the pocket of his blue-gray Oxford shirt, identified him as Ned. Abby noted that the shirt was exactly the same color as his eyes, or what she could see behind his gold-rimmed glasses. She smiled timidly.

"Is it too late to take the tour?"

"No problem," Ned replied cheerfully. "Take your time. It's self-guided, and you can wander anywhere on this floor, but not upstairs. Let me know if you have any questions."

Abby drifted into what must have been the main parlor. With her newfound architectural expertise, she observed that the dropped ceiling was not original, but the wavy glass in the many windows was. The room had been furnished in a cheerful chintz in light colors, and the woodwork was painted white. It had probably been much more somber a century ago. She crossed back through the spacious entry hall to a small sitting room opposite. This was more charming, intimate. There was a small fireplace surrounded by pretty decorative tiles, with a mirror inset over it. This would have been where the family spent most of its time, she decided. On the far side of the fireplace was a door; passing through it, Abby found herself in the kitchen. Nothing of great interest here. At the back of the house, it was dark, and it had clearly been remodeled, in the 1930s, she guessed. The house was surprisingly small, Abby mused; it had appeared much larger from the outside. Maybe that was the point of all that gingerbread.

If the house was as square as it had appeared, there should be one more room on this floor: the dining room. She chose another door out of the kitchen and crossed through a small, richly paneled hall, from which she could see the front hall. She stepped into the dining room. Plainly this room hadn't been modernized. Her eyes followed the soaring lines of the elegant woodwork to the original coffered ceiling, then to the elaborate carved mantel at the far end. She laid one hand on the doorjamb—and then something changed.

So much anger, so much pain.

She knew she was standing in the same place in the same room, its tall windows draped in opulent swags of peach-colored damask, its fireplace surrounded by colorful tiles, flanked by columns. She could make out the gleam of polished silver on the sideboard, the colorful arabesques on the fireplace tiles.

But now there were people in the room, and Abby strained to hear any words. An older woman—in her fifties, maybe?—sat at the broad mahogany table in the center of the room, her hands flat as if to stop them from trembling. Without wavering, the woman watched a man pacing nervously on the opposite side of the table. He was slight, with a receding hairline, balanced by a luxuriant mustache. His suit collar was stiff and high, a stickpin anchoring his broad tie. He looked both sheepish and belligerent. She—who was she?—looked down to see a blanket-wrapped baby in her arms.

"Miss? Are you all right?"

Abby nearly jumped out of her skin at the touch of a hand on her elbow. The man from the hallway had come up behind her.

"You look like you've seen a ghost. Maybe you should sit down."

Abby was fighting between embarrassment and the lingering remnants of the irrational fear that had swept over her. "I, uh . . . I'm fine. It's just that you startled me. I'll go now." Abby wanted nothing more than to escape from this stranger's kind attention.

He still held her elbow, watching her face. "Please, no. There's no rush. Why don't you sit for a minute, just to be sure you're all right? Come on." When she didn't resist he led her not to the parlor but to the smaller sitting room. Apparently he agreed with her that it was a friendlier room, she thought. He settled her into a wicker chair plump with cushions. "Now, just stay there for a moment. I'm going to make a cup of tea. All right?"

Bewildered, Abby nodded. She sank back into the chair. Ned disappeared toward the kitchen, and she could hear the sound of water filling a kettle, the clink of china, a refrigerator opening and closing. She closed her eyes and made a conscious effort to relax. What on earth had happened? And then the memory came back. She shut her eyes: to remember it better or to blot it out? She wasn't sure.

She opened them again when Ned reappeared with a silver-plated tray bearing a teapot in a tattered cozy, two cups, a sugar bowl, a milk pitcher, spoons, and a delicate flowered china plate with some store-bought sugar cookies. He set it down on a low table next to Abby's chair, then took the chair on the other side of the table. Leaning forward, he studied her face.

"All right, now. I wish I could say you were looking better, but you're white as a sheet."

Abby stared at him for a moment, and then to her horror she burst into tears. Even as she attempted to control her sobs, she felt a moment of pity for poor Ned, stuck with this dripping female that she didn't even recognize as herself. He was trying so hard to be helpful, and she just kept making things worse. Wordlessly he handed her a small napkin from the tea tray, then sat back to wait out the storm. Finally, Abby swallowed a few times, blotted her eyes, and ventured a watery smile.

"I'm sorry. This is so not like me. But . . ." She hesitated, afraid that if she went on, he would think she was loony. Oh, well, what the heck—she didn't have anything to lose. "When I walked into the dining room, something weird happened. It was like I was watching a film of people in that room, except . . . they weren't real. They weren't there, were they?"

She looked at Ned to see how he was taking her odd statement. He didn't look contemptuous. In fact, he looked curious.

"Interesting. Was there something that triggered it, or did it just start up out of nowhere?"

She gave an inward sigh of relief. He wasn't going to laugh at her. "All I know is, one moment I was about to walk into the dining room, and the next minute I was watching some kind of melodrama. There were three people there, and one of them—the one I was seeing through or something— was holding a baby, and they were all upset. Well, not the baby, but the others were."

"Did you recognize anyone?" Ned asked, concentrating on pouring two cups of tea. "Sugar?"

"And milk, please. No. They were dressed like people were a hundred or more years ago. Is that part of the house tour? Some hidden projector shows you what life used to be like in the house?" That would be such an easy solution—but it hadn't felt like that. She accepted the cup of tea that he held out to her, and when she took it, she realized her hands were trembling. She tightened her grip on the cup and sipped cautiously. It was hot and delicious. "Is this Darjeeling?"

He nodded.

"It's good." Now that Abby was feeling almost normal, she was beginning to wonder about this man. "Don't you have to watch the door or something? And how come you know where all the tea things are? Do you live here?"

Ned laughed. "It's okay. It's nearly time to close up, and I doubt that anyone else is going to show up today. Saturday's usually the big day. Anyway, I've done this for a couple of years, so I know the house. Actually, no one lives in it these days—it belongs to the private school next door, and they use it for functions, entertaining, and such, so they keep it stocked with basic supplies. Not that I've ever had to deal with a problem like yours until now, but I'm glad that I was prepared. Tea and sugar make most problems better, don't you think?"

He has a nice smile, Abby thought.

"You sure you're all right?" he asked again.

"I'm fine. I probably tried to do too much today, and it caught up with me. I'm just embarrassed about causing you so much trouble." She sipped again at her tea, at a loss for words.

"Well, don't hurry. We can sit here until you're sure you're all right. Do you live around here?"

"I just moved to Waltham last month, and I read about the house tours, and I thought it would be nice to see some of the big old places like this. They're beautiful."

"They are grand, aren't they? This city's had its ups and downs—there was a lot of industry here in the nineteenth century. Watchmaking, mostly. You've heard of the Waltham Watch Company? This was the place. You saw the Paine house? A lot of that was built by H. H. Richardson, and Frederick Law Olmsted designed the grounds. You know—Richardson's the one who designed Trinity Church in Boston, and Olmsted laid out Central

Park in New York." He looked at her expectantly, and Abby wondered if she was supposed to know what he was talking about.

"Yes, I started with the Paine house today. It's gorgeous. But I guess I didn't do all my homework. You certainly seem to know a lot about the houses. Are you from around here?"

"More or less. I work in Lexington, and I've lived in the area for most of my life."

"What do you do?" Not an original question, but it was the best Abby could do.

"I work for a company that does DNA analyses—that's my day job. But my avocation is historic architecture, and New England history. That's why I help with the house tours, things like that. It means I get to see more of the behind-the-scenes stuff than I would if I was just a visitor. You know—attics, basements. The bones of the old houses."

Abby was silent for a few beats. Then she said slowly, "What's the history of this place?"

Ned lifted the teapot, and when she nodded, he refilled her cup, and his, then sat back. "Well, it's kind of interesting. For most of the nineteenth century, it belonged to a family named Hawley. They had a nice big farmhouse here. Then in the 1890s, a successful businessman named Flagg bought it and started making some major changes, at least to the way it looked. The structural core is still the farmhouse, but everything that you see, inside and out, is late Victorian."

"He certainly threw himself into the decorating part—I've never seen so much gingerbread in one place!" Abby said, smiling.

"Yes, he was determined to put his stamp on it. I can show you some of the newspaper articles about it. William Flagg brought in woods from all over the country, and if you look around, you'll see that every doorknob is different. There's some really beautiful work here." He took another sip of his tea. "And then something happened—after about ten years, he ups and sells the place to the school next door. After all the fixing up he'd done."

Abby's curiosity was piqued. "Did he lose all his money or something?"

Ned shook his head. "He may have—I haven't done any detailed research. But I do know that he stayed in Waltham—in fact, he ended up living in a smaller house about a mile south of here, for the rest of his life, and he's buried here."

"Did he have a family?"

"Yes—a wife and two daughters. The younger one went to the school here. His wife outlived him, but she's buried next to him. Don't know what happened to the girls."

Abby shut her eyes for a moment, trying to remember. "Was one of the girls a lot younger than the other?"

Ned looked at her quizzically. "Yes, I think so. Why do you ask?"

"Because that's what I saw. There was a man and a woman, and I think they were fighting, or at least they were very angry. And there was a younger woman with a baby. I didn't think the baby was hers, from the way she held it. Like she wasn't used to babies." *Was that baby the one they raised as a daughter? And why was the wife so angry?*

Ned gave her a long look. Finally he said, "I see. That's intriguing."

"You don't think I'm crazy? Or at least hallucinating?"

He shook his head. "No. I've seen—or felt—too many odd things in old houses to brush off experiences like yours. Have you ever had an experience like this before?"

Abby shook her head vehemently. "No, never. In fact, people have accused me of having no imagination. I'm usually the practical one in any group—you know, the designated driver, the one with the maps and all. That's why this is so weird."

Ned was silent. Abby watched him anxiously and wondered what was going through his mind—like calling in professional help to take her away. She was relieved when he finally spoke.

"Miss, uh—you know, I don't even know your name?"

"Oh, right. Abigail Kimball—mostly Abby."

"I'm Edward Newhall, mostly Ned. Well, Abby, you've certainly come up with a pretty puzzle."

"Why? What do you think that . . . experience was?"

"At a guess, I'd say you stumbled on a past scene that somehow got stuck here. No, that doesn't make sense. You had a vision of something from the past? Or you have an extremely overactive imagination that filled the room with people, like it was a play. Are you sure you've never been here before?"

"Never. I've never even been in this state before, or at least not since I was a kid, and then it was just passing through on the way to somewhere else. I've only been here a few weeks, and I've been so busy getting settled that I haven't seen much of the neighborhood, much less Boston."

"What brought you here, if you don't mind telling me?"

"I came with my boyfriend. He got a job offer, and in a couple of weeks, here we were." Was it her imagination, or did Ned look a little disappointed when she mentioned the "boyfriend"?

If he had, he recovered quickly. "Well, Abby, do you want to explore this phenomenon a bit further, maybe find out who you were seeing, or would you rather just go home and try to forget the whole thing?"

Abby thought for a moment, teetering in indecision. And then it seemed as though she heard her own voice: *No, I'm not just going to forget about this. I want to know what happened, and why.* "If I wanted to learn more, what would I do?"

He smiled. "Well, first of all, you could go to the library in town here, find out as much as you could about this place, and about the family. You should talk to Jane Bennett. She runs the local history section, and she's very good. And there are a lot of local records—microfilms, city directories, that kind of thing. Unfortunately only a portion of it is online, but the library's a nice place to spend time. There might even be pictures of the people who lived here—maybe you'd recognize someone."

Abby shivered. "And if I found pictures and they really were the people from my dream? What then?"

"Well, at least you'd know something, that what you saw was real. Look, why not stop in at the library and see what you can find—if you have the time, that is. Do you have a job yet?"

Interesting that Ned assumed she'd be looking for a job. Well, she did plan to, once she and Brad were settled. Their current apartment was merely a stopgap until they could find a house—or one they could afford. "No, I've got the time right now."

Ned looked pleased. "Then maybe we could get together over the weekend and compare notes? If you're not busy."

Abby thought about her own total lack of plans. No, she was not busy. Brad had already declared he would be gone, playing golf with his buddies. "Sure. Where?"

"How about we meet at the library, on Saturday at ten?"

"All right. Oh, I should get your number, in case something comes up." Like Brad's foursome was canceled.

He pulled out a wallet and extricated two cards. "Write your name and number on the one—you can keep the other one. I'll put my home number on the back." He scribbled on the back of one, then handed the two to her. She wrote her number on the back and handed it to him, and he carefully stowed it in his wallet.

Abby stood up and looked around. No strange figures lurking in the sunny corners, at least in this room, which caught the light of the setting sun through the big front windows. She didn't want to go back to the dining room and see if there was anyone there. Brad would be wanting his dinner. What was she going to tell him about this little misadventure?

"I really should be going now. But I will go to the library, I promise."

Ned stood as well. "So I'll see you Saturday. And you can tell me then if you've seen anybody else during the week."

"Like a ghost, you mean? I hope not. Saturday, then."

He saw her to the door. *I didn't ask him if there was somebody waiting for him at home.* She didn't remember a wedding ring. But it didn't matter: this wasn't a date, this was a history consultation. And she had something to do now—a trip to the library to do research, and then the meeting with Ned on Saturday. Things were looking up.

Chapter 2

Abby was putting the finishing touches on dinner when Brad walked in. She'd set the round table with placemats and candles. He didn't seem to notice. "Smells good, babe. New recipe?" Without waiting for an answer he sat down and began to eat with enthusiasm as she slid into her seat. In between hearty bites of food, he regaled her with the events of his day: what his boss had said about him, or to him; which colleagues he'd managed to ace out of something desirable; how well he was doing. Abby nodded, smiled, made appropriate noises at the right times. By the time the salad was gone, he was winding down.

"Hey, great dinner, hon. What've you been up to today?"

For once she had something to say. "It was such a nice day, I just had to get out. So I went on a house tour here in Waltham."

"Oh? Like what—houses for sale?"

"No, Brad, some of the local mansions, up on the north side of town—they open them up to the public for a week each year. They're really beautiful. I guess they were built by some of the local industrial barons. I went through four of them."

Brad was swabbing the last of his food off his plate. "North side—oh, you mean beyond the railroad tracks? Yeah, some of those guys did all right for themselves."

"Well, the houses were beautiful. Nobody puts that kind of architectural detail in modern houses. It's a pity. I mean, some of those doorknobs alone are works of art."

"Hey, sounds great. Glad you got out. You should do more stuff like that."

"I thought I might go to the library tomorrow, see if I could find out some more about local history. You know, the people who built those places, how they lived."

"Yeah, sure, good idea." His mind was already on something else. Abby allowed herself a small flare of resentment. She'd done what he wanted her to do—she had gone out exploring. Couldn't he show a little interest? She sighed, stood up, and started clearing away the dishes.

Later, as they were getting ready for bed, Brad said, "You know, I think it's great that you're getting out of the house more, but wouldn't you like to meet more people, do some group things?"

"I'll get to that, Brad." *But I did meet someone today, someone who was actually nice to me.* Funny—she hadn't mentioned Ned to Brad, much less about her nearly passing out. But she knew that if she did, Brad would decide that she needed to see a doctor, no, several doctors, and only the best ones, probably in Boston, or at two or three different places in Boston, and, honey, I don't have time to drive you there, so could you take your ailing self to all these wonderful appointments that I suggested but that you have to set up? No, it was simpler to say nothing to Brad. She really didn't think there was anything physically wrong with her.

In fact, she was pretty sure this was something else, but at the same time she was afraid to look too closely at what had happened. What she had seen had been extraordinarily vivid and detailed—but it wasn't there. Was she nuts? Who were the people in that room, the ones she had dreamt about? Would she be able to find them, find out who they were? Did she want to? And if she did, then what?

Ned had been so solicitous when she'd had her . . . spell, for want of a better word. He didn't panic, but he had made sure that she was all right. And then he had listened to her, and he hadn't made fun of her or told her she was imagining things. He had believed her. That was as helpful as the hot, sweet tea. Well, she was going to hold up her end: she was going to find out as much as she could about the family and the house, and see where that led. And then on Saturday she could tell Ned what she'd found.

• • •

The Waltham Public Library was located in the middle of town, on the main street. Abby drove around the block once, looking for parking, and finally found a space in the half-empty lot behind the building. Resolutely she marched up the stairs and entered through the back door. She stopped to ask directions at the main desk, where a cheerful woman directed her to a room at the front of the building that housed the local history collections. On the threshold she stopped to take it in. It certainly didn't look too imposing. There were two oak tables with chairs in the center of the room, and the rest of the floor space and the perimeter were occupied by elderly oak bookshelves. A high counter ran along one side of the room, and behind that were more books locked away behind grilles.

A librarian seated at the desk looked up as Abby approached hesitantly. "Hi. Can I help you find something?"

The librarian looked to be about ten years older than Abby and was wearing comfortable jeans and a sweater. Not intimidating in the least. Abby summoned up a smile. "I hope so. You see, I was on a house tour yesterday, and I really fell in love with one of the places and I wanted to know more about it."

The librarian smiled her encouragement. "Yeah, isn't that a great tour? I've been through the houses any number of times. Which house were you interested in?"

"The one near the school, the, uh, Flagg house?"

"All right. Let's see, where to start . . . Oh, I'm Jane, Jane Bennett. I'm the library archivist and unofficial town historian. How familiar are you with library research?"

"Abby Kimball. I haven't done much since college, but I've used computers a lot."

"That's a start. Are you interested in the architecture or the people?"

"People, I guess. I was wondering who built it, who lived in it, that sort of thing."

"So, part local history, part genealogy. Well, you've come to the right place." The librarian looked around her. There was nobody else in the room this weekday morning. "Why don't we sit down at the table, get comfortable?"

"Great." Abby followed Jane to one of the rectangular oak tables and they sat side by side. Abby dutifully pulled out a pad of paper and a pen.

Jane stopped her immediately. "Whoops! First rule: no pens in here, only pencils. Basic rule for all archival collections."

Abby flushed. "Oh, sorry. I didn't know."

"That's okay—a lot of people don't. So, to get you started, I'll check my files to see what there is about that Flagg house. Since we know it's on the tour, somebody's bound to have done something on it. In the meantime, you know the address, so you can check the city directories over there, see when the family first appears there, and when they left. What else are you looking for?"

Abby was nonplused. "Well, I guess I want to know more about the people—how they made their money, why they bought that place, what they did with it. And I understand that they moved out pretty fast, which seems odd. What happened to the family after. That sort of thing."

"At least you've got the owner's name, for a start. You can follow him through the censuses."

"You have them here?"

"No, but they're on microfilm at the National Archives, which is only a few miles from here. And we have online access here at the library, or you can get a subscription and read them online at home. You can go either way, depending on what you're comfortable with. The online versions are easier to print out, if that matters to you, but the microfilms can be easier to work with, especially if you're hunting—you know, want to know who the neighbors are. Your choice."

"Ah." Abby was beginning to feel overwhelmed, and then disgusted with herself. What had she expected? That a nice librarian like Jane was just going to hand her the entire history of the Flagg family? So she was going to have to do some digging on her own. Fine: she had the time. "Well, since I'm here, let's start with what you have here, and then maybe I'll know what else to look for."

"Great. Oh, and we do have microfilms of births and deaths in Waltham itself, and of local newspapers, which might tell you a bit more. Obituaries are great for information like you're looking for." Jane stood up. "City directories and local histories are on those shelves there. I'll go get the folders." She headed for the desk, then disappeared behind it.

Several hours later, Abby's head reeled with new information. She felt like she had been in another world, another time. What Ned had told her, she had confirmed: William Flagg had bought a simple farmhouse and transformed it to a model of High Victorian opulence, sparing no expense. Plainly he had wanted a showplace. He had made his money through some shrewd business dealings, having played an important role in the formation of a local electrical power company in another town north of Boston, which had quickly gone into new markets and had grown rapidly and profitably. He had moved to Waltham just at that time but had not stayed long with the company, taking over the management of one then another local manufacturing company. He was steadily employed up until his death in 1914, so maybe it wasn't money that led him to give up the grand house on the hill. His wife had outlived him and had stayed on in town, in the more modest house down the hill. From the obituaries that she had found, Abby gleaned that William had been involved in a wide range of local civic activities, such as the Grand Army of the Republic, and had even run unsuccessfully for national office once.

One of the old obituaries had included a photograph, and Abby had to admit that it was the man in her dream or vision or whatever. The grainy image showed a William Flagg who was a middle-aged man with a receding hairline, balanced by a luxuriant mustache curling on the ends. His chin was soft and dimpled, but he looked intent and very serious. When she had seen him in her vision or hallucination or whatever it was, he had been younger, with more hair, but there was no mistaking the face. He looked . . . sweet. Abby almost laughed. That was an odd way to describe an industrial magnate who had been dead for a century, but she liked his eyes—they seemed kind.

She shut her eyes and tried to remember more. William Flagg had been upset, apologetic, on the defensive. And his wife—Elizabeth, was it?—had been righteously angry.

Abby stood up abruptly and went searching the microfilms for Elizabeth's obituary. It proved to be less effusive than her husband's, and this time there was no picture. Abby could sense the writer straining to find anything to say about her, and in the end he had largely recited her late husband's achievements. She had been survived by two daughters, Olivia and Isabel. Abby noted that at the time of her death, she had been living with the younger daughter. *Isabel. The baby.*

Jane interrupted her musings. "We're about to close up. Did you find what you wanted?"

Abby nodded vigorously. "Oh, yes. You've got some great stuff here, and I can't thank you enough. Can I get some copies?"

"Sure. Show me what you need and I'll do it. These old documents can be fragile, you know."

A half hour later Abby emerged from the library and stood blinking in the late-afternoon sunlight. She had photocopies of pictures of the house as it once had been, and of William Flagg, with the kind eyes. She knew she wanted more. She wanted to see the face of the wife; she wanted to know what had happened to the daughters, so far apart in age. She should go home and see what she could find on the Internet. She should visit the local cemetery. She almost giggled out loud: she was really excited about this and she couldn't remember the last time she had felt that way.

She couldn't wait to show Ned what she had discovered.

Chapter 3

Brad was in a grumpy mood when he came home that night. In general, Abby noted that his spirits soared and plummeted based on trivial interactions with his new colleagues and his bosses, and apparently he felt he had not been given his due that day.

"I told him from the beginning that we were going to have problems with bond counsel. And then the municipality wanted to bring in one of their own pet firms, so now we've got two batches of people screwing up the same documents. Waste of time, if you ask me. But that's politics." He grumbled on and off through dinner, barely tasting it as he vented his frustrations to Abby. Abby tried to follow, but she didn't know the people involved, she knew very little about investment banking, and she knew that tomorrow everything would have changed anyway, and Brad would be complaining about a different group of people. She listened with half an ear, but in her mind she was trying to map out a research plan, to fill in the gaps in the story of the mysterious Flaggs.

Brad broke into her reverie. "Hey, where were you today? I tried to call you, see if you wanted to see a movie tomorrow night or something."

"Oh, I went to the library. I told you, I wanted to look up some more information on the houses that I saw yesterday."

"Oh, yeah, right." Brad's interest died quickly. "Well, what about the movie? I need to know so I can work out my schedule. And I'll be out all day Saturday, remember. Maybe we should wait until Sunday for the movie. I want to be on my game Saturday—these guys play for keeps." He didn't seem to notice that she hadn't answered his question, but then, he had answered it for himself anyway.

"That's fine. Whatever you want. I was going to do some more research tomorrow, maybe Saturday too."

"Babe, I think it's great that you're interested, but can't you find something where you can talk to people, maybe get out and get some sunshine?"

"I *am* talking to people. I had a nice chat with the man on the house tour"—*sure, after he scraped me off the floor*—"and I met a really nice librarian today." Obviously these did not count as "people" to Brad—they weren't anywhere near important enough.

"Well, as long as you're happy," Brad replied dubiously.

"I am," Abby said firmly. "Oh, are you going to be using the computer tonight? I wanted to look up some stuff online."

"Sure, go ahead. I've got some more documents to review anyway. You'd think a room full of lawyers could figure out where the commas should go, wouldn't you?"

He went off to the living room, muttering under his breath, but Abby didn't care. As she washed the dishes, she was making mental lists of what she needed to look for.

The next morning she booted up the computer as soon as Brad left. Her sojourn into online genealogy the evening before had been both exhilarating and frustrating. She had caught glimpses of her targets through the electronic underbrush, but there were gaps. Worse than that, sometimes there were conflicting details about the same person, and she had no way of figuring out which were correct. *Patience, Abby,* she counseled herself. *You've just started. Some people spend years on research like this, and sometimes they never find what they're looking for.* It was like watching a picture developing in a darkroom—the vague outlines would emerge, and then as you watched, the details would fill in, until you could see the whole picture. Of course, she chided herself, if you didn't stop at the right moment, the whole process would just keep going and the picture would turn black and be useless. She wondered if she'd know when to stop.

Well, not yet—that much she was sure of. What did she want to know? Well, for a start, where William Flagg had come from. Who was he? If she looked at censuses, she could figure out where he had been born, and where Elizabeth had been born as well.

She found William and his family listed in Waltham in 1910 and 1900. The 1900 census yielded a prize: a notation next to baby Isabel's name that she was adopted. Abigail smiled to herself. She had been right in guessing that the tension in that room had had something to do with the baby.

The 1890 census did not exist, except for a Civil War special pension list, but there she struck gold: not only was William listed, but the record gave his address, and it wasn't the house she had seen. So he had bought the place after 1890, or at least he hadn't occupied it yet. Abby wondered how long the remodeling of the building would have taken in those days. Unfortunately, the members of William's household were not given in the limited 1890 record, so she turned back to 1880. No William in Waltham, but she found him in Lynn: age thirty-three, with wife Elizabeth, also thirty-three, and daughter Olivia, age thirteen. So by 1890, he would have been all of forty-three, and not yet fifty when he bought his "mansion." In 1880 William had been a retail bookseller. How on earth had he parlayed that modest occupation into something that enabled him to buy the handsome Hawley place just over ten years later? Abby shook her head. There was too much she didn't know about . . . well, lots of things. Housing costs in the late nineteenth century. Relative salaries or income for various professions. The demographic mix of Waltham at that time. What the neighbors would say about a rather late baby. Would tongues have wagged if that baby had been born "on the wrong side of the blanket"?

Then Abby stopped herself. What did it matter? What was her stake in this? She really wasn't sure. She'd had this dream, or vision, or something, and it had turned out to be about real people, who had lived and died within a mile of her current home. She'd never heard of them before. She'd never been to Massachusetts before, much less Waltham. They weren't famous, so she couldn't have read about them somewhere and then forgotten about it. Then why did she know their faces, know what their dining room had looked like in eighteen-ninety-something?

So these unknown and long-dead people had popped into her head when she'd walked into their house, and kind of taken over. What did it all mean? For a terrifying moment, she felt as though she was standing on the edge of a vast black roaring space, someplace that terrified her. And then it passed, and she was back staring at her scrawled notes. She was not ready to think about what it all meant. She would take her little pile of information to Ned tomorrow and maybe he could explain it for her. That was all she could do for now.

• • •

On Saturday morning Brad aimed a haphazard peck at Abby's cheek as she lay cocooned in the bedsheets, after he'd woken her by bumbling around the bedroom getting himself outfitted for his golf excursion. Abby would have welcomed an extra hour of sleep, but at least Brad seemed cheerful, whistling as he filled his pockets.

"Bye, babe—gotta go. We've got an early tee time. And we may hang around after—I don't know yet. I'll give you a call later when I know what the plan is."

Abby thought briefly about reminding him that she had research plans today but decided it wasn't worth the effort. She lay in bed, following the sounds of his noisy exit process. Finally she heard the door slam, and he was gone. She gave a small sigh of relief and sat up. Maybe Brad's plans didn't include her, but today she didn't mind—for once she had plans of her own. She was looking forward to meeting Ned and showing him what she'd found. *Not a bad haul for a novice,* she thought.

She showered, dressed, and made her way to the kitchen, where she brewed a pot of coffee, heated up some cinnamon rolls, and laid her notes out on the table. As she went through them, trying to keep cinnamon sugar off them, she made a list of key dates, until she had a pretty fair outline of William Flagg's life in Waltham and before. She sat back, sipping her coffee, and studied the list. William had been born, raised, prospered, and died in Massachusetts. That had nothing to do with her: she had never seen Massachusetts before this year. The decision she and Brad had made to move to Waltham had been prompted by economic factors more than anything else, not some vague historical attraction. She shook her head; her little episode, whatever it was, made no sense.

She was early for her rendezvous with Ned. She waited on the front steps of the library, hugging her notes to her chest, turning from side to side to watch in both directions along the main street. On Saturday morning it bustled with both auto and foot traffic. She'd heard there was a farmer's market somewhere in town and made a mental note to check it out, if it was still open this late in September. She checked her watch nervously, but that didn't make the minute hand move any more quickly.

Finally she spied Ned half a block away, walking toward her. She studied him before he spotted her: middle height, middle coloring. No one who would stand out in a crowd. He walked purposefully toward where she stood waiting. She found herself comparing him to Brad, who always walked in public with a bit of a swagger, as if he was announcing to the world "see how important I am." Apparently Ned didn't feel any need to do that.

When he was in earshot, he called out to her, "Hey, you made it." He bounded up the shallow stairs two at a time until he stood next to her. "You look better than the last time I saw you. What luck did you have?" He eyed the stack of papers she was still clutching.

"A lot, I think. I want to show you—"

He interrupted her. "You look cold. I said we could meet in the library, but we'd have to be quiet there, and there're probably a lot of high school kids in there today. There's a place we can get coffee just down the block, and we can snag a booth and get comfortable. Sound good?"

Abby realized that hot coffee was an appealing idea. "Sure. Lead the way."

He went down the stairs and waited for her to follow. They chatted until they reached an unprepossessing diner a block away. Ned opened the door and held it for her, letting her pass. Inside, he raised a hand to the man behind the counter, then made a beeline for a booth at the back. At mid-morning, the place was not crowded. As Abby slid into the booth, the proprietor deposited two steaming mugs of coffee on the table.

"Thanks, Tom," Ned threw after his retreating form.

"You must come here often," Abby commented, struggling out of her jacket. Ned reached over to hold a sleeve, helping her disentangle herself.

"On and off. It's convenient to the library, and the coffee's good."

Abby took a cautious sip and was pleasantly surprised. "You're right—it is." She sat back and relaxed her shoulders.

"You want something to eat?"

"No, I'm fine. I'd really like to start looking at the stuff on William Flagg. If that's okay with you."

"Sure. You go first." Ned sat back on his side of the booth and watched as Abby pulled out her materials and laid them out on the table. "You've been busy," he said approvingly.

"Well, I had the time, and it was sort of interesting. I haven't done any kind of research for a while, and I've rarely used original documents, so it was fun." She surveyed the piles in front of her, organizing her thoughts. "All right. First of all, I think I was right, that the younger daughter was adopted. She's listed that way in the censuses." She saw for a moment the scene in the house that she had somehow called up; was the argument about the baby? Was the man—William—trying to convince his wife that they should adopt her? Was the baby William's child from an illicit relationship? Evidence for those would be hard to come by.

"Good call," Ned said. "What else?"

Abby pulled out her timeline. "As near as I can tell, William was living in Waltham by 1890, but not in that house. He had moved there by 1895, according to the city directories. But by 1903 he was living at another address in town. He stayed there until he died, and his widow lived there until she died fifteen years later. The older daughter, Olivia, when she married, lived a few blocks away, but then she and her husband disappear from the local directories after a couple of years—I'm not sure where they went yet. The other daughter—the younger one—stayed around, and married a local man. In fact, once I looked at a street map, I realized that after she married, she and the Flaggs lived at adjoining properties. And when Elizabeth Flagg died, it was in her adopted daughter's house. So they must have gotten along, at least."

Ned nodded. "Interesting. Maybe Dad bought the house for her—might be interesting to check local property records. But the rest fits with what I know. I talked to the person at the school who keeps the archives there. They have a great map of the property, and it looks like William owned the house and land by 1893, although he might not have moved in right away if he was busy remodeling the place. And the younger daughter went to school there. Did you look at the obituaries in the library?"

Abby shuffled through her pile of papers. "Yes, I've got William's and his wife's here somewhere. Mostly I was looking at city histories, directories, maps. And then I found the census stuff at the archives. Oh, and William had a military record, in the Civil War. He was from the western part of the state then, not around here. But Elizabeth collected a widow's pension when she was living here."

A plate of Danish pastry materialized on the table, and Tom refilled their coffee mugs and disappeared. Ned helped himself to a pastry and chewed contemplatively, lost in thought. Abby felt deflated: she was not sure if all her findings got her any nearer to understanding why she had "seen" these people. Maybe "seen" wasn't the right word, but she wasn't sure what to call her experience. In fact, she wasn't sure what to do next. Finally she decided she might as well get things out in the open, right now. Then Ned could tell her she was barmy and walk away.

Not that she wanted that to happen, but better sooner than later. "All right, we now know a lot more about William's family history. But we still don't know why I . . . saw him. And it was him, because I found a picture of him in an old newspaper at the library. Before you ask, I had never seen him before, until that thing in the dining room."

Ned looked at her speculatively. "You're sure about what you saw?"

Abby felt a stab of dismay—was he going to doubt her now? But she knew what she knew. She took a breath. "Yes. I know it sounds absurd, but it was incredibly clear, like I was standing there. And I could hear them arguing. I could . . . feel the baby I was holding. It was like I was inside Olivia, watching." She glared at him, challenging him to contradict her.

Ned was silent for several beats, looking at her face, assessing her. Finally he nodded. "All right. What do you want to do next?"

Abby stared at him as a surge of relief flooded her. "You believe me? Really? This whole thing seems so weird—I'm not like that, not usually."

"Like what?" Ned looked amused.

"Woo-woo. Fey. Call it whatever you want. I don't see things. So I'm kind of lost here. What do *you* think I should do?"

Ned took his time answering, idly swirling his spoon around his coffee, not looking at Abby. At last he said, "It seems to me you have two choices. One, you say *Gee, what an interesting thing that was,* and then forget about it. Two, you decide you want to know why William Flagg, who's been dead for a century, and his family have suddenly shown up in your head."

Abby's mouth twitched. "And if I go for door number two, what would I do?"

Ned sighed and selected his words with great care. "Abby, I don't know you very well, so I'm not sure how you're going to react to what I'm about to say. And you have every right to decide I'm the nutcase here and walk out. But let me lay out this idea: maybe what you saw was a true vision of something that really happened, and somehow you picked up on it. And that may mean that you have some sort of, uh, psychic sensitivity—maybe just for William and his family, or maybe it goes beyond that. You said you've never had anything like this happen before? Maybe a sense of déjà vu, someplace you've visited? A feeling that you knew what was going to happen, or what had happened?"

Abby shook her head. "No, nothing like that. My mother always said I had no imagination at all. Maybe no empathy either—I don't even cry at sad movies, they just seem silly and predictable. So I'm the last person I'd expect to be having visions of the dead. Is that what you think is going on?"

Ned smiled, more to himself than to her. "I wouldn't go that far. Heck, maybe you're growing an imagination, just a little later than most people. Maybe you were imagining that room with people in it."

"And the guy just happened to look exactly like William Flagg?" Abby demanded.

"There is that. The question is, do you want to forget about it, pretend it never happened, or do you want to explore this and see where it takes you?"

"I don't know." If she allowed herself to stop and think, she knew this whole thing would appear strange. Maybe she was just adrift in a new place where she knew no one. Maybe William Flagg was her new imaginary friend. *Yeah, right.* Then she was struck by an awful thought. "Ned, you're not some sort of weird cultist or something? Or a sci-fi nut? Is that why you're encouraging me?"

He laughed. "No, I'm a perfectly ordinary science geek who happens to like history. I can give you references, if it would make you feel better. But—" He paused, looking a bit sheepish. "Even though I'm a scientist, I told you I like old houses. And I find I keep running into things in those houses that I can't explain through any logical processes. So call me curious. I try to keep an open mind. I'm not going to tell you you're losing your marbles because you are seeing people who aren't there—at least, not there in the here and now. But we know they were real, and they've been there, sometime in the past. So"—he sat up straighter in his seat—"let me propose that we take this a step further and see where it leads us. I believe you saw what you saw, but I can't explain why you saw it. The question is, will it happen again? Can you make it happen, or at least go looking for it? Or does that idea scare you?"

Abby thought about that. When William and family had appeared in front of her, she hadn't felt scared; what she had felt was the anger and sorrow in the room. Theirs, not hers. She did not feel threatened by the people she had seen; they weren't haunting her. Maybe if she was prepared for it, if she was expecting it, it wouldn't be a problem.

Ned had said "we." So he wanted to help? *Could* he help? In spite of her misgivings, Abby was intrigued. "If I wanted to do that, what would I do? Or we?"

He smiled. "We can try some experiments. How about we start with checking out a few other places where we know William has been, see if that triggers anything, if you see him again? Or anyone else from that room? Or maybe even someone you haven't seen? If you've got the time, that is."

Abby thought about her bleak apartment, and about Brad out playing golf with his buddies, and about her total lack of purpose. This was clearly the most interesting thing that had happened to her since she had arrived in Massachusetts, and maybe even before. "Sure, I've got the time. Where do we start?"

Ned gave her a true grin this time. "How about the cemetery where William's buried? It's only a couple of miles from here."

Abby grinned back. "You're on."

Chapter 4

Ned tucked a couple of dollars under his coffee cup and stood up. "Ready?"

Abby was startled. "Now?"

"Why not? It's a beautiful day. Did you have other plans? We could do it another day, or you could go when you have the time."

Time she had plenty of. And she realized she would like to have a buddy, so to speak, for her foray into seeking the dead. Damn, she was going to have to come up with a good term for this. It wasn't exactly ghost hunting. She didn't think she could talk to anyone she was seeing, and they didn't see her. As far as she knew. One episode was pretty slim data to base any conclusions on.

She realized Ned was still waiting for an answer. "Okay, let's do it."

"One car or two?"

Abby looked at him critically. This was her last chance to decide that he was a demented serial killer and run away. Standing there in the shabby coffee shop, Ned looked perfectly ordinary, a little rumpled maybe. In fact, he looked like a Boy Scout. Just because he'd invited her to go look for a . . . formerly living person in the local cemetery didn't mean he was dangerous. Did it? She decided she trusted him. "Why don't you drive? You can drop me off at my car after. You know where you're going, and I don't."

"Great." Once again he led the way, holding the door open for her. His car was parked in front of the coffee shop. It resembled him: sturdy, dependable, a little frayed, and definitely not flashy. Brad would scoff at it. Abby smiled at her thoughts as she climbed in on the passenger side. Ned pulled out carefully, waving cheerily at a mother in an SUV who stopped to let him merge into traffic, and then went around the block. They followed the main street away from the library, out of town. A mile or so beyond the end of the commercial district, they came to a cemetery that covered several acres. Ned pulled his car through the gates and into the narrow road. Luckily there were no other visitors, so he stopped and parked on one of the one-lane roads.

"This is it."

Abby looked up the shallow rise at the varied tombstones. Even to her unpracticed eye, she could tell that the ones on the side near town were earlier—scraggly rows of dark slate, like so many she'd seen while driving through the towns around here. The stones grew newer as the cemetery filled toward the east, and the latest ones looked to be mid-twentieth century. The site was surrounded by an iron fence supported by sturdy stone piers, and the grass and shrubbery were well-tended. There was no living being visible, unless you counted the squirrels, but she could hear voices of children who were playing in adjoining backyards.

She turned to look at Ned. "Now what?"

"We look for William. Do you feel anything?"

She shook her head, feeling foolish. "No. Am I supposed to feel some magnetic attraction to him or something?"

"I don't know. Let's get out and see what happens." He opened the door, then came around to her side. She was out of the car by the time he reached her side, and for a moment they stood side by side, looking at the stones.

Abby felt foolish, looking for something she couldn't begin to identify. Would she know it if she saw it? "For the moment I'll settle for reading the names on the tombstones. I know how to do that." She started toward the gate.

Net laid a hand on her sleeve to stop her. "Wait a minute. Seriously. Give yourself a chance. Just stand here for a minute. Close your eyes, if it helps. Or not. But try it."

Dutifully Abby closed her eyes and tried to relax, empty her mind. She was conscious of the steady stream of passing cars on the busy road behind her, and of the wind whistling through the maple trees in the cemetery and the crisp leaves that had already fallen. She could still hear the young voices somewhere in the distance, and a dog barking.

Finally she shook her head. "Sorry. Nothing."

Ned was quick to reassure her. "That's okay. Don't worry about it. We can do it the usual way." He led the way deeper into the cemetery.

"That way." Abby pointed off to the left.

"Why? You feel something?" he said eagerly.

"No, but those stones look like the right time period—they're bigger, and they're mostly granite. The slate ones that direction are too old."

"Oh. Right." He veered off to the left. Abby followed more slowly, scanning the stones. She passed a few rows of respectable family markers and suddenly found herself standing in front of a handsome granite stone with the single name *Flagg* inscribed on one side. Ned was still hunting a few rows over. Before calling out to him, she walked around to the other side. Yes, this was the right one. William Flagg, his dates, and his military rank—that Civil War service must have mattered to him. Below him, Elizabeth Flagg, with her dates.

"Ned? Over here."

He looked up from his aimless rambling and joined her. He stopped beside her, reading the stone. "Right. And look." He pointed to the next stone. Abby looked at it and saw the name: Isabel Flagg Whitman. The stones, side by side, were nearly identical.

"So they stayed close. Interesting." Abby stared at the two stones, wondering what she was supposed to make of them. Before her—or maybe beneath her—were the mortal remains of the man who had owned that lovely house up the hill, at least for a time. And the child he—no, they— had taken in. Was it his child? Abby wondered. Was that why there was so much pain in that room? How had Elizabeth felt, taking in her husband's little mistake? In 1890-something, in their social circle, it would have mattered. And yet they had done it, and seen her well educated, and apparently Elizabeth had stayed on good terms with the adopted daughter even after William's death.

She looked around her, her hand on the Flagg stone. Ned had wandered off again, probably to leave her to her own musings, and was up the hill reading inscriptions on the older stones. In the opposite direction, she noticed a bench some twenty feet away. There was an old woman sitting there. Abby looked away quickly, to give her the privacy to mourn her own dead, and then, troubled by something, looked back again. The woman was wearing a long black dress, shapeless and fusty, and as Abby studied it, she realized that the style was far from current, even among old ladies. Nearly against her will, Abby looked at the woman's face, and then couldn't turn away. Elizabeth Flagg. Older, but unmistakably the same woman Abby had seen at the house.

Elizabeth didn't appear to see her, although she was looking directly at the headstone. Abby was afraid to look away, afraid that Elizabeth would disappear or turn into something else. She wondered whether, if she looked at the tombstone under her hand, she would find that Elizabeth's inscription on it would have disappeared, or if Isabel's stone would not be there at all. Standing stock-still, Abby studied the woman, who sat, oblivious, hands folded neatly in her lap, back straight despite her age, hat firmly set on her head. Abby tried to remember when William had died— 1914? So what she was seeing—if she was really seeing it—came from a different era than what she had seen in the house.

"Abby?" Ned's voice startled her. She had been so focused on the woman that she hadn't heard him approach. Involuntarily she turned to look at him, and when she turned back, Elizabeth was gone. As if she had never been there. Which in fact she hadn't for most of the last century.

"What's up?" As Ned drew closer, his expression shifted to concern. "You okay? You look kind of pale."

"She was here—or there, over on that bench."

"Who?"

"Elizabeth Flagg." She found she was trembling.

"Hey, maybe you should sit down."

"All right. But not that bench."

Ned nodded and led her to another, more distant bench. They sat. Abby blessed his silence—at least he wasn't peppering her with questions. She needed to get her head on straight. Had she been hallucinating? Was it just wishful thinking, wanting to please Ned by finding something new to entertain him? But everything else around her had seemed normal, real, tangible. Ned had seen the bench, so presumably that was really there. But he hadn't seen the woman. And if she had really been an eighty-year-old woman, she couldn't have moved fast enough to disappear completely in the time it had taken Abby to turn her head away and back. So she couldn't have been real—or at least, corporeal.

Was it really Elizabeth? Somehow Abby had no doubt of that. Was she losing her mind? She took her emotional temperature. No, she didn't feel like she was crazy—she was just seeing things that weren't there. Great.

Ned sat patiently, watching her, waiting for her to speak. She turned back to him.

"I did see her."

"I believe you," Ned replied.

"Why?" Abby burst out. "I wouldn't, in your shoes. Why are you even here? This loopy woman comes in to that house and practically faints on you, and starts telling you all these weird stories, and you buy it? Maybe you're nuts too!" She stopped, trembling, shocked at her own outburst.

Ned took his time in replying. He pulled one leg up on the bench and laced his hands around his knee, looking off across the cemetery. Even when he began to speak, he kept his eyes on the cityscape in front of him.

"You know, Abby, you really are trusting. You don't know me from Adam's off ox, and I could be the type of person who preys on helpless women. But I think you've got good instincts, and you trust them, whether you know it or not. Maybe you need to listen to them more closely." He sighed. "But that doesn't answer your question, does it? I told you I was a scientist, and that's true. I like science. It's quantifiable, precise. But sometimes I wonder if there's more. No, I don't belong to any group of peculiar people looking for alien invaders. Heck, I don't even go to church, unless my mom makes me at Christmas. I just . . ." He struggled to find the right phrase. "I guess I try to keep my mind open to other possibilities."

Abby, watching his face, could tell that he was troubled. She decided to cut to the chase. "Have you ever seen anything, anyone?"

He looked at her briefly, then turned away. He didn't answer immediately, and then he launched into what she thought at first was a tangent. "When I was little, my folks moved into a new house. Well, a different house—the house itself was old, but I was a kid, maybe five, and I didn't know the difference—I just knew it was new to me. It was probably close to two hundred years old when we moved in, and it sounded like it— creaked all the time. You'd think I would have been scared, a kid like me in a strange place, but it never bothered me."

Ned glanced at Abby, to be sure he had her attention. "I started kindergarten in the local school that year, and I'd come home and tell my mother all about what I'd done every day, who I'd played with. One day after a couple of months she asked me, 'Who's this Johnnie you keep telling me about? I don't remember any Johnnie on the class list.' And I said, 'Oh, he's not in my class. I play with him here, at the house.' And she looked blankly at me. 'He lives on this street?' And I said, 'No, he lives *here*.' And she just stared at me. And then she changed the subject, and we never talked about Johnnie again. Much later, I figured that she must have assumed that Johnnie was an imaginary friend I had made up to keep me company, in a new place—lots of kids do that, I know."

He smiled at the memory. "But she was wrong. Johnnie was very real. He was a couple of years older than I was, and he wore funny clothes, and he never said anything. He used to just pop up now and then—I'd look up, and there he'd be. After a while, I noticed he never showed up when anybody else was around, but I figured he was just shy around adults."

He stopped, apparently lost in his memories. Abby had a funny feeling that she knew what was coming, but she had to ask. "What happened with Johnnie?"

Ned turned to look at her. "He just sort of stopped coming around. I didn't really notice, at least not for a while. I got busy, made new friends, and didn't think much about it. I just forgot about him, over time. Until high school, I guess. We were studying the Revolution, and I looked at a picture in our textbook and I recognized the clothes Johnnie had worn. No wonder they looked odd to me—they were two hundred years out of date." He smiled ruefully.

"So what did you think?" Abby asked carefully.

"I tried not to think about it at all. You know high school kids—they don't want to appear different, you know? A couple of years later I decided that maybe I should do a little homework. I was writing a paper for an American history class, something about daily life in the colonies, so I had an excuse to do some research on our house. And I found Johnnie. He lived before the government started keeping censuses and such, but there was a mention in the town records of a death by drowning—a kid named John Phillips. The Phillips family built our house." He fell silent.

"Wow," Abby said softly. She studied her hands, clasped together in her lap. She didn't know what to say.

After a couple of minutes, Ned came back to the present. He shifted on the bench, turning toward her, and he gave her a bigger smile. "So you can see why I don't write you off as a crazy lady. Welcome to the club."

Abby shook her head. "Now I just have more questions."

"Ask away."

"Did you ever feel, I don't know, frightened by Johnnie, or uncomfortable around him?"

"No. He was just another kid. There was never anything scary about him."

"Did he ever come back, once you knew who he was?"

"No, I'm sorry to say. I would like to have seen him again, when I was older, and I did look for him, but he was never there. But I figured that seeing him was a product of that, I don't know—openness?—that kids sometimes have and then lose when they grow up."

Abby was warming to the subject. "Have you ever seen anyone else?"

"Not really. Oh, now and then, in some houses or places, I get this odd feeling that there's someone there, but I've never seen anyone. But that's one reason I got involved in some of the local historical societies—it gives me the opportunity to spend time in old houses, where I can find out the history of the places, and then wait and see."

"Until somebody like me wanders in." Abby smiled. "You mean you've never seen the Flaggs? Are you jealous? I mean, here you've had these places staked out for, what, years? And I waltz in and hit a ghost on the first try. And I wasn't even looking."

"'Ghost' is kind of a loaded word. From what you told me, you were seeing what you called a mini-movie from one person's point of view, right?"

Abby searched her memory, then said slowly, "I think so—Olivia's. She was the one watching. So you think I was seeing through her when I saw Elizabeth today? Even though it was years later?"

"I can't tell you. You think you're channeling Olivia? Or you've been possessed by her?"

Abby shook her head vehemently. "It's not like that. I mean, it, or she, is not *inside* me—I think I've been seeing whatever it is from inside her. It's not like I've been taken over. If I had been, wouldn't I be seeing a lot more? I mean, if Olivia lived here in Waltham all of her life, wouldn't there be lots of memories here?"

"Maybe she's having trouble getting you to focus? Or there's a loose connection or something. Look, Abby, I'm no expert. I can't tell you what's happening to you. But you've told me that it doesn't scare you. Maybe this is just the beginning of something, and maybe it will get scarier later. Are you willing to keep looking, to try to understand what's happening?"

"I think so," Abby said tentatively. Then in a stronger voice she said, "No, I want to." Nothing like this had ever happened to her, and she was tired of being dependable, predictable, boring Abby. Maybe there was something inside her begging to be let out, and there was only one way to find out. She looked at the rows of headstones, and then back at Ned. "Now what?"

"Got me, lady." He flashed her a grin, then turned serious. "Depends on what you want. Do you want to hang out in Waltham and see if any of the Flaggs come back to visit you? Or do you want to be a bit more, uh, proactive—reach out to them?"

Abby thought, then said slowly, "What I really want is to understand this. I want to know why I see them at all, what it means. They don't scare me—it's not like they're threatening me or anything. But I have to think it means something, that dead people are suddenly appearing in my life, here and now. And I don't like them just popping up randomly. It's kind of hard to live if you're worried that someone dead is likely to appear at any moment."

Ned sat up straighter. "I may be wrong, but I'm guessing that it's more specific than that. Anyway, we need a plan. First of all, have you found out if there's any connection between you and William Flagg? What do you know about your family's history?"

"Not a lot, actually. I think my mother's parents came from New Jersey, but nobody ever talked about it much."

"What, deep dark family secrets? Skeletons in the closet?"

Abby laughed briefly. "No, everybody was perfectly respectable, thank you. They just weren't very interested in the whole roots thing, I guess."

"So ask. See what you can find out. At least get a starting point. Do you have family documents—birth certificates, wedding licenses, that kind of thing?"

"My mother would, I suppose," Abby said dubiously. "Why?"

"So we can start working backward."

"Oh. Um . . ."

"What?"

"You said 'we.' We're doing this together?"

Ned looked taken aback. "Well, yes, unless you'd rather not. Is that a problem?"

She was going to have to tell him about Brad. "I, uh, have a boyfriend, fiancé really—that's why I moved up here, because he did. I don't know what he'd think . . ." *If he even noticed I was gone,* Abby thought before she could stop herself.

Ned looked faintly amused. "I'm talking about helping you with some research, in my spare time. I'm not hitting on you."

"I know." Abby was annoyed at herself. "I just wanted to make it clear . . ." She was just getting herself in deeper. "Okay, sure, let's do some more research. But don't you have to work?"

"Yes, of course. But you can do the grunt work, and we can get together and confer on weekends, now and then. Your boyfriend won't object to that, will he?"

"No," Abby replied, more firmly than she felt. "That's fine. He plays golf and does other stuff most weekends."

Ned looked at her speculatively, then said, "Look, from what you've said, you haven't seen a whole lot of this area yet. How about I give you the quick tour? You know, the obvious stuff like the Lexington-Concord road, some of the other towns around here? You need to know the lay of the land. And I can at least point you toward where the documents are stored. Tomorrow good for you?" He looked at his watch. "I've got to take a shift at the Flagg house this afternoon."

"Yes." Brad could think whatever he wanted. After all, he had left her on her own today, hadn't he? And wasn't there a football game on tomorrow? *Abigail, it's not like you have to ask his permission to do something.* "Could you come by and pick me up? Then you can meet Brad." That would keep things out in the open.

"No problem." He stood up. "Let me take you back to your car."

As they left the cemetery by the front gate, Abby turned for one last look. Nothing had changed—there were no ladies in black lurking behind the trees. Yet in a way, everything had changed.

Chapter 5

After Ned dropped Abby off at her car, she stood on the sidewalk watching as he pulled away, raising a cheery hand to her. Back at her car she sat for a moment, trying to figure out what to do. She still had a lot of the day left, and Brad wouldn't be back for hours, but she didn't feel like going back into the library. And she was torn between wanting to sort out just what had happened in the cemetery today and avoiding thinking about it at all. For all her brave talk to Ned, this whole seeing thing had really rocked her boat.

Get a grip, Abigail! she ordered herself sternly. Maybe she was just stressed out. Maybe this move thing had been more difficult than she had admitted to herself. Brad had so much to keep him busy—work, and now a group of buddies to hang out with. She was happy for him, really. But what did she have? She had been just sort of drifting along, and then this weirdness had started. Swooning, visions in cemeteries? She had gone on a simple house tour and ended up seeing things. *Abigail, you have far too much time on your hands!* Feeling more resolute, she put the car in gear and pulled into traffic.

She stopped at the grocery store on the way home. Somehow she whiled away the afternoon. About six thirty, she realized that Brad had never called to say what his plans were—not that that was anything new. He was out playing with his new buddies, doing guy things, like hitting small balls around, or watching other guys hit balls or throw balls or drive machines. She didn't share those interests, but they made him happy. Funny, where she was concerned, with him it was "out of sight, out of mind."

Finally she decided to scramble herself some eggs, and ate sitting at the small table in the kitchen, catching up on forwarded magazines.

Saturday night. Nothing on television she wanted to watch, even on cable. She dug out one of the mystery novels she'd been saving as a treat and curled up in Brad's oversize easy chair, a wool blanket draped around her shoulders for warmth. But she found she was having trouble concentrating: she would read a page and realize that she hadn't absorbed anything, and have to go back to the top of the page and start over. She was annoyed at herself, since she really liked this author and had been looking forward to reading the book, and now something kept getting in the way.

But what? She had walked into a local house and found herself looking at dead people. She had done her best to explain it away, and she had almost succeeded—until she had seen the picture of William Flagg and recognized him. And then his wife Elizabeth today. So much for rationalizations. Poor Ned—he had been so kind, without making too much of a fuss. And she still felt embarrassed—she must have looked like a complete idiot that first day.

But he had listened to her and had taken her seriously, which was nice of him. He even had given her some helpful suggestions, and now she knew more about the Flagg family of Waltham and the house, but nothing she had found explained why they had showed up in her head. Then Ned had taken her to the cemetery and she had seen Elizabeth Flagg. Why her? Why not William, or both of them—or the whole damn lot of them, dancing on the graves? Was she hallucinating? She shut her eyes, better to recall the old woman on the bench—old, dumpy, unfashionable. Abby had to smile at herself: apparently she had harbored the fantasy that an apparition would be young, attractive, and wearing ethereal white garments that billowed softly in a cosmic breeze. She certainly had not expected to see a squat old lady.

Maybe a glass of wine would soothe her. Abby unwrapped herself from her blanket and padded in stockinged feet to the kitchen, where she poured herself a glass of white wine. Maybe cocoa would have been a better idea, but she wanted something stronger. She returned to the chair and settled in again, sipping slowly. The two "sightings" represented different time periods, maybe separated by decades. Did that mean anything? Abby shook her head. The really big question was, did she want to see any of the Flaggs again?

Yes. That answer came loud and clear to Abby, and she almost laughed out loud. The one thing she was sure of was that whatever this was, it didn't frighten her. She had no sense of malevolence, of evil, or of anyone wishing her harm. She hadn't been sure about moving forward when she'd told Ned, but now she was. All right, she was going to have to find out more about the Flagg family.

But what did she want or need to know? Elizabeth's maiden name, for one thing. When she married William, when their daughter was born, when the second, adopted daughter had somehow appeared on the scene—and where she had come from, if possible. What had happened to the daughters. Maybe they, or their descendants, were still around, and Abby might be able to track them down and find out something more. Maybe they even had family pictures. Would that help? Abby realized that she had to be careful that she wasn't going to try to tailor her ideas to fit someone else's pictures. She would have to be very clear about what she saw, before it got muddied by outside influences. She should start writing these things down.

When Brad finally showed up at nine, Abby was still sitting in her chair, staring into space, her book forgotten on her lap.

Brad dropped into the one other chair in their living room. "Whew, what a day! Those guys are something else." Then he bounced up, headed for the kitchen, and found himself a bottle of beer. He planted a sloppy kiss on Abby before slouching back in the chair.

Abby smiled abstractedly. "How was the golf?"

"Amazing. Those guys are really good. I'm going to have to sharpen up my game if I want to keep up. And I'll need some new clubs. Geoff told me about this place . . ." And he was off and running, talking about people and things that meant nothing to Abby. She smiled and nodded at the right times. At the same time she studied him, as he slouched in his chair. She'd always been attracted to his warmth, his enthusiasm. He was somehow larger than life—certainly larger than she was. She had fallen in love with him because he was everything that she was not—self-assured, ambitious, energetic—and she had hoped to absorb some of his energy. But she was beginning to think the opposite was happening: when she was with him, he leached the energy from her, leaving her paler than before. Like a ghost of herself.

"Hey, Earth to Abigail!" Brad's voice interrupted her thoughts. "You even listening?"

"Oh, sure. Golf. Then you watched some football, right? And you all decided to get a pizza?"

He stared at her a moment. "Yeah, right. Sorry I didn't let you know about dinner, but it was hard to break away."

She knew she should have been annoyed that he had forgotten about her existence, but it wasn't worth the effort. Besides, she didn't want to start an argument. "That's okay—I scrambled some eggs, and I was looking forward to reading this." She held up her book.

Brad ran out of steam. "So, what'd you do today?"

"Went to the library, did a little research around town, picked up some groceries." *Abigail, you sort of forgot to mention meeting Ned.* Better remedy that. "Uh, you remember the guy I met at the Flagg house the other day? He's

33

really into local history, and he volunteered to show me some of the sights around here—you know, where the battle was at Lexington, that kind of thing. Tomorrow. Unless you'd rather do something else?"

Brad had turned on the television and had to drag his attention back to her. "Tomorrow? Oh, sorry—one of the guys has a big-screen TV, and he said we could all come over and watch the Patriots game. I know you hate football, so I figured you wouldn't want to go. You go ahead, make your plans." Belatedly he took in what Abby had said. "Uh, what's your friend's name?"

"Ned Newhall. He was the docent on that house tour I took. I told you about him." Abby hoped her vague description would let Brad classify Ned as harmless.

"Huh." Brad had already lost interest. His eyes were back on the screen, and he scrolled through the cable listings looking for some sports event. "Well, how about we go out for dinner tomorrow night? Just the two of us?"

"I'd like that." She stood up. "If you're going to watch TV, I'll go to the bedroom and read." When he didn't respond, Abby left the room with her book.

She had managed to get through another three chapters but had lost the thread of the plot yet again, when Brad came into the bedroom and threw himself down on the bed next to her.

"A hundred and twelve channels, and not a damned thing to watch." He nuzzled her neck. "I think I'll grab a shower. Then maybe we can find something better to do?" He looked at her with a grin plastered to his face.

Ah, yes, the obligatory Saturday night roll in the hay. Abby tried to look enthusiastic. "What'd you have in mind?"

"We'll think of something." He stood up, peeled off his clothes, leaving them in a heap on the floor, and headed for the bathroom. Abby admired the view of his retreating backside. Brad had been a football player in college and still had the shoulders to prove it. So far he had managed to avoid running to fat, although Abby could imagine that a few years down the line that could be a problem. But right now, he looked good. And she found she was looking forward to concentrating on something real and physical and in the moment, because that meant that she would not have to think about what she had seen today: the woman who wasn't really there.

Chapter 6

The phone rang at ten, just as Abby was clearing up the kitchen after fixing Brad his favorite Sunday-morning pig-out breakfast of pancakes, bacon, and sausage. He was sprawled in the living room reading the newspaper, with his third cup of coffee. Abby grabbed the phone.

"Hello?" she said tentatively.

"Abby?" It was Ned. "I just wanted to check if you were still up for a tour today?"

"Sure—I'm looking forward to it." *And I even got permission from Brad,* a snide voice added in her head. "Can you pick me up here, or do you want me to meet you somewhere?"

"I can come there—it's easier for you."

"Thanks. Why don't you come up, and I'll introduce you."

"Great, just give me the address." After Abby recited their apartment address, Ned said, "Eleven okay? We can pick up some lunch somewhere, if you like."

"That sounds good. See you then."

Abby put down the phone and wandered into the living room. Brad looked up at her from the sports section.

"Who was that?"

"That was Ned, just confirming for today. You sure you don't mind?"

"Heck, no—this way I don't have to worry about you sitting around the apartment all day, moping. And you can check out the neighborhood, let me know if you think there's anything I should see around here."

But Abby knew that Brad had little patience for anything from the past. He lived in the present, with one eagle eye on the future. The rest was dead and gone. Well, her conscience was clear; she wasn't hiding anything. Not that there was anything to hide. Except that she hadn't managed to say anything about her "visions," if that's what they were. She could wait a little longer, until she had put a name—and an explanation—to them, before telling Brad. She didn't want to say anything and have him look at her like she was deranged. Because she didn't really think she was. And Ned believed her, didn't he?

Anyway, today should be a fun excursion—being driven around, looking at some of the prime historic sites of Massachusetts. If the local newscasters were right, this was a peak "leaf-peeping" weekend, so it would be a pretty drive. The weather was cooperating—the sky was an intense unflawed blue that would set off the wonderful glowing colors of the leaves. The air was crisp enough for a light jacket. That thought reminded Abby that she'd better shower and change before Ned appeared in less than an hour.

Abby had pulled on jeans and a turtleneck and was tying the laces of her most comfortable walking shoes when she heard the doorbell. She could hear Brad heave himself out of his chair and open the door, and the rumble of male voices. She went to the closet to find a sweater and then joined the men in the living room. For a moment she looked at them objectively. They looked as though they belonged to different species. Brad was large and substantial, and he wore loose sweats that inflated his bulk still further. Ned was slight, almost wiry, and looked even more so standing next to Brad. He had rolled up the sleeves of his long-sleeved dark shirt, which he wore over naturally faded jeans. The two men were involved in some arcane male greeting ceremony, figuratively sniffing rumps, trying to establish whether the other was friend or foe. Apparently Brad had tossed out the sports card, and Ned had passed. Brad had moved on to occupation, and somewhere they had found common ground talking about computer systems. Ned was the first to notice that Abby had appeared.

"Hi, Abby. Ready to go?"

She nodded, then turned to Brad. "Do you have any idea when you'll be home?"

He shook his head. "Nah. The local game's on early, and we might watch the second game. I'll give you a call, okay? Got your cell?"

Abby nodded. She gathered up a windbreaker and her bag and stood on tiptoe to give Brad a kiss. "See you later, then. Have fun."

"You too." He had turned away before she and Ned were out the door.

Ned stepped aside to let her go down the stairs first. He unlocked the car door for her but didn't say anything until they were seated. Abby wondered if Brad had made him uncomfortable, and sneaked a look at his profile, but he appeared unruffled.

"So, what's the plan?" she asked brightly.

He hadn't turned the car on yet. "Depends on what you've already seen. Have you driven much around here?"

Abby shook her head. "No, first we were busy getting settled, and then I really didn't know where to go. That house tour was the first thing I did just for fun since I've been here. Tell me what I should see."

Ned started the engine and pulled out of the parking lot. "I thought we'd head more or less west, out along the Battle Road, toward Lexington and Concord. It's pretty country, and maybe the tour busses will have thinned out. You do know something about American history?" He looked doubtful.

Abby laughed. "Of course. I mean, I took the usual high school courses, but when I knew we were moving up here, I did some reading too. Quite a lot took place in a very small area, and I'm looking forward to seeing where it all happened. Now, if I remember right, the battle started at Lexington and then moved toward Concord, then the British troops were forced to turn back toward Boston?"

"That's it in a nutshell, but there's more . . ." They chatted amiably as Ned drove. She found him easy to talk to. He clearly knew and loved his subject, but he wasn't at all condescending to Abby in her ignorance. He would have made a good teacher, she thought—patient and precise, but he still made things interesting. "Oh, and then there's the house where the Alcotts lived, in Concord, and of course Walden Pond."

"That's what I meant." Abby laughed. "An embarrassment of riches. Look, can we use this as a sort of general scouting expedition? There's no way we can tour everything in one day, and I hate to have to choose, or to dash through a lot of places. Why don't you show me where things are, and maybe we can pick one or two? And it's such a lovely day—can't we stay outside?"

"Good idea. Then I vote for the Battle Green in Lexington, Walden Pond, and the Battle Bridge in Concord. All very scenic, all with plenty of pretty trees and fresh air."

"You're mocking me. But that's all right—it's too nice a day to argue about it." Abby settled back in her seat and watched the scenery unfold. They headed north to Lexington.

"You live this direction, right?" Abby asked.

"Yeah, at the east end of Lexington. I bought a fixer-upper Victorian a few years ago, but I never have enough time to work on it."

"I'm sorry—here I am dragging you away from your house projects to play tour guide."

"Hey, I volunteered, remember? I love showing off how much I know."

It didn't take them long to reach Lexington. Ned drove slowly through the town, whose main street was crowded with people running errands. When he reached the western end of town, the road split around a triangular open space. Ned pulled over and parked.

"First stop: Battle Green."

Abby climbed out of the car and looked at the empty grass. She turned and looked at Ned quizzically.

"Come on." He led the way to one of the benches that dotted the perimeter. "Quick history lesson. You do remember Paul Revere's ride?"

"Of course."

"Well, then, Paul Revere, as you may not remember—and most people don't—actually got stopped by the British on his way to warn the towns, but they let him go—minus horse—in the middle of the night. Early on the morning of April nineteenth, John Hancock and Sam Adams were staying up that road a bit"—Ned pointed—"and were persuaded to remove themselves for the good of the cause. The minutemen were called out and met here about four thirty—one company under Captain Parker, seventy-seven men—and lined up to wait for the British, over on that side. In the meantime, Paul Revere and Sam Adams were scurrying around hiding a trunk full of papers that John Hancock had managed to leave behind. Can you see the scene, so far? It's not even first light, and all these men—old men, boys, whoever—were standing around in the cold and dark, on their own doorsteps, waiting for the British army to descend on them."

Abby cleared her mind and tried to see it. She tried to put fewer than a hundred men, armed with whatever weapons they could scrounge, on the muddy grass in front of her. They would have been swallowed up by that space, and they had no idea what they would have to face.

Ned had resumed his narrative. "So about five o'clock, the British, under Major Pitcairn, marched into town along that road there." He pointed back toward the road that ran through the town. "There used to be a meeting house at that corner of the green—the patriots couldn't see what was coming, and the British couldn't see what they were up against, until they came around the building. And when they did, and Pitcairn saw how few people he was facing, he told them to lay down their arms and go home. Parker knew he was outnumbered and ordered the men to leave—but somebody fired a shot. No one has ever figured out who, or which side it came from. And that started the whole thing. Eight patriots died, including Jonathan Harrington, who lived in that house there." Ned pointed again. "He managed to crawl that far, and died on his own doorstep. And then the British set off down the road that we're going to take, headed for Concord, where they thought the patriots had weapons and ammunition stored." He fell silent, contemplating the peaceful scene of the modern day, lost in his own thoughts.

"It's all so small," Abby half whispered.

Ned turned to look at her. "This was all it took, to start something that started a significant war that shook the British Empire."

Abby looked back at the green. "I remember the first time I took a tour of Independence Hall, in Philadelphia. Have you been there?" Ned shook his head. "I felt the same way. Our tour group walked into the room where the Declaration of Independence was voted on—you know, there are all these stories about how they kept the windows shut, even though it was June and July and hot as blazes, because they wanted to keep things secret? And here were all these men, wearing eight layers of their best wool clothes—you'd think they would all have died of heatstroke. Anyway, I looked around the room, and it was so, I don't know, human in scale. Just a handful of men, gathered in that one room, and they wrote something that changed the world." She also fell silent. There was something about seeing the real places that put things in perspective. And it made her appreciate how few people it took to make a difference. Were people different then? Did they know what they were doing? Did they have any idea what was going to follow?

Ned was watching her. "Had enough? There's no rush."

Abby stood up. "Can we walk around it?"

"Sure." He stood too, and they moved slowly around the green in companionable silence. When they had made the circuit back to the car, Ned said, "Ready for more?"

Abby nodded. "On to Concord."

They took off along the road on the south side of the green. They drove at a leisurely pace, despite the impatience of other drivers, and Ned pointed out various landmarks along the way. "A lot of these houses are open for tours, if you're interested. And there's plenty of documentation about the battle—you know, who did what where, step by step. I can find it for you, if you want."

Abby nodded noncommittally, watching the trees flow by. Before they reached another town, Ned took a left fork, and a couple of minutes later pulled off the road. "Walden Pond," he said, pointing off to the left. "Want to get out and walk?"

"Sure." Abby clambered out again. "Do we have to go all the way around?"

"Not if you don't want to." They crossed the road and descended the hill to reach the water. "Henry David Thoreau's cabin was over at that end." He pointed toward the far end of the pond. "It's long gone. There's actually a public beach on this end now."

"Not exactly wilderness, is it?" Abby mused. "Was it more isolated when Thoreau was camping out here?"

Ned smiled. "Not really. The popular mythology has got it wrong. Downtown Concord is about half a mile from here. Thoreau neglected to mention that he could walk over to Ralph Waldo Emerson's house for dinner whenever he wanted to. He wasn't exactly roughing it in the wilds."

Abby laughed. "One more cherished myth shot down in flames." She looked out across the water in time to see a train speeding by at the far end. "Civilization is too much with us. How about Concord?"

"You up for some lunch?"

"Sure. Lead on." Abby was surprised to find she was hungry. And that she was having a good time.

Chapter 7

After a short drive into town, Ned led Abby to a small restaurant. She was absurdly pleased that it wasn't a chain, but there didn't seem to be any tacky fast-food places in downtown Concord. In fact, all the shops looked very upscale. After lunch, they strolled the main street, mainly window-shopping. Ned described the town as it had looked in 1775 and pointed out the two old cemeteries in eyeshot.

"Ready for more history?"

Abby sighed. "There's more?"

He laughed. "We've barely scratched the surface. Come on, just one more stop—the bridge."

"Yes, sir." Abby allowed herself to be escorted back to the car for the short drive to the bridge. They pulled into the parking area.

Ned scanned the scene and said, "Thank goodness, no tour busses. This place is much nicer when there aren't a lot of people around."

He led the way across the road onto a broad, tree-lined path. Abby could see a statue on a pedestal, and beyond it an arched wooden bridge. When they reached the statue, Ned spoke again.

"The statue's by Daniel Chester French—he had a studio here in Concord. The bridge isn't original, of course—that one's long gone—but the general shape is all right. The British approached from the town, the way we did. The patriots were on the other side of the river, there."

"Were the odds any better here?"

"Somewhat. The British didn't really want a fight. They just wanted to seize or destroy the rebels' munitions and supplies and go back to Boston. But the rebels hid as much as they could, and then fell back that way, to wait and see what happened. There were about four hundred of them by nine o'clock in the morning, and more kept trickling in from the surrounding towns, as word about what had happened at Lexington got out. They could see smoke from the town, but they couldn't see what was burning. So the patriots decided to move toward the bridge. By then, they actually outnumbered the British troops. The colonists were ordered not to shoot, but the British fired first, and our side let loose. By the time they reached the bridge, the British were spooked—they turned around and headed back to town. The battle here took about three minutes."

"Wow. What happened next, teacher?" Abby grinned at Ned.

"The British hightailed it back for Boston, harried by local militia all the way. And more militia kept showing up as the word spread. Amazing how fast the word got out, considering the state of communications in those days. You could almost feel sorry for the Brits, except that they were so arrogant. They didn't expect a fight—they thought they'd just march in and intimidate those pesky rebels and be done with it. They weren't ready for resistance. What made it worse was that they had been embarrassed by a ragtag bunch of amateurs. That did not sit well with the powers that be. So we got a war, and we won, and here we are. That's the CliffsNotes version, anyway."

"It certainly is different, seeing the real places. Knowing just how long it would take to walk from here to town, for instance. How far is it to Boston?"

"Fifteen miles, maybe?"

"And in modern wars, we just push a button and kill people a whole lot farther away than that. Doesn't seem right, somehow."

Abby meandered around a bit longer, looking at the view, and at the sluggish, leaf-clogged river. "What's that house?" She pointed up a low rise.

"The Old Manse. Lots of the local literati spent time there. Most of them are buried in Sleepy Hollow Cemetery, if you're interested."

"What do you mean?"

Ned ticked off on his fingers, "The Alcotts, the Hawthornes, the Thoreaus, and the Emersons—all very chummy, on Authors Ridge. Want to meet them?"

"Sure, why not?"

"You mean you aren't off cemeteries now?"

This was the first time he had mentioned what had happened the day before. "No. I don't expect to run into anyone I know. Although it might be kind of fun to chat with Louisa May Alcott." Abby figured she might as well test her radar here, on neutral ground. In any case, it sounded like an unusual place.

Back in the car, Ned retraced their earlier route, but then went around the small green with its war memorials and ducked down a road between the old Town Hall and a church. When the road emerged, there were cemetery gates in front of them. He passed through and drove slowly along the narrow winding roads. Although they had passed some old slate stones near town, clearly most of this cemetery was newer, Abby realized. As though he had read her thoughts, he said, "Sleepy Hollow was founded in the later nineteenth century. It was one of the earliest of the 'garden' cemeteries—created almost as a park, where people could wander and contemplate their mortality. Some have fountains, and benches so you could stop and ponder."

"Death as entertainment? The Victorians were a creepy lot, weren't they."

Ned wound through the cemetery, over a small hill, then around to the left. The road dead-ended in a tiny cul-de-sac with parking for at most three cars. He stopped there.

"This is it."

A discreet sign pointed up a flight of steps. Abby climbed up and found herself surrounded by some of Concord's most famous dead, as Ned had promised. She knelt down for a moment for a closer look at Thoreau's stone, which had been ornamented with a collection of offerings, apparently from children: she noted a drawing of a pumpkin, a pencil, and a few pennies. Curious, but kind of touching. She strolled a bit further along and came upon Ralph Waldo Emerson's stone, a pompous chunk of natural pink quartz that only reinforced her opinion of Emerson. What a time they must have had, living cheek by jowl in nineteenth-century Concord! What fascinating dinner-table conversations they might have spun. For a moment, Abby wished that she *could* channel the past, just to eavesdrop on the locals. She laughed inwardly: *fat chance. I'd probably end up in the wrong household altogether and find out how the local butcher was cheating his customers.*

She looked out over the cemetery beneath her. The label did not lie: the authors and their families lay together on top of a ridge, and below stretched a garden of Victorian and twentieth-century stones. At least the place looked well-filled, and certainly well-tended. Ned was lost in contemplation of another group of stones, and Abby aimlessly wandered down a convenient pathway toward the little valley below, stopping now and then to read an inscription or to admire a particularly elaborate carving. On this fine autumn day, there were no other tourists here—most of them were probably out chasing leaves somewhere.

She reached the row of stones at the bottom of the hill, bordered by the road, and laid her hand momentarily on a large granite stone to steady herself. Suddenly the air around her was filled with figures—men, women, children, who overlapped and flowed through each other. Abby was frozen in place, yet she knew she was invisible, as these insubstantial figures swirled around her. She grabbed at what order she could: she noted that the people appeared to belong to different eras, judging by their varying dress. And she didn't think they could see each other. There were layers of them, if layers could be three-dimensional. And temporal: it was as though she was seeing a series of events, all superimposed, existing in the same unreal space. With a start, she realized that she recognized one of the faces: it was her great-grandmother, whom she barely remembered from her childhood, but whose face she had seen in many family pictures. But she was dressed in a style that would have been appropriate in the 1930s, and she was young, barely older than Abby was now.

And this time there was more. At the cemetery in Waltham, the grief she sensed had been old, muted; here the pain was palpable. It came in waves as she watched generations come together to bury their dead, the dead whose remains now lay under Abby's feet. It was as if the pain had soaked into the hard granite of the headstone and was now seeping into Abby through the hand that she had no power to move.

"Abby? Are you all right?" Ned's voice was sharp behind her and cut through the swirling fog of half-seen people. Abby realized she had closed her eyes, and with an effort forced them open again. And somehow found the strength to tear her hand from the stone. Ned's hand on her elbow steadied her, and, eyes open, she saw nothing but the peaceful scene of the cemetery.

Without letting go, Ned came around to face her. "Here, sit down," he said gently, guiding her to the high stone coping of a nearby plot. She sat without protest. "What happened?"

Abby swallowed and tried to collect her thoughts. "I don't know." She realized her face was wet with tears. "I was walking along and I put my hand on that stone, and then . . ." She was having trouble putting into words what she had seen. It was like a fever dream—fragmented, incoherent. "I saw people, lots of people. I saw my great-grandmother. And there was so much sadness . . ." She realized she was still crying. Silently Ned handed her a clean handkerchief. Poor Ned, he kept having to scrape her off the floor, one way or another. Finally she was able to give him a watery smile. "I'm sorry. I keep doing this."

"It's all right, Abby."

"Maybe I should see a doctor. Maybe I've got some neurological problem, or I have a brain tumor. Or I'm completely losing my mind."

"Abby, you can do that if it will make you feel better. You should certainly eliminate any physical causes. But . . ." He fumbled for words.

"I should see a shrink?" she asked, hating the edge of hysteria to her voice.

"No. No, that's not what I was going to say," Ned protested quickly. "I just think we should look into all explanations."

"Like what?" Abby sniffed, but at least she had stopped crying.

"All right, I'll say it, if you won't. Like some psychic connection."

"But I'm not psychic!" Abby protested.

"How do you know?"

She looked at him mutely and shook her head.

"Look," he pressed on, "I'm not going to try to sell you on some mumbo-jumbo about astral links or whatever. I just think we should do some basic research on how all these people are connected to you—the Flaggs, and whoever is here. And on psychic phenomena in general. Can't hurt, right?"

"I guess not," Abby admitted, feeling like a sulky child.

"Do you know who's buried in that plot?"

"No, I came up from behind—I never even saw the name on the front."

Ned stood up and peered at the stone. "Reed. Does that mean anything to you?"

"Not a thing."

Ned sat down beside her again. "Abby, I promise I will tell you if I think you're going off the rails. I know you don't know me very well, so there's no reason you should trust me or believe me. And I know you're going to say that I don't know you very well, so how I am supposed to know what normal is for you? But I don't think you're demented. I think something is happening to you, something you don't understand. Maybe it was there all along and the recent changes in your life just brought this to the surface. Or maybe it's new—I don't know. But before you panic, can we just look at it a little more closely? You can set a deadline, whatever you're comfortable with, and if we don't find anything useful, then you can go find a shrink and pour your heart out. But I think there's something more going on here. And I'd like to help, if I can."

Abby didn't respond immediately. She was calmer now, and she could look at what had just happened more rationally. She took a deep breath and looked around her. Then she looked at Ned.

"Thank you. You've been very kind, especially in not telling me I was loony tunes and running the other way. And like I said at the Waltham cemetery, this doesn't feel like any kind of mental illness. It's breaking in, from outside of me. And I want to know what, know why. I wouldn't say yes to what you're suggesting if this scared me. I mean—*they* don't scare me, but the way this is happening does. But somehow, even when there are strange things milling around my head, I don't feel scared. This time, I felt sad. There was a lot of pain there, but it wasn't mine—it was all those other people's. They don't threaten me, but I want to know why they're suddenly in my life. So let's find out."

"Good for you." He looked at his watch. "The day's about shot. Do you feel okay now? Should I take you home?"

"What time is it? Good heavens, it's nearly five." *And Brad hasn't called, even though my cell has been on all day.* "I suppose I should get home. We're supposed to be going out for dinner tonight."

"Fine." Ned stood up and Abby followed suit. He waited to be sure that she was steady on her feet. "Let's go."

Driving back to Waltham, they were both largely silent. Halfway there, Ned spoke.

"Have you said anything about this to Brad?"

Abby considered her answer. "No," she said slowly, "because I don't think he'd believe me. He'd tell me I needed a pill, or more exercise, or a job. I don't think he'd consider any other possibilities. And I don't want him to laugh at me. You might have noticed, he can be a rather . . . dominant personality."

Ned laughed. "I understand. But if this is a problem for you, you really should talk with him—he should know."

Abby sighed. "I know. But can we find out a bit more first?"

As he pulled into her parking lot, Abby prepared to jump out. "You don't need to come up. And, Ned? Thanks again."

He gave her a long look. "I'll give you a call in a couple of days. You can start doing some digging on the Reeds of Concord. And I think you really need to find out something about your family history. Who knows, there might be a witch somewhere up the line." With a smile and a wave, he pulled away.

Witch, indeed, thought Abby. But this was Massachusetts. Maybe it came with the territory.

Upstairs there was still no Brad, so Abby decided to take a shower. Brad arrived an hour later, full of apologies but bubbling over with good cheer after his hefty dose of NFL football. "Where do you want to go, baby? Your pick."

"Let's explore Waltham. There're a couple of places that look interesting."

"Okay. Let me put on a clean shirt. Hey, how was your day with what's-his-name?" He disappeared into the bedroom.

"Fine," she called out. "We went to Lexington and Concord. And Walden Pond. I learned a lot. Ned's a good guide."

Brad came out of the bedroom, buttoning his shirt. "Seemed kind of wimpy to me. Is he gay?"

Abby stared at him. "I don't know. It didn't exactly come up in conversation, you know."

Her sarcasm was lost on Brad, as he replied, "Well, I'm glad you had a good day. Let's go!"

Chapter 8

Brad had already left the next morning when Abby awoke. They had spent a pleasant evening and had been happily surprised by the restaurant they had stumbled upon. It was definitely one they would revisit. Brad had been attentive—having apparently had his fill of "guy stuff" for the weekend—and Abby had had as much fun as she could remember since they had moved.

But now it was Monday, and she was on her own again, and she had to figure out what she was going to do about the strange visions she was having. Ned had suggested a two-pronged strategy for research: tracing the people she had been seeing and investigating the general idea of psychic phenomena. She wasn't sure which one was more difficult, or more interesting.

It might not have been a psychic connection, but Abby received an answer of sorts when the phone rang. She picked up quickly and found it was her mother.

"Abby? I didn't wake you up, did I? I know it's only eight, but you've always been an early bird."

"No, Mom, I was just getting up."

"You mean Bradley has left already?"

"Yes. He wants to be the first one in the office to impress everybody. He's still the new kid."

"But he's enjoying his work?" Why was it everything her mother said came out as a question?

"Yes, he likes it fine."

"And you like your new place?"

Abby tucked the handset of the phone between her chin and shoulder and wandered out to the kitchen to start her coffee. "Well, it's not permanent, but it'll do for now."

"Have you had any luck finding a job?"

"No, Mom, I've been busy getting settled, and getting to know the area. I haven't decided what I'm looking for, anyway."

"I'm sure you'll find something. You're such a smart girl, and so talented."

Yes, Mom, thank you. Nice that somebody believes in me.

Mom's chirpy tones went on relentlessly. "And what have you been doing for fun?"

"Well, we eat out, and I've met some of Brad's friends from work. Oh, and yesterday I took a tour of the Revolutionary battleground sites in Lexington and Concord. And Walden Pond."

"Oh, that sounds lovely, dear. I know you always liked history."

All right, Mom, why are you calling me now? "Mom, did you call for a reason?"

"Oh, well, yes. Well, it turns out your father has a meeting in New Jersey, and I thought I'd go along with him, so we decided to drive down. I wanted to drop something off at your place on the way, if you're going to be around?"

"When, Mom?" As if she wouldn't be around—where else would she be?

"Tomorrow? If we start real early, we could be there by mid-afternoon. Now, don't you worry about feeding us or putting us up. I know you're not settled yet. But I'd love to see you, and your father would too, and it seems like such a good opportunity . . ."

"Sure, Mom, I'll be here. I'd love to see you too. Why don't you let me cook you dinner? Give me a call when you know you're getting close, and I can give you directions to get to our place from the highway." If she could figure them out herself.

"That would be wonderful, sweetheart. We'll do just that. Now, I'll save all my other chitchat until we see you tomorrow. You take care now. Bye!" She rang off.

Abby heaved a sigh. She loved her mother, but she sometimes wondered about the vagaries of genetics. Her mother was short, round, and bristled with energy and good cheer. Abby was taller and more slender—no one had ever called her round. Or energetic and cheerful. She was more likely to be described as cautious, meticulous, and boring. More like her father, she supposed—but her father and mother had been together over thirty years and still they were very happy together. Oh, sometimes her father would get this glazed look in his eye, and Abby knew he was thinking about something entirely unrelated to what her mother was talking about—at great length. And then he'd catch Abby watching him, and wink at her.

When Rebecca and Marvin Kimball had first met Brad, he and Rebecca had hit it off marvelously. Brad took delight in teasing her, and she gave back as good as she got. Abby's father, Marvin, had just sat back and watched them banter, as though they were both fractious children. Later, though, he had taken Abby aside and asked if she was happy. She had assured him she was, and he hadn't pressed any further.

So now they'd be here—tomorrow. The place was clean, so that was no problem. She could cook them dinner, which meant she might need to shop . . . which would cut into her research time. But then she realized that this would be a perfect opportunity to ask her parents about their family histories. Maybe they wouldn't know all the details, but at least she could get started, and at this point, any information would be a plus. And then maybe she could go back to the library, or look online, later in the week, if she found something she could follow up on. So maybe today she could focus on learning more about psychic phenomena involving dead people.

• • •

Her parents arrived right on schedule, late on Tuesday afternoon. Abby opened the door to their knock to find them juggling between them a strangely wrapped bundle that was nearly as big as one of them.

"Hi, darling," her mother puffed. "We made it!"

"I can see that. And what on earth did you bring?"

"Here, Marvin, set it down in the living room. There." Her mother surveyed the room. "Oh, this is sweet. Not real big, but it's just the two of you. And I know you'll be looking for a bigger place soon, right?"

"Sure, Mom—we just wanted to get to know the neighborhoods, what the commute is like, things like that, before we started looking. We've got a month-to-month lease." She hugged each of her parents. Her mother, as always, felt like a bundle of energy, but Abby thought her father looked a little frailer, a little more stooped. "How are you, Daddy?"

"I'm fine, sweetie. I'm just happy to see my girl."

She turned back to her mother. "Okay, Mom, what is that thing?" She pointed toward the bundle, which was wrapped round and round with bubble wrap, clear plastic, and tape.

"Well, I thought now that you and Brad have a place together, you might like something nice for it. So I brought you your grandmother's rocking chair."

Abby was touched. It was a piece of furniture she'd always loved as a child, a graceful wooden rocker made of mahogany. Her favorite part was the carved swan heads that formed the curve of each arm. "Oh, Mom, I love that chair! And it's perfect for here—not too big, and a sort of timeless style. It's wonderful! Thank you!" She hugged her mother again, much to her mother's surprise.

50

"Well, I knew you loved it, and it's only right that it should pass down through the family and go in your first real home." Her mother took another visual tour of the room. "So, are you going to show me the rest of this place? And what smells so good? What time will Brad get home? You said he takes the train? Is that far?"

Abby let her mother's relentless chatter wash over her as they walked through the small apartment, Abby's father trailing quietly behind. They had just wrapped up the tour when Brad came in, and they had to go through the elaborate greeting rituals: Brad pumped Marvin's hand several times, slapped him on the shoulder, and endeavored to look sincere when he inquired about Marvin's health; then he grabbed Rebecca Kimball in a warm bear hug, and they beamed at each other, and everyone was happy. Then Brad offered to get everyone drinks, and Abby retreated to the kitchen to put the finishing touches on dinner.

Dinner was a cheery affair. Brad sincerely liked his prospective in-laws, which pleased Abby. Rebecca didn't bring up whether they had managed to set a date yet for the wedding, and Marvin just smiled quietly at all of them. They had reached dessert—Brad having uncharacteristically volunteered to clear the dinner plates away—when Abby remembered what she wanted to ask her parents.

"Mom, Dad, what can you tell me about your family histories? We never talked much about your grandparents and their parents, where they came from, when I was growing up. But there's so much of a sense of history around here, it makes me curious. Were any of them from Massachusetts?" There—she'd cast her nets.

Predictably, Rebecca spoke first. "Well, goodness, I don't know that I've ever thought much about it. I know there's a lot of popular interest in genealogy-type things, television shows and such, but I can't tell you a whole lot about my side." Her face darkened. "You know, I guess we didn't talk about it much because of your great-grandpa. When he up and left my grandmother—your great-grandmother—it was like she erased him from the earth. She never would talk about him after that. So that left kind of a black hole on that side."

"I'd forgotten about that whole story. Did he ever come back?"

"No, not in person. A long time later, Nana got a letter from somewhere out west saying that he was dead, but he didn't leave much of anything. She just told whoever it was to go ahead and bury him out there, and that was the end of it. She might have gotten a death certificate—I think he was a veteran, and she wanted to collect his pension. But I have no earthly idea where any of that information might be."

"Weren't you ever curious?"

"Well, sure, but she was so closemouthed, she discouraged any interest. So I never found out anything, I guess."

"Do you know his name? I know you said Nana took back her maiden name after he disappeared."

Rebecca shook her head. "Can't recall at the moment, but maybe it'll come to me. He might have come from Massachusetts, but don't quote me on that. Well, now, what about that dessert? We've got to get to the motel, 'cause we're off early tomorrow."

Refusing to be diverted, Abby turned to her father. "What about your side, Dad?"

He smiled fondly at her. "Nobody special, as far as I know. I think there's a chart your aunt Elsie put together—maybe I can dig that up and have your mother send it to you."

"Thanks, Dad." Abby went to the kitchen to dish out apple pie and scoop ice cream, but her mind was somewhere else. She was troubled. Her mother hadn't given her much to go on. There had to be more, somewhere. At least, she hoped so. Maybe she could try her mother again, after they got back from New Jersey. It would be kind of hard to find her mystery great-grandfather's name, with so little to go on. She didn't even know where her great-grandparents had been married. Ah, well, it didn't have to be a dead end, and it certainly was a challenge.

The Kimballs left shortly after nine. Much as she loved them, Abby sighed with relief when the door closed behind them. It took a lot of energy to keep up with her mother. When she turned from the door, she found Brad industriously unwinding the wrappings from the chair.

"Hope you don't mind, babe—tomorrow's trash pickup day, and I wanted to get this stuff out."

"No problem. It's been a while since I've seen it, but I thought it was wonderful when I was growing up. Mom always made me be careful when I sat on it because it was old."

Brad had the wrappings off in short order and bundled the scraps up, stuffing them into a plastic bag. Abby studied the chair, now revealed. It looked much as she remembered it, although maybe a bit smaller. Her mother had reupholstered the seat, but Abby recalled how proud her mother had been that she had preserved the original horsehair stuffing. *And now it's mine,* Abby thought. It really was lovely, free from the excesses of High Victorian taste—simple and elegant. In fact, it made the functional Ikea furniture she and Brad had collected so proudly look tacky.

Brad emerged from the kitchen clutching several trash bags. "I'll just go stick this in the Dumpster, okay? Hey, are you going to stand there all night admiring it, or are you going to sit in it?" He wrestled the bags out the door.

Abby walked up to the chair and reached down to pick it up and move it to a more convenient position. But when she touched the polished wood, she felt as though she had been slammed by a baseball bat. Fragmented images buffeted her. She snatched her hands away, and the images stopped. Abby stood transfixed, staring at the chair. She'd grown up with this chair, sat in it hundreds of times, and nothing like that had ever happened. What was going on?

Well, Abby, there's one way to find out. She turned and carefully sat down on the seat and laid her hands on the arms of the chair.

Pain. Joy. There was a child in her arms. It was a rosy gurgling baby. No, it was still, straining to breathe, and then it stopped breathing. The same child? Two children? The images flashed back and forth, back and forth. Abby felt as though she was being torn in two as her emotions seesawed. Finally she couldn't stand it anymore and lurched out of the chair. She stood in front of it, shaking, tears running down her cheeks.

"Abby? Abby! What's the matter?" Brad had come back and she hadn't even heard the door.

"I don't know," she whispered.

"Is something wrong? You're crying."

Abby wiped the tears from her cheeks. Part of her yearned to turn to Brad, have him enfold her in his strong arms and comfort her. Another part of her wanted to keep quiet until she had even a vague idea of what was happening. And she knew that Brad would not understand. She took a shaky breath.

"Oh, I'm just being silly. It was so nice to see my folks, and they were so sweet to bring me the chair, and they know I love it. I'm just happy, that's all."

Brad didn't look convinced, but Abby knew that he wasn't about to delve into that "emotional stuff" if he didn't have to. "Look, I'll finish cleaning up, all right?"

"Thanks, sweetie—I appreciate it. Oh, and could you move the chair over between the windows?" No way was Abby going to try to touch it again, not right now.

"Sure." He picked it up easily and carried it across the room. "Here?" Apparently nothing happened when he touched it, as far as Abby could see. "Hey, this is a really nice piece. Wonder what it's worth?" He rubbed his hand appreciatively over the smooth wood of one of the swan heads.

"That's fine there. I think I'll go take a shower now." Abby wanted nothing more than to be alone, to try to sort out what had happened. *And I'll have to tell Ned about this. Tomorrow.* And tomorrow she was damn well going to find out who her great-grandparents had been.

Chapter 9

A bby slept without interruption—no visitations in the night, and no lingering aftermath of her confrontation with the chair. Wednesday morning she watched Brad pull on his working gear—shirt, tie, suit, lace-up shoes—and gave him a sleepy smile when he bent to kiss her good-bye.

"Have a good day, kid. I should be home early-ish."

And he was gone, bustling with self-importance. Abby lay in bed for a while, thinking. *I need to make two piles,* she decided, *one for things I know and one for things I don't know.* Even before she began, it was clear that the first one would be a lot smaller than the second one. All right, she would limit her immediate efforts to her family and let Ned deal with abstract paranormal questions. Any maybe what had happened with the chair the day before.

What did she know? Her own name, of course. Her father's name, and her mother's maiden name. Wait—wouldn't their marriage license have their parents' names on it? What about her mother's birth certificate? There must have been a father listed, and her mother must have needed her own birth record at some point—passport? Driver's license? No, that wouldn't work, because her great-grandmother, when her husband left, had made every effort to erase his name from her life, including formally changing her daughter's name to her own surname, Pendleton. She'd been very stubborn, and very thorough.

Well, at least Abby had the Pendleton name, and it was not as common as, say, Johnson or Williams. She had no idea where Ruth Pendleton had come from, but she was pretty sure it was somewhere in New England or the Mid-Atlantic states. Abby had known her great-grandmother for a few years, and she didn't remember any accent that would suggest otherwise, or any hints of mountains, prairies, horses. So that narrowed her search, sort of. Now, where could she find marriage records?

She looked at the bedside clock: 7:30. Was it too early to call Ned and tell him about the chair incident? Maybe he could see something about it that escaped her. But was it fair to turn to him? She wavered, and then decided that it was a piece of information he should have. Energized by her decision, she got out of bed and went to search for Ned's card in her purse. She dialed, and he answered on the second ring.

"Edward Newhall." His voice was abrupt and businesslike.

"Ned?" Abby said tentatively, intimidated by his brusque tone.

"Oh, Abby, hi. Sorry I was so curt—I was just on my way out the door."

"I'm sorry. I won't keep you long. But this strange thing happened last night, and I thought you should know about it—maybe it would make more sense to you than it does to me."

"Uh—can we talk later? I've got a meeting at eight and I really need to get moving. Or, how about lunch? Can you find your way back to Lexington?"

"Sure. Just tell me where and when." Abby felt a surge of relief. She hated carrying all this around inside. This was followed by a flash of guilt, since she kept dumping the problem on Ned, who really had no reason to help her, and here she was dragging him away from his work, just to make herself feel better.

"There's a place in the middle of town, near the stoplight . . ." He proceeded to give her directions. "About twelve fifteen?"

"Great. See you then."

He hung up. She hoped she wasn't going to get him in any hot water, distracting him from his job. She promised herself that she would handle the next steps on her own—whatever they turned out to be.

She spent the morning roaming around the Internet to see what she could find about Pendletons, but there was such a bewildering array of sources that she couldn't make sense of them. She arrived early at the restaurant, found a table, ordered a coffee and waited, fidgeting. Ned was late. She saw him as he came into the restaurant and looked around until he found her. He dropped into the chair opposite Abby's.

"Sorry—back-to-back meetings, and they all ran late. Why these people can't operate in something other than crisis mode, I really don't know. I'm sorry—I'll have to get back fast, but you sounded kind of spooked. Have you ordered?"

His words tumbled out in a rush, and Abby had no time to respond. Finally she shook her head. "No—a sandwich will be fine. I just wanted to fill you in on something that happened last night."

Ned flagged a passing waitress and ordered two grilled chicken sandwiches, and coffee for himself. Then he turned back to Abby. "Okay—I'm all ears."

Abby described her parents' visit and the chair they had brought. "While Brad was taking out the trash, I decided to sit down in the chair, sort of claim it. But I think it possessed me. It was like at the cemetery,

Sleepy Hollow, when I kept feeling all this sadness sort of swirling around me. But this time, it was two completely opposite emotions, joy and sadness, but they kept shifting back and forth, back and forth. There was a woman, holding a baby, and it was dying, or maybe it was two babies and one of them died and the other one was fine. It was all just fragments. But it was so strong!" Abby realized she was trembling again.

"Whoa! Slow down, take a deep breath. First of all, Brad unwrapped the chair? And he didn't notice anything?"

Abby shook her head.

"And when you sat down in it, that was the first time you touched it?"

"No, I touched it once and backed off fast. Then I pulled myself together and sat down in it. But, Ned, that chair was always at my folks' house—I've sat in it hundreds of times before, all my life."

"Whose chair was it?" He was watching her intently.

"My grandmother's, as far as I know. That's what my mother said."

"Okay." Ned sat back in his chair and stared over Abby's head. Their food arrived, and he picked up his sandwich and took a bite, chewing pensively. Finally he said, "Did your grandmother ever lose a baby?"

"Not that I know of. I could ask my mother, but I don't think so. My mom talks a lot, and I think it would have come out sometime."

"You sure it was your grandmother's chair? Did she buy it, or inherit it?"

Abby stared at him. "I don't know. It never came up. I can't ask her because she's gone now—and before you ask, she's buried in Maine. I can ask my mother, but I'm not sure she knows. You see, we grew up with this kind of strange situation: my great-grandmother got married in her twenties, and had my grandmother, and then the Depression hit and her husband ran out on her, just disappeared one day. She finally heard that he was dead, years later. She was so angry at him that she took back her maiden name, changed her daughter's name, and refused to say anything about him. Ever. So there's this big blank in our family tree, and we all grew up knowing that there were some questions we weren't supposed to ask."

"Interesting." Ned took another bite of sandwich. When he had swallowed, he said, "Okay, let me summarize what we've got so far. Up until a couple of weeks ago, you've never had anything like a psychic experience, right? No ghosts, no voices, no premonitions?"

Abby shook her head. "Never."

"And since you moved to Massachusetts, you've had four episodes, in different places, with different people. One," he counted off on his fingers, "was at the Flagg house, and apparently the people who lived there at a particular time; two, at the Waltham cemetery, with the same people but a different time; three was the cemetery yesterday, with a tombstone for some Reed family; and four was last night, with a chair that's been in your family for, what, at least fifty years? Does that cover it?"

"Yes, I think so."

"Can you think of anything that these places and things might share?"

"No." Abby suddenly felt a wash of despair. "Except for the two Flagg ones, they're all completely unrelated, as far as I know. There's no warning— I touch something and wham, there they are. I'm beginning to get scared. The first time, seeing the people in that room at the Flagg house, it was kind of interesting, once I got over the surprise. The second with Elizabeth Flagg was kind of sad, and then by the third, I was feeling the pain that a lot of people were feeling, at different times—kind of cumulative, you know? But last night it really hit me hard, when I wasn't expecting it—it was so strong." She shook her head, as if to rid it of the memory. "At this rate, I'm going to be afraid to touch anything. How am I supposed to explain to Brad why I won't go near a chair I said I loved?"

"Got me." Ned looked at his watch. "Look, Abby, I'm really sorry, but I've got to go. I know I haven't been much help, and that this is difficult for you. Did your parents have anything useful to say about the family tree?"

"We didn't really have time to talk about it, and they're driving to New Jersey today—I'm not sure how long it will be before they get back home. Or if they have anything back there that can help. For now, maybe it's easier to assume that I'm on my own, starting from scratch."

Ned nodded. "All right. Then this is what I suggest: put together a family tree. See if you can find a software program and download it—it'll make it a lot easier to keep your information straight. Then fill in everything you know. Write down all the family stories you can remember— sometimes there are clues there—dates, places, other names. Then when you know where the gaps are, start checking online resources. You can find a lot of vital records, censuses, stuff like that. But not everything—a lot of stuff isn't online yet, and some other information, like for people in the twentieth century, isn't available to the public yet. So you're probably going to run into some roadblocks. But do the best you can."

Abby was disappointed that he couldn't offer more help, but he had a job—one that did not include babysitting her. "That makes sense. At least it's something concrete that I can do."

"Great." Ned stood up and laid some bills on the table. "Sorry I've got to leave so fast, but it's a crazy day. Maybe we can get together over the weekend and see what you've got. If you want to."

"Hey, thanks for showing up at all." Abby struggled to summon up a smile. "I think I just wanted you to tell me again that I'm not insane. I'll get started on this stuff today. I don't know what our plans for the weekend are, but we can talk later."

Ned gave her one last look, then turned and headed for the door with a backward wave. Abby watched him go, then continued to sip at her now-cool coffee. Ned had given her a project, one that might keep the wolves of weirdness at bay, and which might even give her some answers. If she wanted them: too much of what she'd "seen" involved pain. It didn't make sense to go looking for pain, but then, she'd have to look just to know how to stay away from the pain. She wasn't sure there was any way she could win.

She paid for her lunch and wandered out onto the main street. There were fewer people around today, since it was a workday, and she could stop and try to visualize what it would have been like, as the redcoats, no doubt equipped with drums, marched toward the small green with their ragtag group of untrained soldiers. Why the heck couldn't she "see" interesting historic events like that, instead of being blindsided by tombstones and furniture? What was triggering these episodes? And why her, why now?

The only thing she could do was to go back and build a family tree, as Ned had suggested. Did he have a theory about this? She'd have to ask, the next time they met. Soon.

Chapter 10

A bby drove back to Waltham in a pensive mood. When she entered the empty apartment, she cast a wary eye at the swan chair. It didn't do anything—didn't send out sparks, or start rocking mysteriously. It looked just the way it always had, sleek and modestly elegant, its aged wood polished by years of loving hands, her own included. Abby sighed and turned to the computer. She was using Brad's old laptop, since he had graduated to a sleeker and faster tablet. It was set up on a table in the already-crowded living room. Abby didn't mind: she was more familiar with the older model anyway. She booted it up and waited for the apartment building's Wi-Fi to kick in.

Two hours later her head was spinning. Following Ned's suggestion, she had done a search on genealogy programs and had quickly been overwhelmed. They offered to insert photographs of all her loved ones, and print books for her. They even suggested including voice recordings of oral histories. All she wanted was a simple outline program that she could stick names and dates into and be able to turn out a basic family tree. Finally she settled on one that appeared to be relatively no-frills and, ignoring the much-trumpeted add-ons (for an extra fee), she put in her credit card number and waited for the program to download and install. When it had, she opened it to a blank form.

Where to start? With herself, she guessed. Name, birth date, birth place. Parents' names. Then she stopped. She knew their birthdays, from twenty-plus years of cakes and presents, but she wasn't quite sure which years they were born, and she knew her mother had a tendency to shave a bit off her age. And where? She couldn't even swear to the towns, but she put in the states. For her grandparents her information was even less complete. After half an hour or so, she printed out a basic skeleton report with her three generations, and looking at it, felt depressed. There were so many empty spaces and question marks. How was she supposed to take this back any further?

She sat back and stretched, easing her stiff back. The apartment was quiet, as was the entire building—most people were at work and wouldn't be coming home for another hour or so. The swan chair sat silently behind her, waiting . . . Should she see if last night had been a fluke, a hallucination, or find out whether the chair was really trying to tell her something? She almost laughed at that idea—the chair was trying to communicate? Ridiculous.

Or was the chair just a conduit for something—someone—else? *Come on, Abby, grow a spine, will you?* She stood up resolutely and walked over to stand in front of the chair, looking down at it. It was lovely. The years of hands sliding over the arms had lent a rich patina to the carvings. Maybe that was why she'd always loved it—because it gave her the sense that people had been sitting in it for a long time, and she was the latest of a long line. That idea had never frightened her, until now.

What had happened yesterday? She touched the chair and immediately she had been overwhelmed by . . . She wasn't sure what. *All right, Abby, try to put it into words.* She would have to say that it had been a combination of emotions and images. She shut her eyes to reconstruct it. The images first, because they were easier. She, or that other person, had been sitting in the chair. In her arms there had been a child, no more than a year old. Abby couldn't remember anything noteworthy about what the woman or the child had been wearing. No, that wasn't exactly true: the baby had been wearing a long white cotton gown. Not a terry-cloth onesie and disposable diaper, that was clear. So, it wasn't a modern baby. She hadn't thought it was, somehow.

Boy or girl? That hadn't been obvious either. Or—Abby recalled saying to Ned that maybe it had been two different babies, which would explain why she had such a muddled idea of its gender. One boy, one girl? And one dying or dead. Which? Why? But if one had lived and one had died, that would explain the wild mix of emotions that had swept over Abby as she took the seat: joy *and* sorrow, mixed, overlapping, all at once. It made a strange kind of sense.

So, Abby thought, *I seem to be saying that it's one woman sitting in this chair at different times, with two different babies.* And one child lived and the other died. Who were they? Would she know if she sat in the woman's place again? There was only one way to find out. Abby took a deep breath, turned around and gingerly sat down. She carefully laid her hands over the graceful swan heads and braced herself for the onslaught.

Which didn't come. Cautiously she relaxed into the seat, tried to loosen her muscles, empty her mind. And only then did she catch an echo of what she had experienced the day before. Before, she had been in the midst of the storm; today she felt as though she were looking through a cloud. She could tell that she was looking *through* the woman, because she was seeing

61

the baby through the woman's eyes. One baby cooed and waved its little arms; and then as though a slide had been changed, it was the other baby, whose small chest rose and fell in labored breathing, until it stopped breathing at all. And Abby felt the pain again, but as a soft sweet ache. For this baby had died a long time ago, as had its mother. Only the sadness lingered.

Abby didn't know how long she sat there, her mind catching at wisps of the memory as it faded quietly and then was gone. It wasn't her pain—thank God. But she felt the mother's pain, loss, helplessness, as the baby slipped into death. Nothing to be done, not then, not now.

Why was she feeling this now? Rocking slightly, Abby thought about it. It was as though somehow the chair had picked up an electrical charge from the event, or series of events, and stored it, and had only now discharged that energy to Abby. As a child of the computer era, she found it made a sort of sense to her. What were programs, emails, pictures on-screen, other than a complicated cluster of electrical impulses? The brain somehow recorded memories through electrical changes in cells, didn't it? Couldn't she extend that logic to say that what she was picking up and feeling were just saved images? That somehow, this particular group of impulses or memories had been held, perfectly preserved, until Abby had somehow inadvertently called them up? Abby shook her head. She didn't have the technical terminology to explain it clearly, but intuitively it made sense—to her, at least. Maybe not to anyone else—but then, other people hadn't lived inside the event, hadn't "felt" it, the way she had. Did this happen to other people? She had never seen any kind of reference to it, even in the popular media, but then, she'd never looked for it either.

Now the memory was gone, the charge, if that was what it was, dissipated, dispersed. Abby now felt only the comfort of the familiar chair, its old wood satiny beneath her hands. Maybe she'd exorcized the demons, or maybe she'd just absorbed them, but it was safe to sit here again. She rocked. *Good for you, Abby,* she congratulated herself—*you faced down your fears. Maybe you haven't solved anything, but at least you've learned something.* The thought energized her. Time to get up, time to start dinner. Brad had promised to be home "early-ish," which for him probably meant seven. She stood up and then an idea struck her.

She knelt in front of the chair, then lay full length, and stuck her head under it. There was an old paper label stuck to the inside of the frame. Abby twisted and turned until she could read the faded print. It was the maker's label, some furniture store in . . . yes, Massachusetts. And it had a date stamped on it. She strained to decipher it: 1892. Older than she had thought. Older than her grandmother, certainly. Interesting. One more thing to think about.

• • •

Saturday evening Abby reluctantly agreed to accompany Brad to a party she didn't want to attend.

"Brad, do we have to go?" Abby knew she sounded like a whiny child, but she couldn't stop herself. She wasn't even sure why. She should have jumped at the opportunity to spend a night out in the city with Brad. Shouldn't she?

"Hey, babe, we haven't seen the gang in, what, a month? You need to get out more. Besides, it'll be fun." He was rummaging through his closet, trying to find a shirt.

They had been invited to a party thrown by one of Brad's new friends, and Brad was really excited about it. Abby had met all of them before, singly and in groups, in the time they'd been here, but she still couldn't tell them apart. All the men were much like Brad—young, attractive, ambitious. Taken as a group, they reminded her of a bunch of high school football players, which they probably all had been. All alpha males. She knew they had to be smart: they had all gone to name schools and had all fought for the coveted entry-level slots in their prestigious banking firm. But most of their conversation was dominated either by sports or by the minutiae of deals they were working on, neither of which interested Abby. She wondered if they ever read a book, saw a play, visited a museum. She had no idea what to say to any of them.

Not that she fared any better with the women. She'd met most of them too, and heard more about them from Brad. They all did something important and productive. As she pulled on a cowl-necked sweater and zipped up her good black wool pants, Abby wondered idly how Brad described her to his cronies. Former schoolteacher, foundation flunky. No, he wouldn't put it like that, because that wouldn't make him look good. "Oh, Abby's in educational management, funding resources, that sort of thing." She could almost hear him saying it. Problem was, tonight she was going to talk to all these people face-to-face, and she couldn't glibly toss off all those tidy phrases the way Brad could. But she couldn't stay home either.

The party was being held at a town house on Beacon Hill. "Isn't that kind of expensive?" Abby ventured timidly as they drove over dark streets toward the heart of Boston.

"Bill's folks helped out with the down payment, and Nancy's making pretty good money." Brad concentrated on navigating the narrow one-way streets on Beacon Hill, searching for a parking place.

Unfortunately neither Abby's nor Brad's parents had offered that kind of assistance, and Abby wasn't bringing in anything right now, much less "good money." *Don't start, Abby.*

She tried to say something cheerful. "This neighborhood's so pretty at night—all the lights glowing in the windows. So who's going to be there tonight?"

Brad muttered a curse as a quicker driver darted into an impossibly small parking space in front of him. "Just the guys, and some friends. Don't worry—it'll be fun. Ah!" He executed a deft maneuver and shoehorned their car into a parking space. "Only three blocks away!"

Brad led the way to Bill's house, Abby trailing behind, stumbling on the uneven brick sidewalks, made more slippery by fallen leaves. "Brad, slow down! I can't keep up in thesc heels."

He looked back as if surprised to see her, trailing behind like a clumsy puppy. "Oh, sorry." He waited, then extended his elbow to her in a mock-courtly gesture. Whatever the intent, Abby was glad to slip her arm through his. He felt large and warm and steady. They covered the last block at a more decorous pace and stopped in front of a tall, slender brick building. Abby could see a crowd of people standing around in the parlor through the bow-front windows facing the street. When the door opened, a gush of chatter billowed out.

"Yo, Brad, you made it. Hi, Abby. Come on in." Bill welcomed them, then stood back and let Abby pass, then punched Brad on the arm as he followed her. "Hey, pal, did you see the Penn State game today?" And the men were off, exchanging details about plays and coaches.

Abby slipped out of her jacket and looked around for a place to put it. There was a heap of coats on the stairs, so she added hers to the pile, then, summoning her courage, headed for the noise and light. She paused for a moment in the doorway, looking for an opening. Some faces she recognized, others were new to her. Everybody looked smart and thin and vivacious, talking eagerly, gesturing widely, laughing. They made Abby feel small and pale to the point of invisibility. *Like a ghost,* she thought. *I'm here, but I'm not here.* This would not do. Maybe Brad was right: maybe she'd just been spending too much time by herself, with no one to talk to. Maybe she just needed to practice her people skills more. Maybe her next best friend was somewhere in this room. She squared her shoulders and marched in.

There was an informal bar set up on the far side of the room, and Abby waded through the crowd and helped herself to a glass of wine. Sipping, she studied the people. They looked just the way they should: confident, happy, energetic. Everything she was not. She spied a woman approaching her. Abby knew she'd met her; what was her name? Susan? Sally?

"Hi. Abby, right? I'm Shanna—we met at the office, a month or so ago. You're with Brad."

"Yes, hi, and yes." Abby could never think how to phrase personal questions politely. She knew Shanna was in some kind of relationship with Rich, but she wasn't sure what; she had the vague feeling that "what do you do" was both dated and politically incorrect, but wasn't sure what had replaced it. Thank goodness Shanna didn't notice Abby's confusion.

"So, how're you settling in?"

"Fine, I think—it's all new to me, so I've got lots to explore."

"You're out in the suburbs somewhere, right?"

"Yes—Waltham."

"Oh, yeah, right." Shanna dismissed Waltham with a contemptuous sniff. "Brad said you were looking for a job? What're you looking for?"

"I'm not sure—I taught elementary school for a couple of years, and then I worked for a foundation. I haven't quite figured out where to start. Did Brad say you were at the art museum?" Abby couldn't for the life of her remember what Shanna was supposed to be doing there—taking tickets? Restoring paintings? Running the place?

"Yes—curatorial assistant. I have a degree in art history, so I'm a happy camper. Busy place these days, what with all the expansion plans—they're probably going to be looking for help on the fund-raising staff. If you're interested, I could ask around."

Abby plastered on a smile. "Sure, that would be great." Heck, she liked museums, and she'd heard Boston had a good one, not that she'd seen it yet. Brad didn't like to waste precious football time going to museums. "What does a curatorial assistant do?" She pitched the softball to Shanna and watched her run with it. *Oops, Abby, mixed metaphor.* But in any case, Shanna looked very enthusiastic about it. Abby wondered what it would take to feel that same rush herself. Shanna waved to some other people in the room, who came over to join them. They all knew each other, and gradually Abby came to feel invisible again. They were all talking about people and places she didn't know, great restaurants in the city or Cambridge, a terrific new Belgian movie that was playing only in obscure art houses. How was she supposed to get to know them? Chicken and egg problem—she couldn't share interests with other people until they shared theirs with her. But she kept on smiling, and nodding, and pretending very hard that she belonged with these bright happy people. Maybe it would rub off.

Sometime after one o'clock, Brad made his slightly unsteady way over to the corner where Abby had spent the last half hour trapped in conversation with someone whose name she had long since forgotten, but who had insisted on regaling her with the entire history of the software industry in Massachusetts. Abby's eyes had glazed over after the first fifteen minutes, but her companion hadn't noticed. Indeed, he was still warming to his theme.

"Hey, babe. Time to head for the 'burbs," Brad said, after a contemptuous glance at her captor.

"Fine. Let me get my coat. Sorry I can't stay to hear about . . ." Abby noticed that Mr. Software had already moved on to another unwitting audience.

Outside the night air was cool and crisp. Almost October now, and Abby could feel winter lurking. She wondered where she had packed her winter coat. She looked down at the sidewalks. "These must be nasty when they get icy."

"Huh?" Brad seemed lost in his own thoughts. "Oh, yeah, I guess. Nice neighborhood, though. Wonder what a place around here goes for?" He seemed to see her for the first time since they'd left the party. "Hey, have a good time? I saw you talking with Shanna."

"Yes, she came over and introduced herself. She said she might know about some jobs at the museum."

"Great. You'd like that." It wasn't a question. As though he knew anything about museum management.

Abby sighed. What was it about these people that drained all the color out of her? They *were* nice people—smart, hardworking. Some of them had even made an effort to talk to her, to include her in their conversations. She had nothing to complain about—except herself. It was her own fault if she didn't fit in with them.

"Maybe. I'll give her a call next week, to follow up."

"Great idea."

Riding home through the half-empty streets, Abby wondered: what *did* she want to do? Was it worth it to make the effort to fit into Brad's gang of friends? There was nothing wrong with them—but they were wrong for her. But what did that say about Brad, and why he and she were together? She shook her head. It was late, she was tired. Things would look better in the morning.

Chapter 11

Brad and Abby slept in on Sunday morning and then pottered companionably for a while, reading the paper, making and clearing up breakfast. Abby was sorting laundry in the bedroom when Brad came in and started putting on his jeans.

"Going somewhere?" she asked.

"Rich wanted to get together and watch the game at his place—I thought I mentioned that last night. We didn't have anything planned, did we?"

Abby didn't know if she felt disappointed or relieved. "No, nothing in particular. That's fine. I've got stuff to keep me busy. You will be home for dinner, though? Or at least give me a call if you're going to be late." *Again,* she added to herself.

"Sure. The later match-ups suck, anyway." He whistled to himself as he pulled on a sweatshirt, ran a comb through his hair, and filled his pockets with keys, change, and other guy stuff. "See ya later." Abby heard the door slam, and he was gone.

Up to her elbows in dirty laundry, Abby wondered if she was supposed to be annoyed. No, she didn't want to go watch football with the guys, but it would have been nice if Brad had at least asked if she had anything in mind for the day. They spent very little time together during the week. Well, they had been to the party last night—but that was Brad's friends, the ones he saw at work. On the other hand, she had no friends. *Cut the pity, Abby. You've got things to do—like working on that genealogy.*

She needed to call her mother and decided to do it before she lost the impulse. She was happy to find that her parents had returned to Maine from their trip to New Jersey. Abby made the necessary chitchat, and then got to the point.

"Mom? You remember we were talking about family history stuff, when you were here? And I asked if you could look for anything you've got?"

"Oh, that's right, you did. But we've still got to unpack from the trip, and then I've got to clean this place up, and do some laundry . . . How about this? Let me take a look in the attic tomorrow, see what there is, and if I find anything, I'll send it to you."

"Fine, Mom." Abby sighed with resignation. It was the best she could hope for at the moment. "Let me know when you stick it in the mail—I'll keep an eye out for it."

"Okay, sweetie. Now, tell me all about what you've been doing. And how's Brad? He's always so sweet to me, such a nice boy . . ."

It took Abby another fifteen minutes to get off the phone, after she'd assured her mother that she was fine, Brad was fine, they'd been to a nice party, and everything was hunky-dory. Which was not exactly a lie: it was as hunky-dory as it ever was. Only that wasn't very. With another sigh, Abby turned back to finish sorting laundry, and then the phone rang.

"Abby? It's Ned."

"Oh, hi." Finally, a friendly voice.

"I just wondered what luck you'd had with finding that software we'd talked about, and if you'd made any progress?"

Shifting mental gears, Abby found she could respond with some enthusiasm. "Yes—I did find a program and downloaded it and filled in what I knew. But then I looked at the results and realized how little information I had. I just asked my mother to look for anything she's got at home, but I don't expect a whole lot. She's a real dynamo and loves to clean things out. Which means that a lot of stuff gets thrown out, if she doesn't think it's important." *Including half the relics of my childhood*, thought Abby ruefully. Ah, well, water under the bridge. She could only hope that her mother had some respect for legal and personal documents. "She might get it to me this week—if I'm lucky."

"That's a good sign. Well, I'll let you get back to what you were doing . . ."

"Not much," Abby muttered.

"What?"

She hadn't realized she had spoken out loud. "Oh, I just said I'm not doing much. Brad went to watch football with his buddies, and I've just been cleaning up." God, she sounded pathetic. And did it sound as though she was fishing for an invitation? She felt a flurry of panic.

Ned didn't seem to notice. "You up for some more sightseeing? I've got some errands down your way—I'd be happy to show you a bit more of the area."

Did he mean it, or was he just being polite? Did she sound that wretched? "Well, I don't want to bother you, if you've got things to do."

"Nonsense," he said firmly. "I love showing off my home state. And we can talk about your next research steps, if you want."

"Okay. What time?"

"Say, two? I'll stop by and pick you up, if that's all right."

"That would be great. See you then." Abby hung up the phone

decisively, before she could change her mind. Well, if Brad could go play with his friends, she could play with hers. And Ned was a friend. That was nice to think about—she did actually have a friend of her own.

She'd finished the laundry and was sorting through her notes and the pathetically spindly family tree she'd put together when she heard Ned's knock. Quickly she gathered up a jacket, her purse, and her notes, and opened the door.

"Hi," she said, slightly breathlessly. She held up her pile of papers. "I thought I'd bring these along, if you don't mind. I want to be sure I'm doing things right, before I get hopelessly entangled."

"Not a problem." Ned waited while she locked the door behind her. "I'm parked out front."

"Where are we going today?"

"Well, I thought we could head out toward Wellesley—there's a coffee place there that roasts its own beans, and I like to stop there when I can and stock up. Have you ever seen the college campus?"

"No, but of course I know about it. I went to Swarthmore." In what seemed like another lifetime.

"You'll probably see some similarities, although the Wellesley campus is bigger . . ."

They chatted amiably on the way. It took no more than half an hour to reach the town of Wellesley. Abby fell silent as they crossed the Charles River and passed through Newton Lower Falls.

"Penny?"

Abby jumped when he spoke. "What? Oh. I was just looking at the town. Is that the Charles River we just crossed? The same one as in Cambridge?"

Ned nodded cheerfully. "One and the same. It's a little smaller here."

They followed train tracks into the town of Wellesley, passing an imposing Victorian town hall as they came in. Ned drove through the town, and on the far side turned into the college campus and slowly drove through it. Abby admired the great open spaces and the soaring Gothic buildings, interspersed with more modern additions, including a much newer building on a hill.

"It certainly looks . . . collegiate, doesn't it? Except for that thing."

Ned laughed. "Yes, it does, and if you're wondering, that's the Science Center. And Frederick Law Olmsted designed this campus. He was a busy man."

They reached the far edge of the campus and turned back toward town.

Ned pulled into a small parking lot in front of the coffee store. "Want to come in, have a cup of coffee?"

"Sure." Abby opened her door and climbed out, and he guided her inside. On a Sunday afternoon, the coffeehouse was only half filled, with a mix of students and townspeople. Abby looked around and sniffed appreciatively. The place was filled with blond wood, rich dark colors, and the heady scent of coffee beans. They found an empty table by the front window and Ned went up to the counter to order their coffees, adding a couple of cookies at the last minute.

When he returned he set them on the table. "There. Now we've staked our claim to the table. Show me what you've got."

"I feel embarrassed, it's so little." She spread out her few pages so he could see them.

"No, don't apologize. Everyone has to start somewhere. You picked a good program—it's pretty flexible, and it usually prompts you if you're trying to put in something ridiculous, like a baby born five years after his father died. Not that it hasn't been known to happen." Ned flashed her a grin.

Abby sipped her coffee approvingly. It was good—black and strong.

Ned's voice broke into her thoughts. "So, what do you need to do next?"

She studied the sheets. "Push it back, one generation at a time, right? There has to be some record of my grandmother's birth, or of her parents' marriage. And I may as well start with Massachusetts. Oh, and I found out something about the chair."

"The one . . . ?"

"Yes. Well, let me tell you first about what happened when I sat in it again. It was like the first time, only very, I don't know, diluted. I mean, I saw the same things, but it wasn't anywhere near as intense. It was a whole lot easier to handle. And then, while I was sitting there, it just sort of faded. I'm not sure that's exactly the right way to describe it, but it stopped, and there I was, just me, sitting in the chair. But that's not what I wanted to tell you. I looked under the chair, and it was made in Massachusetts, in 1892— there was a label. That was before my grandmother was even born. So I'm wondering if maybe it was my great-grandmother's."

"Interesting." Ned seemed impressed. "So Massachusetts would be a good starting point." He stopped for a moment. "There was something else I wanted to ask you about."

Abby looked at him curiously. "About my family?"

"No," he laughed, "about the here and now. Didn't you tell me you were looking for a job?"

Abby nodded. "Yes, I guess so. I haven't figured out what I want to do, but I should start doing something soon. Why?"

"Well, a friend of mine works at the Concord Museum—you remember, we went by it the other day. It's just down the road from the Alcott house. Anyway, one of the staff there quit suddenly—medical reasons, I gather, but it was unexpected. So they're looking for someone to step in quickly."

"What's the job?" Abby said dubiously. "I don't have any museum experience."

"That's not a problem—it's the coordinator for the school programs and educational outreach. You've taught, right? And you've done some nonprofit administrative work. You'd be fine. So what do you think?"

Abby was impressed. Not only had Ned paid attention when she'd given her brief life history, but he recognized that her background was a good fit. "It sounds great! What should I do?"

"Give Leslie a call tomorrow—here's her number." He handed her a card with a phone number scrawled on the back. "I'll tell her to expect to hear from you. If that's all right? I don't want to push you into anything, if you're not ready to go back to work."

"No, this is wonderful. It sounds perfect. I *will* call her. And, Ned? Thank you."

He looked abashed. "Just trying to help. If it works out, Leslie will owe me big-time. Are you finished with your coffee?"

Abby looked down. Her cup did seem to be empty. "I guess I am."

They walked out into the sharp October air. The sky had darkened since they entered and the chill wind whisked dry leaves in aimless circles on the road. Abby stopped abruptly outside the door and stared across the street. There was a cemetery there.

Ned had gone ahead to unlock the car but turned to see her standing, frozen. "Abby? What is it?"

"Can we go look at that cemetery? If you don't mind?"

"Sure. I never turn down a good cemetery. Why?"

She didn't answer. With deliberation, she crossed the main street at the crosswalk and climbed up over the low stone retaining wall into the cemetery, Ned following close behind her. She stood for a moment, reconnoitering. The church at the far side was clearly twentieth-century, but the stones that lay in front of her were old, many eighteenth-century, with a few Victorian monuments scattered throughout. The burials were arrayed in untidy rows, not quite parallel to the church. She started walking slowly, toward the middle of the small cemetery. She stopped in front of a row of stones and hesitated a moment. She looked back over her shoulder at Ned, who was watching her with questions in his eyes. He didn't speak, and she turned back and moved forward, reaching out a hand to touch the tallest slate stone. She shut her eyes.

The world dissolved into gray. The modern church was gone, but there was a much smaller wooden building in the corner, and the land around the cemetery was open. But the rows of stones were there, or at least parts of them, and swirling around them were people, layered again as she had seen in Concord. Many people—men, women, children. There was a silent noise in her head, as though all the voices of those people had blended together to create an echoing white din. Across time. These people had died a long time ago.

Abby opened her eyes. Once again her face was wet with tears. Ned moved closer to her and laid a hand on her arm. "Look," he said, pointing to the stone.

For the first time, she read the inscription. *Erected in memory of Deacon Samuel Reed who died June 16th 1807 in his 56th year.*

"Are you all right?"

Ned's voice was so kind. She really had to stop crying. She nodded, since she was having trouble speaking. "It's another Reed," she whispered.

"Then I think we need to know more about the Reed family, don't you? That's the same name as at Concord."

Abby hadn't realized that she'd been holding her breath, but she let it out now with a sigh. "Yes, it is." She looked around and found several other Reeds nearby, in the same row, and in another not far away. "I seem to have some sort of connection with these people," she said, surprised to find that her voice was shaky.

"I think you're right. And maybe that will help you—you can take these names and work forward, and maybe that will tell you something."

"Oh, right. Then I'd better get the details." She pulled a small notebook from her purse and jotted down the names and dates, and then sketched out the relative locations of the tombstones—who lay next to whom. By the time she was done, she felt steadier. Maybe she was getting used to being swamped by ghosts.

That word stopped her. These weren't ghosts. They still didn't see her. She'd prefer to say that these were real people she was seeing, only from the past. How, and why? She had no idea, yet here she was, standing in a cemetery, and she was surrounded by them. This was getting a bit too bizarre.

Ned's voice broke into her thoughts. "Ready to go? You look cold."

"I guess I am."

Ned took her arm again as they crossed the street and helped her into the car. When he was seated, she turned toward him.

"You don't see anything, do you?"

"I believe that you do."

"I wish I knew why. Why me? Why now, why here? It doesn't make any sense."

"Have patience. There's more you can find out. And I'm glad you're not trying to shut out . . . whatever this is."

"I'm not so sure I'm glad. I didn't ask for this." Abby fell silent, and remained silent most of the trip back to Waltham. Ned didn't interrupt her thoughts. It was not until they pulled into her parking lot that she roused herself to speak.

"Thank you, again."

"For what?"

"Well, for the job lead, for starters. But for . . . well, for being there. I don't know what I'd do if I didn't have someone to bounce this off of." Brad would be useless, she knew.

He looked at her for a moment. "I'm happy to help. Look, give me a call after you've talked to Leslie and let me know how it goes, all right? And let me know if you find anything interesting about the Reeds."

She watched him leave. *You'll be the first to know, Ned,* she said to herself. *And quite possibly the only one.* She turned to go up to the apartment.

Chapter 12

B rad had come home in time for a reasonable dinner, pumped up both by the game he had watched in the testosterone-rich atmosphere of Rich's bachelor apartment (Shanna having apparently opted to find something else to do) and by his incredible thoughtfulness at remembering Abby's request to be home early. She had decided once again not to mention her excursion with Ned, not that there was anything suspect about it, but because Brad would probably find some way to misconstrue it. Since things were going nicely and Abby wanted to keep them that way, saying nothing was the safest course. Time enough to fill him in when she figured out what these bizarre visitations were, or if anything came of this possible job lead that had materialized out of thin air.

She called Leslie Monday morning. She wondered whether she should call first thing and catch Leslie before she was fully engaged in her day, doing . . . whatever it was she did; or give her time to settle into her regular Monday routine. In the end, she opted for a compromise, and called at 9:37. Leslie answered on the second ring.

"Leslie Walker." The voice was slightly breathless.

"Uh, hello? This is Abigail Kimball. Ned Newhall suggested that I call you about a possible job?"

"Right, yeah. What time can you be here?"

"You mean today?"

"Yes. How about . . . no, I've got a meeting . . . can't do three . . . how about four o'clock?"

Abby swallowed. "Fine. Where will I find you?"

"You know where we are? Look at a map. Stop at the desk in the lobby— they'll know where I am. Four o'clock." She hung up before Abby could say anything, much less protest.

Apparently she had a job interview. She knew roughly where the museum was. Now all she had to do was fill the next five hours or so, without driving herself into a state of total dither. Back to the computer, then. She printed out a fresh copy of her résumé and then returned to the elusive genealogy, which was proving to be a wonderful way to eat up time. Who were the Flaggs? The Reeds? And why were they drawing her in, all over the place?

It seemed that the next time she looked up it was nearly three, and she needed to shower and change if she was going to be on time for her meeting with Leslie.

She made it to the museum in Concord with five minutes to spare, and then had to wait in the lobby. She hadn't seen the inside of the museum before, although she had noted the discreet sign when Ned had driven her past it. What she could see from her bench in the lobby pleased her: lots of light and air, and modern exhibit cases that made her itch to go exploring. Later, maybe—if she was lucky.

Leslie Walker finally emerged from somewhere backstairs, issuing apologies before she was ten feet from Abby.

"You must be Abby. I'm so sorry, everything just keeps piling up, and I've been falling behind since I got out of bed this morning. Oh, I'm Leslie, obviously. Follow me."

Abby had not yet managed to say a word. She followed Leslie obediently, taking in her unruly blond hair, the handsome suit that hugged her generous curves, and the scuffed leather shoes. It was as though Leslie was fraying in all directions, just a little. She led Abby through an unmarked door, up a set of stairs, turned, turned again, and then threw open another door—apparently her office. She threaded her way through the piles of books, artifacts, posters, extra shoes, and general office supplies to throw herself into the protesting chair behind the scarred wooden desk. "Here, sit. Oh, sorry, that chair's sort of buried—just put the junk on the floor, there."

Abby managed to clear enough space to sit. She stared at the dynamo in front of her. Leslie returned her stare, frankly appraising her. "So, what do you know?" Leslie asked.

"What? You mean about the job? Ned just said someone had left unexpectedly and you needed some help, and he thought my qualifications might fit. Maybe you should start at the beginning?"

"I wish I had the time. Okay, short version: my director of education just found out she has breast cancer, and she's freaked. I think she'd do better staying on the job, keeping busy, but she wants to go smell the roses while she can, and I gave her my blessing. Which leaves me at the start of the school year with no one to manage the school programs. Ned said you have teaching experience?"

"Uh, yes, two years in the Philadelphia school system. Then a year at a foundation in Philadelphia."

"You like it?"

"Teaching? Yes. I taught first grade—the kids were great, but the system was a mess. Like any big-city school district."

"Why'd you leave?"

"My, uh, boyfriend got a good job offer up here, and I decided to come with him. I wasn't exactly on a fast career track where I was, and I've always been curious about Boston."

"Huh. What's your undergrad degree in?"

"English. At Swarthmore."

Leslie gave a discreet snort. "Look, here's the bottom line. You look decent, responsible—although I'm not sure I'd recognize a serial killer if I met one. I need somebody like yesterday. The calendar for the fall term is all set up, but I need someone to stand up in front of the school groups and give the patter about history, the Revolution, all those literary types in Concord, that kind of thing. We've got some good canned texts to work from, so you wouldn't have to reinvent the wheel, but you could tailor them later if you wanted, once you get comfortable. Assuming you last a week— but then, I guess you know about the energy levels of a busload of kids on a field trip, right? You want to give it a shot?"

"Yes." The answer was out of her mouth before Abby had time to think, but she realized that she meant it.

Leslie beamed. "Great. Look, I've got someone lined up to cover tomorrow's sessions, but you could come by, get comfortable with the collections and the layout here, and watch the run-through. Could you start day after tomorrow?"

"Uh, sure." Things were moving very fast, Abby thought.

"Oh, yeah, details. The pay sucks"—she mentioned a number so low that Abby had to stop herself from laughing—"the benefits are lousy, but we've got a really great group of people here, good volunteers, and a supportive board. And it's a nice town to work in, if you beat the rush-hour traffic. You'll figure it out. Hey, look, I'm thrilled that you're willing to give it a shot. If it doesn't work out, you can walk away, sadder but wiser. But I think you'll be fine. Welcome aboard." With that, Leslie stood up and extended her hand. Abby took it and they shook.

Three minutes later Abby found herself in the small parking lot adjacent to the museum. She felt completely bewildered. What had just happened? Well, apparently she had a job. A real job. Just like that. And she had Ned to thank for it. And maybe, she thought, casting a glance over her shoulder toward the other end of town, those Reeds in the cemetery there.

Somebody was looking out for her, anyway. Could the dead Reeds pull strings?

Driving home, she realized that she knew very little about what she was getting into—she hadn't asked a lot of questions. Who did she report to? Leslie, or someone else? What was Leslie's position? What time was she supposed to show up? Still, even with all these questions buzzing in her head, she felt good. Maybe thinking and planning were much overrated and she was just supposed to "go with the flow" here. Besides, the place had a good feel to it. *Hold it, Abby—are you relying on intuition here?* Well, it was as good as anything else she'd tried. And she'd have something to tell Brad. He'd be pleased . . . providing his dinner appeared on time. Although maybe she should inflate the salary, just a little, for now. Abby looked at the clock in the car and accelerated cautiously.

Leslie had been right about rush hour in Concord, and the roads were crowded, although most people were coming out from Boston rather than heading in her direction. Driving back to Waltham, Abby tried to figure out what to tell Brad. She'd found a job. Plus. Was it sufficiently impressive to compete with all the lady friends of his work buddies? Minus, maybe. Would he get on her case about making such a snap decision, without doing a lot of research and planning? Or consulting him? Double minus there. And how on earth was she supposed to explain how she had heard about it and come to interview for it without even telling him first? She'd have to say something about Ned, and the fact that she'd seen him again, but she wasn't sure what.

She bounced from one mood to another. Heck, if it didn't work out, Leslie had said she could just walk away, right? What was the downside? Somebody else had done all the work of setting the programs up, or at least that's what Leslie had told her. All Abby had to do was walk in and take over. Oh, God, what had she been thinking? She couldn't run anything. Would Brad step up to the plate and tell her she could handle it easily? Sometimes she wondered what he really did think of her and her professional abilities. He certainly hadn't held her teaching job in very high regard, even though she'd been happy doing it. She'd gone along when he had told her about that foundation position that he had scouted out for her, which paid better. But she hadn't enjoyed it nearly as much as teaching. She sighed and realized she was already home, with nothing resolved in her head.

She was putting a meat loaf in the oven when Brad walked in. He gave her a squeeze as he passed her on the way to the refrigerator to get a beer. With the beer in hand, he disappeared toward the bedroom to change into his at-home clothes. Abby still hadn't decided how to tell him her news, but decided to wait until they were sitting down at dinner, so she could talk to him face-to-face. That bought her another half hour's reprieve. She set the table, digging out some candles, trying to make things nice. She could hear the sound of the television in the next room as Brad checked the sports news.

Half an hour later she surveyed her handiwork. Food on the table, candles lit. She turned off the overhead light and called out, "Brad? Dinner's ready." She poured herself a glass of wine and sat down.

Brad came in pumped up about something he'd seen on the news. Abby listened with half an ear as she dished up dinner. She smiled and nodded, thinking that she resembled a geisha. She waited patiently for Brad's monologue to subside so she could find an opening for her announcement. Finally he slowed down, but only so that he could chew.

"Brad? I think I've got a job."

It took a moment for her statement to sink in. "What? Hey, that's great. Did you talk to Shanna?"

"No, this is at the Concord Museum, working with school programs."

"Sounds up your alley. How'd you hear about it?"

Here we go, Abby thought. "You remember Ned, the guy who gave me the tour last week? He knows one of the people at the museum, and she told him that someone had left there suddenly and she really needed someone fast, and Ned remembered that I'd said I used to teach, and he gave me her number, and I called her . . ." Abby realized she sounded like a runaway train and really ought to take a breath. She also realized that Brad was staring at her.

"Whoa, babe. When did this happen? You didn't say anything about it over the weekend."

"Well, I saw Ned yesterday, and that's when he told me about the job."

"Yesterday?"

"Yes, while you were off watching television with the guys."

There was a moment of silence. Abby braced herself for Brad's response and watched his face. She could almost outline the thoughts that passed through his head. *Hmmm . . . another guy . . . should I be jealous? Nah, I saw him . . . nothing to worry about there—a real nerd. Job status . . . museum is good, Concord's a nice place, but more towheaded kiddies? Can't pay much . . .*

"What's it pay?"

Abby almost smiled—she'd nailed it. But then she realized she had to answer him. When she told him the truth, she knew he would argue. "Jeez, Abby, that'll barely cover your gas. I'm sure you could do better in the city, and you wouldn't have to work with kids."

"Brad, I like working with children," she said quietly but firmly.

"But some nowhere museum? Why didn't you talk to me first?"

She cocked her head at him. "Why, so you could talk me out of it? Look, I like Concord, it's a nice museum, and Leslie and I hit it off. It felt right to me. I'm the one who'll be working there, so it's my decision."

Brad stared at her as though she had grown a second head. The silence spun out for several seconds, and Abby had to restrain herself from rushing in to fill it with apologies.

Finally he said coldly, "Well, you might as well play out the hand, see how you like it. It'll give you something to do, instead of just sitting here bouncing off the walls. Speaking of walls, Bill was really pissed about the new office layout . . ." And Brad was off on some anecdote. Abby's momentous news had been examined and filed, probably in a folder marked "Irrelevant to Brad." Abby found she was both relieved and disappointed. She would like to have talked a bit more about Leslie, her first impressions of the museum, what it would be like to teach history on the very town where it had happened, but obviously Brad wasn't interested. Oh, well, there would be other opportunities. She listened with one ear to his convoluted story while thinking about what to wear tomorrow. And, oh yes, telling Ned. Should she call him tonight? That way Brad would be sure to see that everything was aboveboard with him. But then she couldn't say anything about her genealogy research. Then she remembered that it was Monday, and there would be football, and Brad would be oblivious. She could call Ned after the game started.

Predictably Brad was ensconced in his favorite chair before nine, ready for kickoff. Abby retreated to the bedroom to make her call. No one answered, until the recording came on. As she listened to the brief message, she tried to figure out what she wanted to say.

"Ned? It's Abby. I met with Leslie today, and she offered me the job—I'm going in tomorrow. I can't thank you enough—you've been a real help." She floundered briefly, wondering if she should say anything else about her research, then deciding against it. "I'll try to get back to you over the weekend, or next week, and let you know how things are going. Thanks again." She hung up reluctantly, dissatisfied, then slowly went into the living room to join Brad.

Chapter 13

The next morning, Abby decided to head for Concord early, erring on the side of caution. She wasn't a blue-jeans-for-everything person, so she chose a modest knit sweater and pale wool pants, with a tailored jacket over it. She was sitting in her car in the parking lot at the museum by 8:30, wondering when she could go rap on the door. Which door, for that matter? She was relieved to see Leslie emerge from another car that pulled in. It didn't surprise her that Leslie was a morning person, given the high energy that she had exuded yesterday. Abby got out of her car and waved tentatively.

Leslie beckoned her over. "Hey! You came back! When I thought about it, I wondered if maybe I'd scared you away. I do come on strong sometimes."

Abby laughed. "No. I just figured you had a lot going on and we'd sort things out as we go. Except I didn't ask a lot of relevant questions, like what time I should be here, or which entrance I should use, or who I should report to."

"Eight thirty is fine, I'll get you a key to the staff entrance, and me. You report to, that is." Leslie kept moving as she talked, and Abby trailed behind, into the building, up the stairs. Instead of following yesterday's route to her office, Leslie turned and led Abby down another hall to an extremely small room. "This is you. Sorry it's so small, but with these old buildings, you use what you can. The computer's pretty recent, and at least you have a window."

Abby stepped into the space, which barely allowed room to move around the old wooden desk. There were modern shelves along one wall, stuffed with books, booklets, papers, videos, CDs, and unidentified junk. The desktop at least was clear—apparently her predecessor had managed to take her personal memorabilia with her, despite her precipitous departure.

Leslie was still talking. "Look, I don't know what kind of shape Marian left things in. I'd say boot up the computer and see what's there, then start with the piles. There must be a schedule there somewhere. Then why don't you come see me about 9:30, and I'll take you around, introduce you. The first tour starts at ten, and you'll want to see that. And we can deal with all that paperwork stuff later. Okay?"

"Right." Abby smiled, but Leslie was already halfway down the hall. Abby sat down in the desk chair and exhaled. She looked around her. *What a mess!* Out of the frying pan, into the fire, it seemed: no sooner had she made some kind of order at home than she was called upon to sort out somebody else's chaos here. But at least it was only one room—and it was her own.

Maybe she should start with the computer. She turned it on and waited, praying that there wasn't any sort of password or code she would need, since she had no idea who to ask, and wasn't even sure if she could find her way back to her office if she left it. Luckily she found herself at the main directory page without any further action. People were trusting here, apparently. She started scrolling through folders.

An hour's effort left her feeling much relieved. There were well-organized files for scheduled events, each with the contact people, group size, special requests for content, payment, parking, and so on. Marian had done a thorough job and left things in very good order. Abby wondered if she would ever meet her—poor woman. She hated benefitting from someone else's misfortune, and she wished her well. After scanning the boilerplate information on the education programs ("12,000 students a year," "over 500 programs and tours," "hands-on activities," "curriculum packets"), she turned to the event scheduled for this morning. It appeared to be a group from a local elementary school, which had requested information on colonial life. Curriculum materials had been sent. Follow-up materials had been promised, and Abby hoped whoever was handling today's talk would know where to find them, because she didn't have a clue. She looked at her watch: 9:25. She'd better start trying to find Leslie's office.

After only two wrong turns she found Leslie in her office and on the phone. Leslie held up one finger, without interrupting the flow of words. Leslie's office was not substantially neater than the one she had just left, but the accumulated things were more interesting. Some of them actually looked antique, and Abby wondered if they were from the museum's collections or belonged to Leslie.

Leslie banged the phone down. "Finally! Some people just won't stop talking! Found everything? Great. Let me introduce you to a few people, then we should head downstairs and help Caroline set up . . ."

Once again Abby found herself trailing in Leslie's wake, stopping at intervals to nod, smile, and shake hands with some new person. Abby made a mental note to find a staff list soon, if she had any hope of keeping all these faces straight; maybe there was one on the computer. Leslie headed down the stairs and into a room adjacent to the main lobby, where another young woman was laying stapled packets of paper on each seat.

"Caroline, this is Abby Kimball—she'll be taking over Marian's job as soon as she learns the ropes. I told her she should sit in today, and maybe afterward you can show her where the materials are, stuff like that? Thanks." And Leslie disappeared; Abby was surprised not to see a cloud of dust swirling behind her. She turned back to Caroline, who smiled.

"Energetic, isn't she?"

"Definitely. Hey, can I help you with anything?" Abby gestured toward the pile of packets.

"Oh, sure, thanks. I need to check that the DVD player is set up. Just put one packet on each chair. If we counted right, there should be just enough." Abby took the stack of materials that Caroline handed her, and then Caroline disappeared behind another door.

She had finished laying out the materials when she heard the unmistakable sound of a bus motor outside, followed shortly by a babble of childish voices in the parking lot. The class group had arrived. Caroline reappeared, threw Abby a bright, brief smile, and said, "Here we go!"

Abby retreated to the back of the room and watched as the school group filed in, and Caroline went into her spiel. First she showed a brief video, then she led the children out of the room and into the exhibits. Abby found she was enjoying herself. Caroline clearly loved her subject, and liked working with the children, who were reasonably well behaved and asked intelligent questions. In the back of her mind, Abby compared these kids to the inner-city Philadelphia children she'd taught not long before. There you could never be sure they'd had breakfast, or even dinner the night before, and you could never count on them to have paper or a pencil. Or even a coat in winter, in some cases. But some of them had been eager and had tried so hard . . . Abby was brought back to the present by the sound of clapping: apparently the tour was over, and the students were thanking Caroline. She checked her watch. Eleven thirty—where had the morning gone?

"So, what'd you think?" Caroline was collecting scattered pages left behind.

"You did a good job—the kids were really paying attention. And you've got some great stuff to work with."

"Think you can do it by tomorrow?" Caroline had a wicked gleam in her eye.

Abby quelled a stab of panic. "Sure—just give me an outline and I can conquer the world."

Caroline laughed. "Don't worry—I'll handle it for a couple more days. But you will be on your own by next week. You'll do fine. Leslie said you'd taught in Philadelphia?" Abby nodded. "Then these kids should be no problem for you."

"Marian left everything pretty well set up, as far as I can tell."

Caroline's face clouded for a moment. "Yeah. We'll miss her—she was great to work with. But if you need anything, just ask—you'll find a lot of help here. Well, gotta go—I've got a class this afternoon. See you tomorrow."

As Caroline left, Leslie came back. "So, how'd it go? Did you find everything? Are you hungry? I usually take new hires out to lunch on their first day—and you never know when we'll both be free at the same time again. What do you like?"

"Fine. Yes, lunch sounds good, and I eat anything. And I don't know much about the town, so you pick."

"Chinese, then—there's a good place by the station. We'd better drive—saves time."

Leslie headed out the door, waving at several people on the way. Once in the car, she pointed to places as they passed them: "good bookstore, independent; nice toy store; real pricy shoe store, but if you're on your feet a lot . . . That's the library—they renovated recently, and it looks great; some nice shops down that way . . ." It took no more than three minutes to reach the restaurant. Leslie was still talking. "Good market, over there, and that's a convenient dry cleaners. Oh, but you don't live around here. Waltham, was it? But you might still want to do your shopping and stuff here."

Abby was beginning to realize that Leslie didn't even expect an answer to most of her comments. She followed her into the restaurant, which was only half full. They settled themselves into a booth and ordered. Finally Leslie sat back and looked at Abby.

"So, what do you think?"

"I'm overwhelmed, but I like it."

"Good. I couldn't believe how you dropped out of the sky into my lap. It's almost enough to make me believe in a benevolent deity. So, how do you know Ned?"

"I met him about two weeks ago on a house tour in Waltham." Should she go into how she had all but collapsed in a heap, and he had revived her with tea and sympathy?

"Oh, yeah, another one of his pet projects. He's really into local history."

"Is that how you met him?"

"No, actually, we met at a college party our junior year. He was at MIT, and I was at Harvard. God, that was a while ago! We were engaged for a while, after college, but then one day we looked at each other and said 'no way.' We're just too different. I figured I'd rather hang on to him as a friend than marry him and drive him crazy. So here we are. You're not married, right?"

Abby was trying to process what she had just heard. Even though she knew relatively little about Ned, she had a hard time picturing him with Leslie. "Uh, no. I've been with this guy—Brad—for a couple of years. Actually, we're engaged, and we moved up here together, and I guess we've sort of talked around marriage, but we've never set a date or anything."

"Ahh, no hurry—you're what, twenty-five, twenty-six? No need to rush into anything. You like Waltham?"

"What I've seen of it. Brad's working in Boston, so I don't know where we're going to end up—we're sort of looking around, getting to know the place. Concord seems nice." *If slightly haunted,* she added to herself, remembering the cemetery.

"Sure. If you don't mind the mild liberal snobbery and the housing prices. Anyway, it's a great place to work. So, here's how I see the education program . . ."

Half an hour later, Abby had to admit she was impressed. Leslie might not hold still for long but she clearly understood her field, even down to the details. *I could learn a lot from her,* thought Abby. *If I can keep up!* At any rate, her enthusiasm was infectious, and Abby found herself popping with new ideas and plotting new directions for the programs.

"Well, we'd better get back. We should get you into the system, if you ever want to get paid, and get you set up with insurance."

Abby sighed inwardly: maybe the salary was low, but she liked the place, she liked the people she'd met so far, and she would be glad to get back to teaching kids again. She was not about to kick serendipity in the shins, if that was even possible.

"That's fine."

"Good." Leslie stood up, paid the bill at the desk, and they were off once again.

The afternoon passed in a blur, and Abby was surprised to find how quickly five o'clock came. She gathered up her belongings and found her way out to the parking lot. It wasn't until she was halfway home that it struck her: if Ned had been engaged to Leslie, he probably wasn't gay. *Guess you were wrong there, Brad.* And the same little voice went on, *And if he held his own with someone like Leslie, he must have hidden depths. Interesting . . .* Abby wasn't sure if she'd mention that to Brad.

Chapter 14

Brad was already home when Abby arrived and greeted her enthusiastically at the door. Grinning like a small boy, he took her hand and led her into the kitchen, where he ceremoniously presented her with a bouquet of flowers.

"For your first day. I thought we should celebrate—you've been kind of quiet, down in the dumps lately. We can go out for dinner . . ."

Abby kissed him. "Brad, that's so sweet! And I'd love to go out. It's been a busy day, but I had so much fun! You want to go now?"

"Yeah, just let me change into something more comfortable." Brad bounded off toward the bedroom, clearly pleased by his little surprise. Abby carefully cut the stems of the flowers and filled a vase with water to put them in. She was touched—she couldn't remember the last time Brad had done anything like give her flowers. She carried the vase into the living room and set it on a table. Brad still hadn't reappeared; Abby could hear him whistling in the bedroom. She wandered toward the door and leafed through the mail Brad had dropped on the table next to it. There was a large padded envelope addressed to her in what she recognized as her mother's loopy scrawl. She must have found something in the family papers! Abby itched to open it, but Brad reappeared at that moment.

"You ready, babe?"

With a regretful pat, Abby laid the envelope down with the rest of the day's mail. It was probably for the best: she should wait and open it when she had time to go through it slowly and carefully. And given how much preparation she had to do this week, she wouldn't have time for it until the weekend anyway. She turned to Brad.

"I'm ready. Where do you want to go?"

"Let's try something new. Bill told me about this great place a couple of miles out on Route 20 . . ."

Abby followed obediently. She was still full from lunch—she wasn't used to eating a real meal in the middle of the day—and her head was spinning with everything she'd seen today and everything she needed to do in the next few days. It was a nice feeling, she reflected, having something real to do again. Leading a class of thirty kids for an hour or two was going to be a whole lot easier than trying to control a room of forty kids for a full day. And she had some ideas about possible grant funding for some of the programs she'd seen go by. She wondered who at the museum handled grant proposals, and if they could work together.

"Earth to Abby!" Brad's voice broke in. "Were you planning to get out of the car?"

"Oh, we're here already? Sorry, I was thinking."

Brad squired her into the restaurant and they were led to a table. He made a great show of asking her opinion about what she wanted to eat, to drink. Usually he just said something or other looked good, and Abby ordered what he did, but tonight she took the time to read the menu and picked a seafood dish.

When the waitperson had retreated, Abby sat back and smiled at Brad. "I had such a great time today. In the morning, I had to get into the computer and find the files for the programs. Oh, and I have my own office, but it's really small. But the computer is pretty up to date, and the woman who had the job . . ." Abby couldn't seem to stop herself, as she recited step by step the events of the day, including her lunch with Leslie. Brad was fairly quiet. In a corner of her mind, Abby watched Brad. In the beginning, he seemed sincerely interested in what she was saying, throwing in a relevant question now and then, making a suggestion, or laughing appreciatively as she described what one of the kids had said during the tour. After about ten minutes of this, she noticed that his eyes were beginning to wander around the room. He interrupted her once to flag down the waitperson and ask for more water, and when were their meals coming? After fifteen minutes he had stopped smiling and was openly fidgeting. When the food finally arrived, he nearly snarled. "About time."

Abby smiled sweetly at him. "Are we in a hurry? After all, it's not a school night. Or maybe it is—we've got two groups coming in tomorrow at the museum. Caroline says I'll be on my own by next week."

"Yeah, sure, good." Brad was very busy buttering a roll. "Too bad it doesn't pay better. Hell, you've got a degree from a good college, and teaching credentials. You should be doing better than that."

Abby felt a chill. "Brad, this is a small nonprofit—none of them pays very well. Besides, it's something I want to do. I'm not in it for the money. I just want something that I enjoy doing, that I can feel good about."

"And you can't feel good while you make money?" Brad's tone was snide.

What was this about? Abby wondered.

"Is there some reason we need money? We've got enough. You're getting a good salary."

Brad's contempt was obvious. "You are so clueless. You've got to think strategically, take the long view. You've got only forty or fifty years until retirement—have you thought about how you're going to save for that? And what about if we buy a house—how much mortgage we can carry is going to depend on our combined incomes. Besides, people judge you by the kind of salary you can pull down. You know that. That's why I left Philly—they flat out weren't going to pay me what I was worth. At least here somebody values me, even if I do get stuck with the scut work for the guys with the corner offices . . ." And he was off and running. Abby studied him as though he was an anthropological specimen: Brad in full rant. It wasn't pretty. He sounded both whiny and self-righteous. She hoped he didn't sound like this at work. But then, how could he, and still suck up to those guys in corner offices who controlled his future? That was where she came in: she was the vessel for all his bitching and moaning, so he could go back to work the next day and smile, his canines gleaming. Funny, she'd never seen her role in that light before.

Wait a minute—wasn't this supposed to be her night? Somehow they'd slipped right back into their usual places at the table, Brad complaining while she smiled and nodded and soothed. Well, she didn't feel like putting up with that, not tonight. It was time to seize the conversational reins again.

"I had some ideas about funding sources for some of the museum's programs—I'll have to see what they've done about that."

Brad looked startled by the interruption. "Huh? Oh, yeah, right. Sure, that's a good idea—show some initiative. Way to go. Hey, this chicken thing is really good." He poked at his plate.

Abby gave up. She'd had her few minutes in the sunshine of Brad's attention. The thought had been sweet, anyway. Maybe he just had a very short attention span. *Or maybe he really isn't interested in me, in what I care about,* a little voice inside whispered.

With a conscious effort, Abby dredged up a smile. "Yes, this is good too. You should tell Bill we tried this place."

Somehow dinner ended. Abby was quiet on the way home, reliving pieces of her day. Brad led the way into the apartment, then locked the door behind her. For a moment, Abby's eyes lingered on the envelope waiting for her. Something to look forward to—later. Brad came up behind her and slipped his arms around her waist, kissing her neck. "Hey, babe, we aren't done celebrating yet."

Abby would really have liked to curl into bed with a book—or one of the files she had brought home from work—and go to sleep early, but apparently Brad had other ideas. Oh, well, maybe the flowers deserved some reward. She turned within his arms. "What did you have in mind?" And followed him to the bedroom.

The rest of the week passed in a blur, albeit a happy one. For the first time in months, Abby felt useful and challenged. She had not realized how flat her life had become until it was suddenly filled with movement and purpose. In her spare moments, she tried to impose order on the mess that Marian had left on the shelves, but mostly she was learning the collections, reviewing the course outlines, getting to know the rest of the staff, trying to figure out the mechanics of contracting with schools and getting the money out of them before the bus arrived at the front door. She was happy, she realized. And she was going to solo on Monday, teaching her first class.

Whatever ghosts there were in Concord, they left her alone.

Friday after work she arrived home at six and didn't feel like cooking. Or doing anything, for that matter. She poured herself a glass of wine and wandered into the living room. Sitting in "Brad's" chair—the most comfortable one, of course—she put her feet up on a packing box and contemplated the shadowed ceiling. How did she feel? Happily tired. Drained. A little numb. Excited. Nervous. She smiled to herself in the growing darkness. Maybe she had made the decision to take this job on an impulse, but so far it had turned out better than she could have hoped. Maybe it had just been luck, or serendipity—but heck, wasn't she due some? It had been a long dry spell. She sipped her wine and relaxed.

Ned. He popped into her head, unbidden. It was so strange, the way she had met him. She'd never had a dizzy spell in her life, and she'd been lucky to have her first without a crowd of witnesses. But Ned had been calm and solicitous, without overreacting. He'd made sure she was all right. Well, maybe he thought he had some sort of legal responsibility, as a tour leader, to see that she wasn't about to sue the City of Waltham for negligence or something. But it hadn't felt like that. He had been sincerely concerned.

And he had listened to her nutty story and he had believed her. She wasn't sure she believed herself—believed that she wasn't just hallucinating—but she was glad that he hadn't laughed at her, or patted her on the head and told her to go home, take two aspirin and forget about it. He had taken what she said seriously, and had offered constructive suggestions instead of empty platitudes. That was nice.

She hadn't had time to think about her "visions," or whatever they were, since last weekend. Was that good or bad? She was pleased that they hadn't upset her enough to interfere with her so-called normal life. As far as she could tell, she wasn't a helpless hysteric. And, she had to admit, there had been nothing frightening or threatening in the visions themselves, just in the fact that they were happening, without warning or explanation, and she was never sure when the next one would happen. Somehow she really wasn't worried that one would pop up in the middle of a lecture at the museum; that building was "safe," or at least not haunted by . . . whatever it was that was haunting her.

So, now the weekend was here. She had some more reading to do, and she wanted to tweak the presentation she was going to make on Monday, but that still left plenty of time. And that meant she could get back to her personal research—starting with the contents of the envelope her mother had sent, which she had resisted opening all week.

She thought about her mother and wondered why she had always been so incurious about her own family. Abby knew her mother lived very much in the present. She was a high-energy, no-nonsense go-getter, the person a teacher always called when she needed a few dozen cookies or help with costumes; the person the local political committee called when they needed someone to coordinate poll activities or stuff a few thousand envelopes. She was a doer, not a thinker. Abby took after her father, who said little and thought much. If he had been a professor, he certainly would have been absentminded, and she had often wondered how he managed to function as an accountant, which she thought would have demanded much more focus than her father possessed. But he was kind, and sweet, and steady. Abby loved both her parents, but she felt closer to her father.

Abby thought about standing up and retrieving her mother's envelope, but she was too comfortable right where she was. Better to start fresh in the morning, with a clear eye. Unless, of course, Brad had made plans. Abby's mind drifted to Brad and their time together. They'd met at a party, she couldn't even remember whose. She had watched him covertly for a while before they were introduced. He had the kind of easy camaraderie that she envied, and he had seemed somehow a little larger than life. He had attracted a cluster of both men and women, and he didn't seem to be posturing for any of them. He'd just been having a good time. It was so unlike her usual party behavior that she had actually been jealous.

And then a friend had pulled them together, and he had spent time talking to her. And had seemed interested in her. Maybe she had seemed like a strange foreign specimen to him; maybe he'd mistaken her silences and awkwardness for subtlety and depth. She still didn't know. They'd been a couple for over two years, and had lived together for over half of that, and she still didn't really understand what he saw in her, what he wanted from her. She gave a snort: part of that answer was easy. At the moment he wanted someone to pick up his laundry, clean the bathroom, cook him meals, and go to bed with him, when and if he wanted to. How much of that was going to change, now that she had a job again and would be commuting, and would probably have weekend and evening commitments now and then? My God, was he going to have to find the washing machine in the basement all by himself? Abby chuckled at the image of Brad, laden with a monstrous sack holding weeks of accumulated laundry, armed with a flashlight, searching the bowels of the building, seeking the elusive machine . . .

She was still enjoying her fantasy when he walked in.

"Hey there. What're you doing, sitting in the dark?" He began turning on lights.

"Relaxing. It's been a busy week."

"What's happening with dinner?"

"At the moment, not a whole lot. You have any ideas?"

He looked momentarily disgruntled. "Pizza, maybe?"

"Fine with me. Why don't you call?"

He gave her an enigmatic look, then went to the kitchen to find the menu for the pizza shop. Abby didn't move. She was not going to feel guilty about not making dinner. Let him sort things out—he was a big boy. He even had an MBA. Surely he could commandeer a pizza. Abby giggled, and then noticed that her wineglass was empty.

Brad came back, holding a bottle of beer. He looked momentarily nonplused that she was sitting in "his" seat, but he crossed the room and sat in the other armchair, signaling his displeasure as he squirmed to make himself comfortable. Abby watched him with little sympathy, waiting for whatever pronouncement he was going to make.

"I've got to go in to the office tomorrow, at least for a few hours. We've got a big IPO coming and the boss wants us all to be up to speed on the details."

"That's fine," Abby said airily.

"And there's football again on Sunday . . ." He looked at her with a challenging expression, as if daring her to object.

"Don't worry about me. I've got to prepare for Monday, and I've got some other things I want to do. Just let me know if you'll be home for dinner."

Was she imagining it, or did a flicker of disappointment cross Brad's face? What had he expected—a scene? Tearful protests? An abject Abby, pleading with him not to leave her all alone with no one to keep her company? She laughed.

"What's so funny?"

Oh, that had been out loud? "Nothing, sweetie. Just something I was thinking. So, how was your day?"

Chapter 15

Saturday Brad was out of the house by the time Abby woke up. She stretched luxuriously, enjoying having the whole bed to herself. Brad took up far more than his share, and he thrashed a lot.

And it was Saturday, and she had things to look forward to. She did the necessary errands—groceries, dry cleaning, gas for the car, liquor store—and all the while that mystery envelope from her mother remained in the back of her mind. She came home, dutifully put away her purchases, and made herself a light lunch. Finally, at twelve thirty, she was ready to delve into her ancestors. She sat down at the desk and, opening the envelope, pulled out a pile of mismatched papers. On top of the pile was a scrawled note in her mother's hand: "Sorry there's not more—don't know where it went. I'll keep looking. Hope this is what you wanted. Talk soon! Love, Mom." Typical.

Abby pulled the pile toward her and began sorting it. There was no particular rhyme or reason to the items—crumbling newspaper clippings, faded notes in old-fashioned writing, a short and sketchy hand-drawn family tree, and a few copies of legal documents. Abby decided to start with the documents, thinking that someone must have thought they were important if they'd kept copies. There were only a few: a marriage license for Ruth Pendleton and one Samuel Ellinwood, from 1921, in Rhode Island. Good heavens—Ruth had been only seventeen! So Samuel was the mystery great-grandfather that nobody ever talked about. Another appeared to be her great-grandmother's birth certificate: Ruth Pendleton was born in 1904, in Connecticut. Of course the form listed Ruth's parents: Samuel Pendleton, and . . . Olivia Flagg.

Abby felt the bottom fall out of her stomach. She stared at the faded document in front of her, incredulous. So Olivia Flagg was her great-great-grandmother? Olivia, daughter of William and Elizabeth? Olivia, from Waltham? Olivia, who had been bouncing the baby in that fateful first vision? Abby sat gazing blankly at the paper, thoughts whirling around her head. Slowly they began to settle. Her first concrete idea was to call Ned. No, she couldn't call Ned all the time with her little finds. *But this is a big find, Abby.* Yes, but . . . had he suspected something like this? He was the one who had told her to check into her family background. Had he wondered if she had some connection to the places and people around here?

She needed more information. She pawed impatiently through the remaining papers. There was another paper, folded, tearing along the folds: the death certificate for Samuel Pendleton dated 1953, of pneumonia, in Montana. There was a short newspaper clipping attached to it with a rusting paper clip, describing the death of a transient identified as Samuel Pendleton, no known kin. Abby wondered how her great-grandmother had ever come by it. Had she known where Samuel was after he vanished? When was that? And why? The more answers she found, the more questions she had.

Abby laid the documents on the desk in front of her, neatly squaring the corners. She thought hard: what else did she want to know, and where was she going to find it? An irreverent thought popped into her head: *just go to the cemetery, Abby, and talk to Elizabeth.* No, that was silly—and unlikely. Elizabeth wasn't really there, only her remains were. She was dead. She wasn't about to sit down with Abby and explain everything. Abby would just have to work it out for herself.

Which meant what? All right, she had proof of her great-grandmother's birth and marriage. Ruth had taken her maiden name of Pendleton back, and Abby wondered what the legalities were for that. She'd given that surname to her daughter as well—had that created problems? She had proof of Ruth's mysterious missing husband's death, at least. Would it be worth her time trying to find his parents? Not right now. Abby had a feeling that whatever was happening went back further, to the Flaggs. After all, it was the Flaggs she had seen at the house, Elizabeth Flagg at the cemetery, and the chair had belonged to Olivia Flagg's daughter Ruth. But whose children had she "seen" when she sat in Ruth's chair? What had happened to Olivia and her husband? Had they stayed in Massachusetts? How had Olivia felt about the sudden appearance of Isabel in her family? Abby could only guess, but it was clear that Isabel had stayed in Waltham and had maintained a relationship with the Flaggs, up until her death and burial next to them.

And where did the Reeds fit in this tree? Because Abby was pretty sure they had to be part of the same line. Why else would she be "seeing" them?

She needed more and the library seemed the easiest place to start: the library would have city directories and other local files for Waltham, and maybe she could trace Elizabeth Flagg back further. She checked her watch—if she left now, she could still get in a few hours at the library before it closed.

• • •

At five o'clock, as the library was closing, Abby emerged, dazed and bewildered. She stood on the front steps of the building and shivered in the October wind. Half of her mind was still lodged in an earlier century and she was trying hard to fit all the fragments together in some coherent way. She wavered, uncertain about what to do next. And then she knew: the cemetery. Would the gates still be open? She might as well find out. She got into the car and drove slowly through town, looking at it with new eyes. Which buildings had been there in 1900? In 1920? She reached the cemetery, where the sign said vaguely that the gates were closed at sunset.

Apparently the sun hadn't set, since the gates were still open. Abby pulled up outside the wall, then walked slowly to the Flagg stone. She approached cautiously, unsure of what she would find. The wind whistled through the branches, sending down a shower of vivid gold leaves. Even the squirrels had retreated.

Abby walked around the stone until she was facing the inscribed side. Was she supposed to say something? Invoke the spirits of the dead? This was foolish. She was cold and confused, and here she was standing in a cemetery at dusk trying to talk to her three times great-grandparents. She took off her glove and reached out a tentative hand and touched the headstone.

Fragments, flashes. She saw Elizabeth again, and for the first time, a younger woman she had to assume was Isabel, standing with her. William's burial? Or visiting his grave? But she knew she recognized them, only that didn't move her forward. And through whose eyes was she seeing?

The spell was shattered by a shout. "Ma'am? I'm closing up now—you gotta leave."

Abby looked around her. Nothing had changed, except that it had grown darker. There was no one else there, corporeal or not. She waved at the man standing impatiently by the gate. "Sorry, I lost track of time. I'm leaving." She passed through the stone piers, and the iron gates clanged shut behind her.

She drove home in an abstracted mood. If she wanted any peace tonight, she'd better make something for dinner to avoid an argument. What she really wanted to do was to set down what she had learned, to fill in some of the blanks in her computer program, to fix the faces in her mind.

And she needed to talk to Ned. Tomorrow, while Brad was out watching football with the guys. She needed to talk to someone who could help her make sense of what was happening, and she couldn't think of anyone else who would fit the bill. So it had to be Ned.

Abby was throwing together an uninspired dinner when Brad walked in. "Where were you this afternoon?" He sounded annoyed.

"When?" Abby said absently, chopping onions.

"About two."

"Oh, I went to the library for a couple of hours. Why?"

"Bill and Nancy were talking about going to a play tonight, and they wondered if we wanted to come along. But then I couldn't get hold of you." Clearly he felt he was the injured party. "What was so important at the library?"

"I was looking up some more local history and I guess my cell was off. Oh, guess what! It looks as though I may have had ancestors who lived in Waltham. Isn't that an amazing coincidence?"

"Yeah, sure. Listen, I can still call Bill, and we could meet them somewhere."

Abby thought about that. Dinner wasn't anywhere near ready; she'd have to shower and get dressed; and she just didn't feel like going out again. "I'm not really up for it tonight. We've already been out twice this week."

"C'mon, it'd be fun. You ought to get to know them better."

"I'd love to, just not tonight. Maybe we could plan something for next weekend." Abby scraped the chopped onions into a sauté pan.

Brad gave her a long look then stormed out of the kitchen, muttering. Maybe he'd had a bad day. Maybe IPOs were difficult beasts to master. Abby realized she didn't really care. She had tried to share what she was doing and he'd brushed her off like a mosquito. Okay, maybe her dead relatives weren't exactly fascinating to an up-and-coming young banking wizard, but couldn't he at least pretend to care? For a minute, anyway? She had certainly spent plenty of time listening to him go on and on about things she knew nothing about, and she had smiled and cooed and stroked . . . It was her turn now. She wanted equal time. Well, maybe 40:60. Or even 35:65. But she wanted to know that he was listening to her, at least part of the time.

Brad's mood did not improve over dinner. He started on a second beer as they sat down, and when he went back for another midway through the meal, he was annoyed that there were no more.

"Damn it, Abby, I told you we were running out of beer. Couldn't you have managed to remember that much?"

Abby considered. Had she forgotten? No, she was good at remembering little things like that, besides which she wrote down errands on the magnetized pad on the refrigerator. "No, I don't think you told me."

There was a moment of silence. While she waited for his reply she had time to wonder: had she never contradicted him before? Questioned his authority? Suggested, even hinted, that he might be wrong? She honestly couldn't recall.

His response was not unexpected, but it wasn't pleasant. "Like hell I didn't. You've just been too busy thinking about this little job of yours to take care of the basic things around here."

Abby stared at him, wondering which part of that attack to deal with first. To her surprise, she found she was angry. Interesting—she wasn't used to being angry with Brad. She mustered her wits. "*Little* job? I don't think that's fair, Brad. Maybe I won't make as much money as you do, but the job matters to me. I enjoy it." She paused to see what effect her words were having. Brad looked mildly stunned, as though a fluffy kitten had bitten him. "And as for taking care of basics around here, I think I've done more than my share. Maybe you could pick up some of the slack, you know. I don't even drink beer. Why don't you buy it once in a while?"

Now he was staring openly. Then he stood up abruptly and threw his napkin onto his place. "I don't need this kind of shit." He stormed out of the room, and two minutes later she heard the front door slam. Abby hadn't moved. She wondered idly where he was going. Back to Boston, to play with Bill and Nancy? To a local bar, to get that beer he so desperately wanted, and to nurse his grievances against her? She sighed. Maybe he'd had a bad day and needed to take it out on someone. But she was getting a little tired of being the target for his venting. She had a life too. Had she been unreasonable? She didn't think so. Had she really never questioned anything he'd said? Abby reflected on that, and then smiled. Maybe she hadn't, but maybe it was time she started.

She stood up and carried their plates out to the kitchen. Funny—she was doing all the cooking and all the cleaning up. Brad's contribution was to call for pizza now and then. Not exactly an equitable distribution of responsibilities, was it? Then she wavered. She'd held her ground at dinner, and Brad had stormed out. If he came back later and found the kitchen in a mess, it would probably just add fuel to the fire. Abby picked up a sponge and started washing.

And when she was done, she went to the phone and called Ned. There was no answer at his place—of course, it was Saturday night, and he probably had a life. But she left a message.

"Ned? It's Abby. Listen, I've found out some fascinating stuff about my family, and I'd like to run it by you. Do you have time tomorrow afternoon? Give me a call."

She hung up, pleased with herself. She surveyed the kitchen one last time, then went back to the desk in the living room, pulled out her notes, and began writing.

Ned called shortly after ten. Abby grabbed the phone quickly, thinking that it might be Brad, and was surprised to hear Ned's voice. And then pleased.

"Hi, Abby—sorry I missed your call. What's up?"

"I went through my mother's papers today, and you know what? It looks like Olivia Flagg was my great-great-grandmother!"

"Wow, that's fantastic! And you had no idea?"

The sincere enthusiasm of his response was unmistakable, and it warmed Abby. "No. She was married to a man named Samuel Pendleton, and they had a daughter, Ruth. She's my great-grandmother. Ruth married Samuel Ellinwood, and he's the great-grandfather who disappeared. Apparently he went out West and died there. My great-grandmother kept his death certificate, and a newspaper clipping."

"That's just great." He was quiet for a moment, and Abby felt a flurry of panic. She really wanted to talk about how this new information fit in with what she had been seeing, but she was afraid that Brad would walk in in the middle of the conversation and ask who she was talking to so late. Luckily Ned went on, "So—you want to get together, go over this?"

Abby heaved an inward sigh of relief. "Yes, I'd really like that. I want to see what that means about . . . you know, the other stuff."

"Sure. How about after lunch tomorrow? I'll give you a call and we can pick a place to meet."

"Great. See you then." Abby hung up with a feeling that combined relief and elation. She found she was too keyed up to go back to her research, so she threw herself into a chair and scrolled through the cable channels, finally settling on an old movie she'd seen before. She fell asleep partway through, then got up and went to bed. Brad had still not come home when she fell asleep.

Chapter 16

B ut Brad was there in bed the next morning when Abby woke up, sleeping soundly, snoring lightly, smelling of stale beer and tobacco smoke. She slid out and went to make the coffee. He appeared a few minutes later, looking rumpled and apologetic.

"Hey, babe, I'm sorry I snapped at you last night. I was in a lousy mood."

Abby smiled at him. "That's what I figured. But it did hurt that you didn't take my job seriously."

He looked at her, and she could almost see the wheels turning in his head: *I apologized and she's still on my case?* Then apparently he decided it wasn't worth fighting about. "Okay, I get it. I'm sorry. What's for breakfast?"

Abby sighed inwardly. One step forward, two steps back, apparently. "How about pancakes?" She began rummaging in the cupboards for ingredients. Without turning, she asked, "You still going to watch football with the guys?"

Brad was leafing through the Sunday paper, tossing aside the sections that didn't interest him. "Yeah, sure. Why not? You want to come?"

"No, you go ahead. I've got to get ready for tomorrow." Abby concentrated on making batter. One problem solved: she was free to meet Ned.

Brad was long gone by the time Ned called. "Are we still on?"

"Sure. Where?"

"I'll come by in about half an hour and we can decide."

When Ned pulled into the parking lot Abby was waiting downstairs, holding her growing stack of research notes against her chest. She climbed quickly into his car.

Ned glanced at her before putting the car in gear. "You must really be excited about the Flagg connection."

"Oh, I am. I was just amazed when I saw that. Uh . . ." She hesitated. "What?"

"I went to the library . . . and then I went back to the cemetery."

"And?" he prompted.

"They were there," she said, in a small voice, not looking at him. "At least, Elizabeth and Isabel were. I could see them standing by the tombstone, but only when I put my hand on the stone. And then I had to go, because the custodian wanted to shut the gates." She fell silent, feeling somehow deflated. It sounded so silly when she said it out loud.

"Interesting." Ned concentrated on driving for a couple of miles. Abby was beginning to wonder if she'd made a big mistake by calling him, when he went on. "So, do you think the fact that they're your relatives has anything to do with your seeing them?"

Abby shook her head. "I don't know. It makes a weird kind of sense, but I can't explain it. So what am I supposed to do now? And that might explain the Flaggs, but not the Reeds." Abby looked out the window. It seemed that they were retracing their path from the prior week. "Are we headed for the coffee shop?"

"Yes, if that's okay. It's quiet, and there's room to spread out, if you want me to look at your notes."

They had left Route 128 and were passing through Newton Lower Falls, when Abby reached out suddenly and grabbed Ned's arm. "Turn right, here," she said urgently.

"What? Why?"

"I don't know—just turn."

He complied, and they followed a winding residential street lined with expensive-looking houses for a couple of minutes.

"What now?" he asked.

"Wait . . . there. Pull over, on the right there."

There was a short line of cars parked along the verge, and Ned pulled in at the end of the line. He turned off the engine and turned to face Abby. He didn't say anything, but waited, his eyes on her face. Abby didn't notice. She was staring at a white colonial house ahead of them. She could see a realtor's sign in the front yard, advertising an open house that afternoon.

"Can we go in?" she asked, her voice tense.

"I don't see why not." Ned got out of the car and helped her out on her side. He led the way along the side of the road until they came to the front door of the house, which was protected by a small, Early Victorian porch, later than the original house. The main door was open, and he pulled open the storm door to let Abby walk into the small stair hall in the center of the house. Abby walked blindly in and laid her hand on the wooden newel post at the bottom of the stairs. She froze.

There were people. She could tell that some were real, like the realtor who sized them up as a nice, upscale young couple in the market for a Weston colonial and made a beeline for them. Abby could vaguely hear

Ned brushing her off politely. There were other "real people" in the house, Abby knew—she could hear them moving around.

But then there were the others. Abby rubbed her hand over the worn wood of the newel post, shaped by centuries of hands to an odd irregular form. She saw two people, mainly, a man and an older woman. They appeared to be arguing, although she couldn't hear them. Damn—if she was going to keep seeing people, couldn't they come with a soundtrack? The man was the angrier of the two; the woman appeared cold and her attitude didn't waver. Abby pulled her hand away from the post and they faded. Without saying anything, Abby turned and walked into the room to the left of the hall. A dining room, with wide plain boards forming the wainscoting, clearly old. Abby gave the room a passing glance but kept going, through a door toward the back, into a long, narrow room that was now a kitchen. She stopped in the middle of the room. "Here," she said, in a near whisper, to no one in particular.

Behind her she could hear the persistent realtor talking to Ned. "And this is actually the oldest part of the house, built before 1800. It used to be across the street, on the other corner, and if you can imagine, the owner just picked it up, moved it here, and built the rest of the house around it, about 1810. There's a lot of stuff in the town records, if you're interested . . ." Her voice faded as Abby moved around the kitchen, looking at the woodwork, and then toward the back corner of the room, where there was a narrow, clumsy stair along the wall. The boards that made up the wall looked like they had come from some ancient barn, and they bore traces of red paint. Abby tentatively reached out her hand and laid it flat against the wall.

The images welled around her. Many people, again layered, as in the cemeteries. One man seemed more in focus than the other people. She turned partway to look into the kitchen, without taking her hand from the wall. There, halfway across the room. Short—maybe her height. Ordinary-looking, brown hair, brown eyes. And his clothes . . . she'd seen clothes like that recently. In the Concord Museum. In the Colonial Life display. He shifted and dissolved, but there were others . . .

And then Ned—real, solid Ned—stepped in front of her. "Darling, this lady wants to know if we'd be interested in making an offer. There's been a lot of interest." With his back to the realtor, his expression belied his cheery tone—he looked concerned. Abby realized that she was panting, taking short, sharp breaths. Reluctantly she pulled her hand away from the wall, and the real world came back in focus. She straightened her shoulders and took a deep breath.

"I don't think so, dear—there's not enough room for a nursery." She was pleased to see one corner of Ned's mouth twitch with suppressed amusement. "But it is lovely. What period did you say it was?" She smiled brightly at the realtor.

"Between 1790—this part here—and 1812, when it was finished. A lot of the original woodwork survives, which is a big plus. And the renovations have been carefully done . . ."

Still smiling mindlessly, Abby and Ned drifted away from the realtor, who shrugged and turned to the next likely prospects. Ned guided Abby toward the front door, and then outside. At the corner the property was bounded by an old dry-stone wall, and he steered her toward that. She sat gratefully, and he sat beside her without speaking.

After a long time, Abby said thoughtfully, "You know, you really are a very peaceful person. Most people would have been bombarding me with questions if I pulled a stunt like that." She turned to look at him.

"I figured you'd tell me when you were ready. What happened in there?"

Abby turned over several answers in her mind before settling on one. "I don't know. I just knew we had to come this direction, and I knew we had to stop, and go in . . . I saw someone. Well, there were lots of people—a man and woman in the hallway, arguing, but then in the kitchen, one man in particular. I know he wasn't real, but he was there, and I could see him. And his clothes were . . . old. I'd say colonial."

"Ah."

"You're going to tell me I have more homework to do, aren't you?" Abby demanded.

Ned smiled. "Well, it would be easy enough to find out who owned the property in 1800. This is Weston—they take their history very seriously, and their records are in good shape."

"Shoot—now I have a job and have to work. Cuts into my research time." Abby realized that this most recent encounter hadn't shaken her. Maybe she was getting used to whatever this was. She returned Ned's smile. "And thank you for the job, too—I'm having a great time at the museum, and I really like Leslie." She shivered—she had almost forgotten that it was fall, at least in this century.

Ned was quick to notice. "You're getting cold. Why don't we go hunt up that coffee and you can tell me what else you've got, and maybe we can figure out what to do about this." He gestured vaguely toward the house.

"Yes, let's." She stood up and took one last look at the house before leading the way back to the car.

She was silent for most of the short ride to Wellesley. Inside the coffee shop, she let Ned get the coffee and sat back in her chair, after nodding a greeting toward the cemetery across the street. "Hi, guys," she said—to them or to herself, she wasn't sure. Ned came back with the coffee and sat down.

"Now what?" he asked.

Abby smiled. "I was going to say the same thing. All right, let's take this one thing at a time. I've got William Flagg's obituary here, and the announcement of Olivia's marriage—actually, that took place in Boston. And the obituary says that Olivia was living in Connecticut when her father died, so I guess that's one more piece. I can look at Connecticut censuses, see what that tells me. I've got her daughter's—my great-grandmother's—birth certification, but I still need to look for my grandmother's birth record."

Ned appeared to be thinking out loud. "Parts of this are pretty straightforward—if something's not online, you can go to a library in the town you're looking at and see what kind of local information they have. Or you can write or email the town clerk, or the county, or the state, for vital records. That's a good start, and you need to do it. But there's another piece to this, and I'm not sure how you get at it . . ."

"What?"

"Well, there are two basic questions here. One: why are you seeing these people? And two: why are you seeing them when and where you are?"

Abby chewed that over for a moment. "You mean, are they trying to tell me something? Communicate somehow?"

Ned shrugged. "Maybe. I don't know. I'm trying to keep an open mind. But it's interesting. And if you assume that there's a logic to it, don't you wonder just what that is?"

"Of course I do, but I'm just beginning to get a handle on it. I have no idea why this started, and I don't know if this is going to just disappear as quickly as it started. I'm pretty sure it's not harmful or dangerous—it's not like I'm going to get sucked into their time or something. I don't think they see me." She fell silent. She could feel Ned's eyes on her face, but she couldn't bring herself to look at him.

"Abby, have you told Brad about any of this?" His voice was kind.

She shook her head. "Brad, uh . . . doesn't have a lot of imagination. Or a lot of patience. He's a pragmatist: if he doesn't understand something, he just brushes it off and moves on. I think he'd just tell me I was broken and I'd better see about getting me fixed."

"I'm sorry."

"Why?" Abby looked at him with curiosity.

He met her look. "Because this can't be easy for you. And I can see how you might doubt your own sanity, and you need someone around to keep you grounded."

"Oh." She was absurdly touched. He hardly knew her, but he was worried about how she felt. Which Brad wasn't. "I figured you'd just see me as an interesting scientific experiment—you know, strange woman starts hearing voices, channeling the dead." She stopped, unsure how to go on.

"I know it's not that simple. I don't know you very well, and I'm not sure how well you can handle it. And you shouldn't have to do it alone."

His kindness brought her near tears, and she didn't trust herself to speak. She stared at the swirling patterns of the oil on her coffee. In fact, she wasn't sure what she would have done if Ned hadn't been there to reassure her. Probably checked in to the nearest mental hospital, or tried to pretend that it hadn't happened—until it happened again. But she did know that she was glad he was there to listen. Finally she managed a watery smile. "Thank you. For believing. For trying to help. I'm glad you're here."

Ned's expression was serious, and for a moment Abby thought he was going to say something more. Then apparently he thought better of it and sat back in his chair. "I'm glad I could help. Listen, I think we've covered enough for today, and you've got to go to work tomorrow. Why don't you put this on the shelf for the week, let it jell? If you've got the time, you can identify the sources for the records you need, maybe write for the ones you can't get to, but don't push it. There seems to be a lot happening and pretty fast, and you need time to get used to it."

"Don't obsess, right?" Abby laughed. "Don't worry. I just want to understand what's happening to me." Abby struggled to find words. "It's sort of like I've been tone-deaf all my life, and now suddenly I understand music. It means I have to rethink some things about myself. But that's not a bad thing."

"I think you're handling it all remarkably well. As you go through your research, think about what connects these people, to each other and to you.

If this were just random, you'd be overwhelmed with them. Massachusetts has been settled for a long time, and there are a lot of dead here."

"Right, figure out the connection." She finished her coffee. "Ready when you are."

As they were driving back to Waltham, a thought struck her. "You ever watch the old *Star Trek* episodes? The originals, I mean?"

Ned grinned. "Of course. I'm a geek, right?"

"The closest thing I can think of is that this all feels sort of like a Vulcan mind meld. I mean, I touch something and suddenly I hear and see things, like the thing was a transmitter of some sort."

"I see what you mean. Interesting idea. Maybe there is something physical about it. One more thing to think about."

Chapter 17

After Ned dropped her back home, Abby tried to put her latest "episode" out of her mind, because she actually did have some work-related material to review. She settled down at the desk and retrieved the course packet for her tour the next day. She was pleased with the overall quality of the materials—not only was the information interesting and well-assembled, but the spiel and the handouts were well suited to a restless elementary school audience. She jotted down a few ideas for possible future changes, but for the moment she was content to work with what she had in hand. Still, she had to admit that every time she came upon a fictional image of the colonial residents of Concord, she recalled the man in the Weston kitchen. She could see him so clearly, down to the buttons on his shirt. *A none-too-clean shirt,* she added to herself. If he had been a fantasy or a hallucination, he had been a grubby one.

Brad came back about seven. Abby had fixed a casserole, and they shared a subdued supper, each lost in his or her own thoughts—or trying to avoid any more conflict. Brad seemed uncharacteristically quiet, but Abby was glad of the peace and didn't prod him. She had enough to think about without adding his complaints, real or imagined.

As her workweek began, Abby came to feel that she had stepped onto a moving carousel, and all she could do was grab a seat and hang on. Not that she was unhappy, but she was so busy she didn't have time to think. And she liked being busy—she had forgotten how much she enjoyed using her mind for something more challenging than how to sort the books on the shelves. The people she met at work were all very welcoming; the surroundings were lovely; the commute was tolerable. She came home at night drained, and she would not have been surprised if Brad had accused her of being a zombie, except he didn't seem to notice anything different. One night he was keyed up, talking about what he had done that day; another night he was moody or outright surly, and nothing was right. But mostly his noise washed over Abby, and she smiled, and cooked, and washed dishes. She did her best not to think about her "seeings," and only now and then would a face from the past flash in her mind's eye. She would get to them, in time, she promised silently.

The bits and pieces she had were busily assembling themselves independently in some dark, quiet corner of Abby's mind. Samuel Ellinwood had married Ruth Pendleton, that she knew. Her grandmother

Patience had been born a year after their marriage. And then, before her grandmother had been old enough to remember him, Samuel had vanished, abandoned his family, never to look back. Why was that? What would have driven him to do that? Everything she knew about her great-grandmother Ruth suggested that she had been a strong-willed woman—hadn't she managed to erase poor Samuel from the family?—but would his desertion alone have been enough for her to push him away forever?

They'd been married in the twenties, but Ruth hadn't been born until the Great Depression had begun. Did that have anything to do with it? Was Samuel a poor provider? One of the many who had found himself out of a job, with no idea how to get back on track? But they'd had only one child to support.

Or had they?

Abby was washing dishes when she reached that question, and she stopped, oblivious to the running water. She knew of only one child—but what about the vision she'd had sitting in what she now knew was her great-grandmother's chair? Had there been another baby, one who died? Had that been the last straw for Samuel? And how was she supposed to find out, if her great-grandmother had never even said where they had lived?

Abby shut off the water, leaving the dishes half done, and went to the computer. She knew that she could access the 1930 census online, so she called up the right website and slowly typed in "Samuel Ellinwood," with no state. There appeared a list with several Samuels, and a few variant spellings, but only a handful appeared in New England, and only one in Connecticut. She clicked on that one and realized her hand was trembling. The record came up on the screen. Yes, it was the right Samuel, and listed wife Ruth, and infant daughter Patience—her newborn grandmother. She had a place for them, where they had been, three-quarters of a century earlier.

Which didn't answer her question about another child, but at least now she could write to the right county and ask if there had been any other children born to Samuel and Ruth Pendleton within a few years of 1930. And she had a feeling she knew what the answer would be, whenever it came—because she'd seen the baby. Almost against her will, she stood up and walked over to the swan chair and slowly sank into it. No, there were no new visions, but she knew what she'd seen, and she wouldn't, couldn't, forget it. *I'm sorry, Ruth—sorry about the baby, sorry that Samuel didn't live up to your hopes and expectations and ran away.*

Brad's voice shattered her mood. "Hey, Abby, you look like someone stole your favorite teddy bear. You all right?"

Abby quickly brushed away a tear that had been trickling down her cheek. "Sure. Just tired, I guess. I was thinking about my family, whoever owned this chair."

"It's a nice piece—bet it's worth something now."

"Brad! It's an heirloom. I don't care what it's worth—it means something to me. How can you put a price tag on it?"

He held up both his hands in protest. "Hey, I didn't mean anything. I was just making conversation. Geez, I can't say anything to you without you biting my head off." He picked up a magazine and pointedly started reading.

Have I been that touchy lately? Abby couldn't think of many examples, at least not since that little blowup they'd had last Saturday. As far as she could tell, she'd been her usual quiet and amiable self. So why was Brad so sensitive about it? She had no idea. Maybe his fragile masculine ego was still smarting from the withdrawal of one hundred percent of her attention. Poor baby—he'd just have to learn to live with less.

She was still at the computer, so she decided to find out where Connecticut state and town birth records were kept and send out that request tonight, while it was fresh in her mind. And then it occurred to her that she still hadn't found Elizabeth Flagg's maiden name, or where she and William had been married. She had a birth year for her, from the tombstone, but that wasn't a lot to go on. Abby turned back to the censuses—maybe she could follow William back through them, at least find out in which decade Elizabeth first appeared with him. After another half an hour she had most of what she needed.

She knew that William had been living in Waltham in 1890, since he showed up in the Veterans Census, but in 1880 he was in Lynn, and in 1870 in Ware, as well as in 1860 and 1850. Further back than that she could not go, since only his father's name would appear, but she had gotten the basic outline. Elizabeth Flagg was first listed as his wife in 1870, which made sense—William would have married after he was discharged from the Union Army. And Olivia appeared with them—they hadn't waited long to have a child. Why hadn't there been any more? Olivia was born barely a year after their marriage, and then nothing. Well, Abby amended, nothing until the mysterious appearance of Isabel. She sighed—how did one ever untangle family stories like this, with so little to go on? But at least now she could look for a marriage in Ware, sometime between 1865 and 1870. It was another step forward—or backward, as it were.

"Yo, babe, you planning on going to bed sometime?" Brad's voice came from the bedroom. Abby looked at her watch—after eleven. Where had the time gone?

"I'll be right in," she replied. She shut down the computer, giving it a final pat, then went around the room turning off the lights. She paused at the kitchen for a moment, contemplating the unfinished dishes. Oh, well, they'd still be there tomorrow.

• • •

After a few more days, Abby felt as though she had been working at the Concord Museum forever. She liked the kids in the school groups that came through, and she found she liked history far better than she remembered. She also felt as though she was harboring a slightly guilty but pleasurable secret: her bizarre link to the past. That was never going to go on a résumé!

But during the week, she had had little time to even think about that, much less do anything about it, apart from a few random stabs at computer research. And she needed to do more, much more, if only to preserve her own sanity. It was unnerving, not knowing when another "episode" would happen. She would like to be able to predict them a little better—to figure out what triggered them, and then at least have the option of avoiding those triggers—or seeking them out. She had to admit she was ambivalent. Part of her wanted these weird happenings to just stop as quickly as they had started; another part of her wanted to see what was going to happen next.

At least she could be systematic. She had a family tree, one with a lot of blanks on it. She needed to fill in the blanks. There were specific ways to do that, and here she was in the middle of all the original sources and later information she could hope for—if she could only figure out what she was looking for. So far she'd been "haunted"—she shied away from using that word—by people from two different families, the Flaggs and the Reeds. The simplest and most logical conclusion would be that those two families were connected, although she hadn't yet figured out how. If they weren't linked, then there was no way of telling if there would be other appearances, and how many. Abby wasn't about to go looking for others.

Right now she needed to sort out the ones she knew about. She'd sent off her query about Samuel and Ruth's other child, but she didn't expect an answer for at least a week.

She was mildly curious about the marriage of Olivia and Samuel Pendleton, but there were no real questions there, so she could put that on the back burner. That left her with the task of finding Elizabeth's maiden name. For that, she needed to find marriage records—but where? William and Elizabeth had been married and were living in Ware in 1870, but how was she going to find time to get to Ware, halfway across the state, when any official records offices were open? That was the problem with having a real job: no time to do all the other interesting things in the world. So she'd have to settle for writing more emails and hoping someone would be kind enough to answer her within a year or two. At least for the Reeds who were buried in Concord, she could use the Concord library, and she could do that on a weekend, or maybe during a lunch hour, if she was very quick. Somehow Abby doubted that any part of this research was going to be quick, but she had to start somewhere, and she was impatient.

Another thing that she could do was check the record for the Reed plot in Sleepy Hollow Cemetery. It turned out that the cemetery was managed by the Town of Concord, and Abby called the office from work early one morning. A very pleasant woman answered, and Abby tried to explain her interest.

"Where's the plot?" the woman asked.

"Uh, how do you describe locations?" Abby hadn't really thought about it.

"Well, lot number, if you have it. No? Well, then, where is it physically? Near town?"

"No," said Abby dubiously, "it's nearer the back gate. You know Authors Ridge?" *Now there's a stupid question, Abigail,* she chided herself. *Of course she does.* "If you go down the hill from there, there's a loop at the bottom of the hill. The Reeds are sort of in the middle, on the side near the Authors."

There was a moment of silence, punctuated by some computer noises. "That's Sleepy Hollow Avenue. Got it. William Reed, died 1899, right?"

"That's the one."

"Okay, we've got the plot record. Do you want me to send you a copy?"

"Could I come by and pick up a copy?" Abby ventured hesitantly. "I work here in Concord."

"Sure, no problem. Give me a few hours to make a copy. And there's a five-dollar charge. I can leave it in an envelope at the desk, if you want."

"That would be wonderful. Thank you."

Abby hung up with a feeling of accomplishment. She wasn't sure what the record would tell her, but it was one step forward, at least.

She picked it up at lunch the same day. Unfortunately, it didn't tell her much. There were eight people buried there, four Reeds and four people with other surnames. She could assume that the women at least were Reed offspring, although why they were buried with Mom and Dad, rather than with their husbands, she couldn't guess. She filed the record away in her swelling folder.

Chapter 18

Saturday Brad was up early, before Abby.

"You look energetic," she said sleepily. "Did we have plans?"

"Uh, no. Bill wanted to get together for some pickup basketball, before it gets too cold, and I said I'd show up. You've got errands and stuff, right?"

"Sure. And I thought I might go to the library in Concord. What time will you be back?"

"Hey, I don't know. Late afternoon, maybe. I'll call you."

Abby lay in bed, watching Brad carom around the small bedroom. "Do you want to do something tomorrow, maybe? We could go look for some pick-your-own place, get some apples. Or maybe see a movie—we haven't done that in a while."

"Sure, babe, whatever you want. I'm all yours. Or, no, wait—the Patriots are playing early tomorrow, and it should be a good game. They're on a roll."

Abby sighed inwardly. "That's what I've read. You want me to pick up some snack stuff for you?"

"Just make sure we've got beer, okay?" He exited with a flurry, and again Abby heard the outer door slam shut behind him. Well, here she was, with another free day on her hands. Good thing she had a plan for it, because obviously Brad didn't want to spend the time with her. Why was that? she wondered. Earlier in the summer she had thought it was because she was just boring, occupied as she was by packing things, arranging for utilities for their new place, picking out curtains—all the minutiae it took to keep daily life going. But now she had a job, and she was afraid that Brad was bored with her because she just wasn't paying enough attention to him. *Damned if you do, damned if you don't. You can't win, Abby.* She threw off the covers and climbed out of bed.

Errands done, she headed for Concord shortly after lunch. At the library, she meandered her way through the historic lobby with its imposing statue of Ralph Waldo Emerson, then asked the woman behind the desk where the local history materials were kept. She was directed to the lower level. The term "basement" would be an insult to the expansive, well-lit space that occupied most of the floor. Clearly there was substantial interest in local history and local families of Concord. Hesitantly Abby approached the woman in charge, who looked up from the papers in front of her.

"Can I help you?" A cheerful smile softened the standard question.

"I hope so. I wanted to find some information about the Reeds who are buried in the cemetery here."

The woman stood up. She was notably taller than Abby. "You came to the right place. What do you know?"

"Not much—only what I've read on the tombstone." *And the faces I've seen,* Abby added silently. *That won't help much.*

"Well, then, I guess we'll start with the basics. When did they die?"

And they were off and running. The librarian explained what the seemingly endless arrays of books covered, including a wealth of histories and records from towns other than Concord. Abby made a mental note to figure out what other places she wanted to investigate—it would certainly be handy if this turned out to be one-stop shopping for all her genealogy needs. On the other hand, there was just so much here, she wondered if she could ever cover it all. She realized the woman was winding down.

"So, why don't you start with the vital records? They might be a bit early for these people, but you never know."

Abby smiled at her. "Thank you. Can I yell if I need help? I'm kind of new at this."

The woman laughed. "Sure. That's what I'm here for. And we get a lot of people like you here. Happy hunting!"

Abby made another circuit of the perimeter and pulled out a few volumes. Taking them to an empty seat at one of the glossy wooden tables, she settled down, laid out her materials, and dug in. Three hours later she knew that William Reed and Mary Ann Corey had announced their intentions to wed in the church in Concord, but there was no record for their marriage—they must have been married somewhere else, then. The banns said William had been from Newton, and Mary Ann from Concord, but Abby couldn't find any other references to those Reeds in Concord. She was surprised: she hadn't thought that people wandered around that much in the middle of the nineteenth century. She supposed she would have to look in surrounding communities—but then, she wasn't even sure which they were. She needed to find a map.

A touch on her shoulder startled her, and she looked up to see the librarian. "Any luck?"

Abby nodded. "At least I've got a start. They seem to have announced their marriage here, but only the wife lived here, and her parents didn't."

"Sorry to kick you out, but we're closing soon."

Abby looked at her watch. "Good heavens, I had no idea it was that late. Sorry."

"No problem. You can come back again—we're open a couple of nights a week."

Abby made a mental note of that information and gathered up her papers. As she climbed the stairs and went out into the bracing autumn air, she reflected that this kind of research was sort of like hunting. You had to believe your target was out there somewhere, but sometimes you got only the occasional tantalizing glimpse of it. Still, it was enough to keep you coming back for more. Abby knew she wasn't anywhere near finished.

The evening began quietly enough. Brad was actually home when Abby returned from Concord.

"Hey, sweetie, you're here!" Abby greeted him.

Brad grumbled something unintelligible, apparently absorbed in reading. Abby shrugged, hung up her coat, and went into the kitchen to look for something to make for dinner. She was still staring into the open refrigerator when Brad came in and reached around her for a beer, and then backed away to lean against the countertop, watching her. Idly Abby reflected that in the past he would have wrapped an arm around her, beer or no. When had that changed?

She pulled an unopened package of chicken parts out of the refrigerator and closed the door. Brad hadn't moved.

"What do you feel like eating tonight?" Abby asked, laying the chicken on the counter and opening a cabinet. "Chinese, Indian, Mexican?"

He didn't answer, absorbed in peeling the label off his bottle with a thumbnail.

"Brad?"

He looked up at her then. "What's with this guy Ned?"

Abby looked at him quizzically. "Ned? I told you, I met him on the house tour a few weeks ago. You met him, remember? He's been helping me with some research."

"Uh-huh. He left you a message on the machine this afternoon, wondered how the job was working out. Why does he know about that?"

Abby eyed him. He looked belligerent, and she wondered just how long ago he'd started on the beer. She reached past him, peeled the wrapping off the chicken, and moved to the sink to wash it. "Brad, I told you all this, remember? My boss is a friend of his, and she told him she needed someone, fast. He told me, I called her and got the job. End of story."

She began chopping onions. If Brad didn't have an opinion about dinner, she would make what she felt like. Brad hadn't moved, and she could feel his eyes on her.

"How many other times have you seen this Ned guy?"

Abby stopped chopping to stare at Brad. Was that what this was about? He was jealous? That was laughable, although she supposed she should be flattered that Brad thought she would be attractive to other men. But she assumed he was just being territorial: he didn't want any men sniffing around "his woman"—even a man he had branded as a possibly gay wimp. Brad was still waiting for her to say something.

"A couple of times. Why? You were out doing something, so Ned's been showing me around. That's all."

"I don't like it. I don't like the way he sounds on the message."

You mean, like he cared? "Well, Brad, what do you want him to do? Grunt? Use words of no more than one syllable?"

"That's not what I mean. You're a good-looking woman, and you don't have a lot of friends around here, so you're, I dunno, hungry for attention? I don't want him to take advantage of you."

"Brad, listen to yourself. You sound like something out of a Victorian novel. What on earth do you mean, 'take advantage of me'?" Some small part of her was warmed that at least Brad still thought she was attractive.

"I just think that his message sounded like more than just a casual 'hey, how'ya doin' sort of thing."

Abby leaned against the counter at a right angle to Brad, and she looked at him. His expression combined sheepishness and anger, but now he wasn't meeting her eye.

Was this the time to tell him about what had been happening to her? Would it help her to explain why she had been spending time with Ned? Or would it only make things worse?

She knew that the longer she went without telling him, the more difficult it would be to explain. He deserved to know, if he cared about her. Before speaking, Abby found a wineglass and poured herself a glass of wine. She took a sip, then began.

"Brad, there's something we need to talk about."

She was not prepared for the explosion that followed.

"Damn it—I knew it! You've been sneaking around behind my back, seeing this guy. What, I'm not good enough for you? You've been mooching around, living off my dime, and you're cheating on me?"

Abby was stunned at Brad's outburst and couldn't even figure out what to answer first. "Brad! It's nothing like that. Why on earth would you even think that?" And if he did think that, he didn't know her very well—she prided herself on her honesty, and she would never, never think of betraying Brad. And "mooching"? She had never counted on him to support her—she'd had a job in Philadelphia, she'd been carrying her own weight. It was only since they'd moved to Massachusetts that she'd been unemployed—and she'd been busy making his life easier for him while he went to his high-powered job in the city. Didn't that count for something?

"Then why haven't you talked about him?" he shot back.

Because I knew you'd react like this. "Because I didn't think you'd be interested in my research project, that's all. Look, can we go into the living room, sit down, talk about this more calmly?"

He glared at her, then turned and stomped out of the room, throwing himself into his easy chair with an aggrieved sigh. Abby followed more slowly, trying to marshal her thoughts. She sat on the couch, facing him.

"You wanted to talk. So, talk," he challenged.

"All right. I told you I met Ned on that house tour I went on, right? Well, it was a little more complicated than that." She took another sip of wine, stalling, trying to decide where to start. "He was the guide, or docent, or whatever, for the last house I visited—you know, the big one on the school grounds, that you can see from the road? Anyway, I got there late, the end of the day, and there was nobody else around. When I walked into this one room, the dining room . . . I got kind of dizzy, almost passed out."

Brad stared. Abby watched a series of expressions flit across his face. "Why? Were you sick? Or . . . pregnant?"

Which scares you more? Abby wondered. "No, nothing like that. It was just that . . . I had something like a hallucination about one particular room, like I was seeing it in the past."

"So what're you saying—you had some sort of déjà vu thing?"

"Not exactly." She couldn't think of any way to explain it that would make sense to him. "Anyway, Ned noticed I looked kind of shaky and made me a cup of tea, and then we started talking about the people who had lived there. And that's when I started doing research—at the National Archives here, and at the library in town."

Brad looked skeptical. "Why?"

Abby shook her head. "I don't know—I just thought I needed to find out who those people were. And I did. I found an obituary for the man who lived in the house around 1895, and there was a picture. It was the man I had seen in that room."

There. She'd laid it out on the table. She watched Brad curiously, waiting for his response. Several seconds ticked away.

Finally he spoke. "Abby, that is the biggest load of crap I've ever heard from you. You're telling me that suddenly you've gone all psychic and you're seeing dead people? Come on."

"Brad, I haven't decided what this all means. I just know what I saw, and I wanted to find out why."

"Bull. You were bored because you didn't have a job, didn't have enough to keep you busy, and you met this guy, and he was nice to you, or whatever, so you've been seeing him ever since, and you cooked up this little psychic fantasy to keep him interested. Right?"

The surge of anger she felt surprised her. "Brad! It wasn't anything like that!" Between her indignation and her need to explain, Abby was having trouble getting any words out. "You know I've been busy since we moved, and you know I was going to look for a job. And I have one now. That wasn't the point. This other thing just sort of happened." Abby stopped, all too aware that her last statement could be interpreted in more than one way.

"And you're going to try to tell me that you haven't seen him since?"

"No, I didn't say that. I've seen him, but as a friend. He's been helping me with research—what to look for, where to find it." Abby wondered if it was wise to tell him about the subsequent episodes and decided that she'd better get everything out in the open now, get things cleared up between them. "And . . . I've seen things—people—a couple of times since, in different places."

Abby couldn't read Brad's gaze, but she knew he didn't look happy. Finally he said, "And you waited until now to tell me anything about this? Were you ever going to, if I hadn't stumbled on the message from your pal Ned?"

"Brad," Abby began, hating the note of desperation that crept into her voice, "I just wanted to understand what was happening before I tried to explain it to you."

"Yeah, right. And handy Ned just happened to be able to help you with all this 'research.'"

Brad stood up abruptly, and Abby shrank into herself. "You know what I think?" he said. "Either you're sneaking around on me with this guy or you're going crazy. I'm not sure which idea I like better." He grabbed his jacket from where he'd tossed it on the table by the door. "I'm going out."

"Brad?" Abby called out, but he was already gone. She sat numbly in the chair as the echoes of the slammed door faded. *You wondered why I didn't tell you, Brad? Because I knew you'd say exactly what you did.* It was so unfair, she thought. Ned was a friend, nothing more. And the visions? Maybe she was losing her mind—but she wasn't going to concede that until she'd exhausted all other possibilities. She didn't feel crazy, just confused.

And a small part of her wondered, *Why couldn't you have just believed me, Brad? Why couldn't you have seen how hard this is for me? Given me a little comfort, support? I didn't ask for this, but it happened. And now all I want to do is figure it out and go on with my life. Our life.*

She wasn't sure how long she sat there, but it was dark when she finally dragged herself out of the chair and went back to the kitchen to put the chicken away. She wasn't hungry anymore.

Brad had not returned when she went to bed, close to midnight.

Chapter 19

She hadn't heard him come in, but Abby found Brad asleep on the couch when she wandered into the living room Sunday morning. He was dead to the world, smelling faintly of stale beer again, and Abby studied him for a moment while he slept on. What was it she loved about him? His energy, his boyish charm, his determination? *And,* she reminded herself, *the fact that he said he loved you.* That hadn't happened very often in her life.

But now she wondered about him. It wasn't much fun when Brad funneled all that energy into his work and didn't save any of it for her. His determination gave him a sort of tunnel vision—and she wasn't in the tunnel. And the charm? It was a tool that he could turn on and off: he used it when it suited him. He'd won her, and he'd flipped the switch to "off." *Face it, Abby,* the small voice in her said, *he's an overgrown kid, impatient, and insensitive to anyone else around him.* He was the center of his own universe, and everything, everyone else was supposed to be an orbiting planet, basking in his warm glow. She should know—she'd been there. So where was she now?

Somewhere outside Brad's solar system. It was a lot colder out there, but the view was very clear. She didn't like what she saw.

In a pensive mood, she went into the kitchen to make coffee. While she was in the kitchen, she heard Brad's cell phone ring—it sounded muffled, so it must have been in his pocket. He roused himself enough to answer it, and said, "Yeah, sure. See you there." A few moments later, Abby heard him lurch toward the bathroom, followed by the sound of running water.

When he came into the kitchen, his hair wet, his chin clean-shaven, his eyes were wary. Abby wondered how he was going to play this. After all, he'd been the one hurling accusations at her; he'd been the one who stormed out and stayed out for hours. She was not going to start out by being defensive, so she waited for him to speak.

"Uh, looks, Abs. Maybe I was a little out of line last night. And maybe part of this is my fault—I've been so busy lately, with work and all."

Which doesn't explain why you run off to play with your friends on weekends when you don't have to work, instead of spending the time with me, Abby added mentally. Still she said nothing.

"But I really think you need to take a look at what you're doing. I mean, this 'seeing things' business just sounds nuts. Maybe you should find a shrink or something."

Fine—now I'm broken, and I have to find somebody to fix me. She'd seen this coming. "Brad, I'm not sure that would solve anything. I'm willing to try, but I'm not about to say that because I'm seeing things I must be unbalanced. That's not what this feels like."

"Then what *is* happening?"

She shook her head. "I don't know. I don't understand it, but I want to. And I wish you'd have a little faith in me." She wasn't sure whether she was referring to Ned or to her "visions" but either one would do. "Although I guess I should be flattered that you're jealous."

Brad still looked doubtful. "Ah, hell, I don't really see you with that Ned guy—he's kind of a nerd. Maybe I'm just overreacting—there's been a lot going on at work, a lot of stress. I didn't mean to take it out on you."

Abby softened. "Can I help?"

Brad shook his head. "Nah, it's just business stuff—in-house politics, that kind of thing. Not a whole lot you can do about it." He stood up straighter and stretched his neck. "That damn couch is useless for sleeping. What's happening for breakfast?"

And I'm supposed to be making it for you, as usual, Abby thought. "How about waffles?"

"Fine. Oh—I'm meeting the guys later for football. Will you be around?"

Was that a challenge? "Yes. I've got some work to do." She didn't elaborate.

He left not long after breakfast. Abby wondered if she should return Ned's call. She wondered if she would tell Brad if she did. Should she tell Ned not to call her at home? That didn't seem right either—he was a friend. Didn't she have the right to have friends? Sure, he was a man, but he didn't seem interested in her as a woman—just as a weird phenomenon who saw things that weren't really there. And she wasn't interested in him as a man. Or at least, she hadn't thought about it. After all, she loved Brad, she was living with him. How could she be thinking about other men? Ned was certainly very different from Brad—quiet, curious, unassuming. At least he listened to her, without criticizing. That was nice.

She decided to let sleeping dogs lie. If he called, fine; if he didn't, that was fine too. She was startled when the phone rang at about twelve thirty. She answered tentatively.

"Hello?"

A man's voice—not Ned, not Brad. "Hi, uh, Abby, is it? Is Brad there? I tried his cell but it went straight to voice mail."

"He's not here at the moment—he's somewhere watching the Patriots game with some people from work. "

There was an awkward silence. "Oh. Maybe I got it messed up—I was just going to ask him if he wanted to get together to watch."

Abby took a wild guess. "Is this Bill? He left here over an hour ago— I'm sure he'll show up soon. Must be fun to watch the game on a big screen."

"Huh? What do you mean?"

"Oh, I'm sorry, I must have gotten confused. I thought you had one of those giant TVs."

"I wish. Well, I won't keep you—I'm sure he'll be here any minute. Nice talking with you." Bill hung up very quickly.

Abby sat back and digested that short conversation. Brad had lied about Bill's TV. Brad had also apparently lied about his plans for the day. The more she thought about it, the more she wondered how many other weekend plans he had lied about. And if he wasn't hanging out with Bill and the guys, where was he?

She stared at the phone, and then slowly hit the speed-dial button for Brad's cell phone, to leave him a message. To her surprise, after three rings he answered. "Abby?" He sounded incredulous.

"Hi, sweetie. Bill just called wondering if you'd like to watch the game with him."

Silence. And then Abby could hear a throaty laugh in the background— definitely female—and a muffled curse as Brad apparently put his hand over the phone and said something. He wasn't with Bill and the guys, he was with a woman. Abby waited for the stab of dismay to shoot through her. It didn't. Why was she not surprised? Because maybe her intuition had gone into overdrive, and she'd already picked up the signs, without realizing it? So that was why Brad had picked that fight with her last night—had tried to turn the tables on her, accusing her of carrying on with Ned, because he was carrying on with another woman. And with a flash of insight she knew who it was.

"Well, Brad, maybe you should give Bill a call and straighten him out. Oh, and say hi to Shanna."

Abby hung up. She stared at the phone, waiting. As she expected, Brad called back immediately, but she ignored the call. She really didn't want to talk to him. He tried again, then a third time, before giving up. She sat in the chair, still staring at the handset of her phone, thinking furiously. Brad and Shanna. How long had that been going on? And how often?

And how did she really feel about it? Hurt. Insulted. Angry. And—if she was honest with herself—relieved. At least now she knew why things had seemed "off" between them for a while—and it wasn't her fault, or at least not entirely. She'd thought it was the stress of moving, new job, change—but in fact there had been a wild card in the hand that she hadn't even seen. What was worse, she could see that Brad and Shanna made a good couple. They were both sharks. They were certainly better matched than she and Brad were.

So, Abby, what are you going to do about it? She contemplated that for a while. Did she want to try to work things out with Brad. *No.* Well, did she want to go back to Philadelphia, where at least she had a network of friends and some professional contacts? She was mildly surprised that her first response to that idea was also "no." She liked this part of Massachusetts. She liked her job, and she liked Leslie. And she certainly had some unfinished business with all these dead people popping up all over. She couldn't just walk away from all that, at least not until she understood it. But she did have to get out of this apartment. The lease was in Brad's name, since he had been the one with the income, but she didn't like the place anyway. She could find something of her own—although, she realized with a moment of panic, she wasn't sure just how far her salary would go if she had to rent her own place. It would be nice to be closer to work, and Concord looked like a lovely place to live, but she was sure the rents were astronomical.

She looked around the room. With the single exception of her great-grandmother's chair, there was little here that was hers, and not much that she'd miss. Maybe she should be looking for a furnished attic somewhere. Maybe she'd turn into a typical old maid with a cat. Maybe now she could get a cat. My, there was a lot to think about.

She wondered when Brad would show his face again, now that he knew that she knew. And Shanna knew that she knew. Would he hurry back to Waltham, try to explain himself, to make things right? And what would right be? Abby had no idea. Or would he stall as long as possible, then slink in after dark?

And what was her role in this silly charade? Was she supposed to disintegrate into a heap of soggy tissues and misery? She almost laughed out loud at that image. Was she supposed to be angry—rant and rave, throw things at Brad, tear her hair, or threaten to tear out Shanna's (obviously fake) blonde hair? Abby tried to visualize that and failed entirely. She was surprised to find that she wasn't anywhere near that angry—despite the fact that Brad had lied to her systematically. Had dragged her across several states and dumped her in an entirely unfamiliar place, and expected her to make things nice for him. And had had the nerve to accuse *her* of cheating. That really was ridiculous.

Brad opted for option two and came skulking in after six. Abby had managed to spend the afternoon on odds and ends, and more than once had found herself walking around the few rooms of the apartment, mentally ticking off which pieces she considered hers and how many additional boxes she might want for books. There wasn't much, which made her sad. After all, she and Brad had spent over a year together, and there was precious little to show for it.

He let himself in and closed the door quietly behind him. Abby had been in the kitchen and came to stand in the doorway. They watched each other across the dark divide of the living room. Brad finally spoke first.

"I'm sorry you had to find out like that."

"Oh, were you planning to tell me?" Abby's tone was quiet but biting.

Brad had the decency to look away from her then. "Well, you must have known things weren't going well with us. Look, obviously you haven't been happy for a while."

Abby regarded him as though he were a bug under a microscope. "And when did you notice that? Before or after we left Philadelphia? Before or after you met Shanna? Before or after you slept with her?"

"Abby!" Brad sounded genuinely hurt. "I didn't do this on purpose. I never planned to hurt you."

"Oh, no. You just sort of tripped one day and fell onto Shanna? And by the way, wasn't she involved with a friend of yours?"

"Look, what's the point of talking about it? It happened. I'm sorry."

"And what do you want to do about it?" Abby was honestly curious to see what his response would be.

"I don't know," he said miserably. "I mean, I feel awful about what this must be doing to you."

Abby gave a short laugh. "Well, that's a first. Let me ask you one thing: do you love Shanna?"

Brad stared at his hands in his lap. "Well, I don't know, maybe—I think so. It's not like it was with you. I mean, you were so soft and sweet, I just wanted to take care of you. Shanna challenges me. She makes me want to do big things. She's exciting—"

"I don't want to hear it," Abby cut him off abruptly. "I get it. You used to love me, maybe, but now you don't. You may or may not love Shanna, but she's a heck of a lot more fun to be with. All right, I'll make it easy for you. I'll move out."

Abby's words hung in the air like bubbles. She wondered where her gumption had come from, why she wasn't fighting to keep him, or at least fighting to buy time. But, she realized, she didn't want time. She wanted it to be over. She wanted a clean break. She could visualize what their effort to reconcile would look like: both of them tiptoeing around, being extra polite and considerate, going through the motions. And they would end up in the same place anyway. Why not just get it over with?

Brad was looking at her as though she was a stranger. "That's it? You don't want to fight about it?"

Abby regarded him wearily. "Why bother? You're a big boy, and you know what you want. I may not know what I want, but I'm pretty sure it's more than this. And I won't fall apart just because you aren't around. I'll move out as soon as I can find a place I can afford."

Sheepishly, Brad said, "I can help you out, if you need money."

"Forget it. I'll manage. But for the moment, I think you can stay on the couch. Now, what do you want for dinner?"

The last thing out of her mouth surprised even Abby, but she realized she actually was hungry—ravenous, in fact—and it seemed silly to cook for just herself. She could be generous in victory. And she did feel that she had won, even though she was walking away from this with no more than a few boxes of stuff in a battered car. *And a chair,* she reminded herself. *And my self-respect.* That brought her up short. Suddenly she felt a new kinship for her unknown great-grandmother, who had had to make a new life for herself when her husband walked out, leaving her in the middle of the Depression with a young child to care for. *I don't know who's channeling who here, Ruth, but thanks.* Abby sure hoped that heredity worked.

Chapter 20

Abby felt far less confident in the cold clear light of Monday morning. As she drove toward Concord, she made mental lists: find local paper with rental listings. Apartment agency? Ask around at work, see if anybody knew of anyplace small and cheap. Figure out what to do about furniture, starting with a bed. Utilities. Change of address forms, again; she wasn't even sure if the first ones had gone through. Tell her parents—ouch. They were certainly going to be surprised. The drive went very quickly as her mind raced.

She parked in the lot and made her way up to her office. She'd left the apartment early, mainly to avoid having to talk to Brad, and there were few people around. In her office chair, she sat and surveyed her little domain, which was still cluttered with someone else's stuff. Well, she had some time, so she decided to dig in and sort out the mess.

Half an hour later she was trying to stuff just one more folder into the overflowing wastebasket when Leslie stuck her head in the door. "Got a minute?"

"Sure." Mystified, Abby followed Leslie back to her office. Leslie handed her a hot coffee.

"Here. This is my nominal staff relations follow-up conversation—the nonexistent manager's handbook says I should have one with all new hires. Congratulations on surviving your first full week. How's it going?"

Abby sipped the coffee, trying to decide how honest to be. She opted for the most direct route. "I love it. I feel like I've found some piece of me that's been missing for a while." She was struck with a bolt of self-doubt. "You aren't going to tell me I'm doing a lousy job and fire me, are you?"

Leslie laughed. "Like hell. I watched a couple of your tours last week—you're doing fine. You jumped right in like a pro. You have a real rapport with the kids, and you make history come alive to them. I've got no complaints. I just wanted to make sure you weren't feeling overwhelmed, or were going to make a dash for the nearest exit."

"No way. But—" Abby hesitated. "I may need to take a little personal time—I think I'm going to have to find a new place to live."

Leslie regarded her with sympathy. "Trouble in paradise, huh? I've been there. What're you looking for?"

Abby shrugged. "I don't think I can afford to be choosy—you know how much I make. Just something quiet and simple, and not too far away

127

from here, if that's possible." Abby noted that Leslie had a distant look in her eye. "Uh, hello?"

Leslie focused on her again. "Sorry—I just had a brainstorm. Let me make a couple of calls before I say anything, okay? And sorry about you and . . . what's his name. Guess I won't need to learn his name now, huh?"

Abby grinned at her. "Nope—I think he's history."

"You okay with that? I mean, you're not about to have a nervous breakdown or anything?"

Not about Brad. "No, I'm fine. In fact, I feel better than I thought I would—it's like I had to spend a lot of energy trying to figure out what would make him happy, and now I only have to worry about making *me* happy. And I'm very glad I've got this job. Which I'd better get back to—there's a tour due at ten."

Abby was grateful for the demands of the busload of children, which kept her mind off her own woes. She kept telling herself that she felt fine, but she wondered if she was kidding herself—that in reality, somewhere underneath there was a festering swamp of pain and resentment and sadness that was going to erupt at a very inconvenient moment. If she felt so little now, had Brad meant so little to her? But she survived the first tour of the day without falling to pieces and retreated to her office to consider lunch options.

Leslie's head appeared again. "Yeah, I know, twice in one day. Listen, I've got a proposition for you."

Abby looked at her expectantly. "I'm all ears."

"Well, I've got this college classmate, owns a house about two miles from here. Also owns a house in Arizona, which is where she and her husband spend their winters—can't take this New England snow, I guess. Anyway, generally she finds some sort of house sitter for the place here, just to have someone to keep an eye on it, make sure the pipes don't freeze, that kind of thing. This year she had somebody lined up but his plans changed at the last minute, and she didn't have time to find anyone else before she left town. I gave her a call and asked if you could fill in. You interested?"

Abby gaped. "You mean, a whole house? For how long?"

"Until May. Don't get the wrong idea—it's not a mansion. But it's plenty big for you. And it's a real nice property—the land behind it is protected, so you feel like you're out in the country. What do you think?"

"It sounds perfect." And another thought struck her. "And it's furnished?"

"Yep, completely. My friend keeps a full set of everything at each end—saves all that messy packing and stuff. All you have to do is pay the utilities."

"Wow." *My karma must really have changed,* Abby thought. "Well, unless I'm allergic to the place, it sounds wonderful. What do I have to do?"

"I'll give the caretaker a call, tell him to meet you after work, and he can show you around—you know, the heating system, the alarm system, stuff like that—and give you the keys."

"It's a deal! And, Leslie? Thank you again, for everything."

At seven o'clock that evening, Abby found herself standing in the foyer of the house she had just promised to care for over the next six months. She hadn't even seen it by daylight. The handyman-cum-gardener-cum-security specialist had handed her a key ring with a bewildering array of keys, and three pages of typed instructions about how to turn things on and off. The list ended with some twenty emergency contact numbers. She felt positively giddy with—something. Joy? Relief? Triumph? Or some happy combination of all of those. Yesterday she had split up with her boyfriend of over two years, without any sort of plan; today she had a great new place to stay, with no strings attached. She could map out the next step in her life while living in the lap of luxury—well, compared to what she was coming from, anyway. And she could fit everything she wanted to bring in her car. She needed to call Brad to tell him she was going to stop by.

She dialed the number at the apartment. No answer. She called his cell, but it went immediately to voice mail. Oh, well, she didn't exactly need his permission to collect her clothes and books. And the computer—surely he wouldn't begrudge her the old laptop? And if he did, she could afford to buy a new one of her own. She set off for Waltham in high spirits.

Two hours later, she had loaded the car, including the laptop. The swan chair she had wrapped in blankets and settled carefully in the backseat. She made one last trip upstairs, and looked around the living room. In spite of all her hopeful efforts, it had never ceased to be impersonal and cold, and removing her few possessions had made little difference. *Brad, it's all yours.* Dutifully she left a note with the details of her new address sitting on top of a small stack of the most recent bills. Let Brad worry about those.

She made her way slowly down the stairs, out to her car, and drove back toward Concord. Even in the dark she was beginning to recognize local landmarks. She went past the museum, past the small town green, and turned right in front of the Colonial Inn. She followed the road past the statue of the minuteman and over the Concord River. A mile or so farther on, she arrived at "her" house. It was set well back from the road, and she was pleased to see that outside lights came on when she pulled around the side to the garage. It was a reassuring touch. And she now had a garage door opener, so she could pull in and unload her stuff easily. Maybe it was for all the wrong reasons, but Abby felt like she was moving up in the world.

The house sat on the slope of a hill, with the garage at the lower level. Her handyman-guide had said that usually the house sitter stayed in the guest suite on the lower level, and she had no complaints about that. To take over the master suite upstairs seemed presumptuous. She opened the door, disabled the alarm, and began to carry her possessions in, starting with the swan chair, which she carefully set in the place of honor in the guest bedroom. It took only a few trips to bring in the suitcases and boxes. Abby made sure that the garage door was closed, then locked the entry door behind her.

She turned to contemplate her new home. Her battered packing boxes looked pitifully shabby in the well-appointed guest room—and pathetically few. Was this really all she had brought with her to start a new life? She walked slowly to the center of the room, listening to the silence. The windows overlooking the back showed no lights, only blackness, but Abby pulled the blinds anyway, shutting out the night.

Unexpectedly, standing in the middle of the unfamiliar room, in a strange house, a rush of emotion overwhelmed her, and she sank to her knees on the carpet in the middle of the room and started to cry. What had happened? What had gone wrong? She and Brad had started out for Massachusetts with such high hopes. Brad had been so charged up about his new job, and she had been honestly happy for him. And it had all fallen apart so quickly. When had the trouble started? Should she have seen it coming? Had she missed something? She couldn't hold back the tears. She felt more alone than she could ever remember, and her life was spinning out of control around her.

She didn't know how long she sat there, tears running down her cheeks, mourning her lost hopes and plans, but gradually the storm subsided. And then a curious thought forced its way into her head: she was the one who was moving on. That was something she never expected. If anyone had asked her, even a week ago, she would have said that she would fight to save their tattered relationship—probably far longer than was good for either of them. But here she was, on her own, after a quick clean break. *Good for you,*

Abby! She sat up straighter and wiped the tears off her face impatiently. All right, she would permit herself this moment of regret, for the last two years of her life, for the lost hopes, and for everything that might have been—and then let it go. *Good-bye, Brad,* she said to herself. *I wish you a good life. Just not with me.*

Chapter 21

Abby woke up abruptly the next morning, momentarily unsure of where she was. She had slept badly, startled by unfamiliar noises—mostly the intermittent rumbles of the furnace and the water heater, but also strange cracks and pops as the house cooled during the night. She crawled out of the ample queen-sized bed and crossed to the window, pulling up the blinds. Then she stared, transfixed. She had not seen this place by daylight, and she hadn't realized just how impressive the view was—what looked like wetlands at the bottom of the slope behind the house, and wooded hills beyond. The house had been placed to take maximum advantage of the topography. From this room at the back of the house, she couldn't see any neighbors, or any houses at all. What she could see were three deer grazing on the lawn below her, no more than twenty feet away. She wondered if there was any way she could set up her computer work space to take advantage of this scene—or if she did, if she'd get any work done with this view to stare at.

Pulling herself reluctantly away from the misty morning spread out before her, she searched for clothes. She'd been too exhausted the night before to think about unpacking, and everything was jammed into a box or suitcase. Oh, well, the kids would just have to live with rumpled Abby for a day or two.

Showered and dressed, she ambled upstairs to the kitchen and put on a kettle for coffee. While she waited, she surveyed the kitchen. As Leslie had said, the house was not large, but everything she could see was top-of-the-line. This was a nice way to live. Abby wasn't sure she could aspire to it as a long-term goal, but she was going to be sure to enjoy it while she could. The kettle whistled and she made a pot of coffee. Seated at the breakfast table in the kitchen, she started jotting down items for her shopping list, stopping to check in cupboards and closets as she went. The larder was surprisingly well stocked, but she found her tastes differed slightly from those of the absent owners and there were some other things she wanted.

Abby managed to avoid thinking about anything substantial for most of the week. She got up early, drove the blessedly short distance to the museum, worked hard, and came home—if her house-sit qualified as "home"—in the dark, tired. She poked around the house a bit, but she still felt like an intruder, wearing a limited path between her two-rooms-with-bath downstairs—which came equipped with a more than respectable television—and the kitchen above. The house, buffered by its deep front lawn, was quiet, as was the entire neighborhood—few vehicles traveled the road in front at night. In spite of the elaborate alarm system, Abby was not yet entirely comfortable being alone in such a large place. It was going to take time to familiarize herself with it and achieve some sort of psychological possession of it.

It was several days before Brad called her cell phone one evening. Abby stared for a moment at the familiar number on the phone before answering.

"Hello?"

"It's me." Brad paused. "You took all your stuff."

"Yes." She wasn't about to make this easy for him.

"Hey, shouldn't we at least talk about this?"

Abby considered, then said slowly, "I don't think so."

"Why not? So I screwed up. But how can you just walk out like that? Don't I mean anything to you?"

Once you did, Brad. And then you started taking me for granted. And then you slept with Shanna. I don't want to talk about it, I just want it to be over. Abby felt achingly old and wise compared to Brad, who really didn't see that he'd done anything wrong. And there was no point in trying to explain it to him, because he would never get it.

"Yes, Brad, you did. But when I found out about Shanna, I guess a lot of things fell into place. You're better off with someone like her anyway. She's more your type that I ever was." *And why did it take me so long to see that?*

Brad seemed bewildered by her response. Had he expected her to plead, to apologize, to beg to come back? Abby was happily surprised that she didn't want to do any of those things.

"So that's it, then? Well, it's your life, I guess." Brad sounded like a spoiled little boy.

"Yes, it is. Oh, if there's any mail for me, can you forward it? I'll put in a change of address card, but I haven't had time yet."

"Yeah, sure." A long pause. "Well, bye, Abby." Another pause. "Sorry." He hung up before she could respond.

So that was that? The end of two-plus years of her life? What was that line, "not with a bang but with a whimper"? Although that line could be interpreted in more than one way . . . Maybe it had been a bang—for Shanna. Abby smiled. Her heart couldn't be too badly broken if she could see that as funny.

By the weekend she was feeling braver, and she needed to stock up on some more things. She added some other errands to her list. All her cold-weather clothes had been sitting in boxes for a couple of months, so she needed to take them to the cleaners. She needed to find the liquor store, the post office, a hardware store. And then she wanted to treat herself to a stroll around town, maybe ending up at the bookstore. She sighed with pleasure at the day before her.

Her reverie was broken by the sound of her cell phone. Where had she left it? In her purse? But where was her purse? This house was far bigger than the apartment, and she kept putting things down and losing them. She followed the sound, but by the time she located her purse the phone had stopped ringing. She checked for her messages and missed calls, expecting to see Brad's number appear. But it was Ned's.

Did she want to talk to Ned? Why wouldn't she want to talk to Ned? Well, for starters, she would have to explain that she wasn't living in Waltham anymore, and why. But she couldn't blame Ned for that, even if his last innocent phone call had precipitated this whole mess. Which was turning out surprisingly well. For which she ought to thank him. Before her thinking got any more convoluted, she hit the recall button. He picked up on the second ring.

"Abby?"

"Uh, yes, it's me. Listen, I—" "I understand . . ." They were talking over each other.

"Ned? Let me go first. I guess you figured out that I'm not in Waltham anymore."

"Yes. I called your place, talked to Brad, and he said you'd moved out." He stopped, and Abby wondered if he was going to ask anything more.

"Well, yes. It all happened kind of quickly. I found out he was involved with someone else, so I split. And Leslie found me this incredible house-sit, so I'm all set."

"Abby, are you all right? I mean, this is just one more thing, on top of everything else . . ."

She was touched that he even thought to ask. She said gently, "Yes, really, I think I am. Anyway, it feels right. Maybe all those people I keep seeing are watching out for me." She smiled at the idea, even though he wouldn't see it.

"Well, if you're sure." He didn't sound convinced. "I just wondered if you'd found out anything else, about your relatives, or about the Reeds."

"I haven't had a lot of time to work on it since last weekend. Oh, that's right—I never filled you in on that. I think I've narrowed down when William Flagg was married, and I think it might have been in Ware, so I sent a request to see if they had a marriage record. I can't exactly run out there while I'm working, and the clerk's office is closed weekends. I really need to find out Elizabeth's maiden name. I couldn't find anything online."

"And no other, uh . . ."

"Visions? No, not since the last one. Not that I've been looking—Leslie keeps me pretty busy."

They both fell silent for a moment.

"Uh, Abby—would you like to do something tonight? I mean, maybe get dinner, or just talk?"

"I'd like that. I'd volunteer to cook, but I'm still not sure how all the gadgets in this kitchen work. Maybe we could meet somewhere?"

"Listen, have you ever been to the Wayside Inn, in Sudbury? Longfellow wrote about it. The food's not spectacular, but there's lots of ambience, and it's a nice drive. Want to try that?"

"Sure, sounds nice. You want to come by here and pick me up?"

"All right. I'll make reservations and pick you up around, say, six thirty?"

"Fine. Let me tell you where to find me." She gave him instructions, which were not difficult, since "her" house lay on the main road between Concord and Carlisle. "See you later."

After she ended the call, Abby sat at the kitchen table, staring into space. And, she had to admit, thinking about Ned. Brad had thought there was something going on between them, which was ridiculous. She would never even have contemplated such a thing while she and Brad were together—it would have been wrong. At least, to *her*; Brad hadn't been troubled by any such reservations. But now they weren't together, and Abby had a feeling that was final. Which meant she was back in the market again.

But—Ned? She shook her head. She couldn't see it. Her feelings were still too jumbled, and this was definitely not a good time to think about jumping into something new. Right now, she'd much rather have him as a friend. She needed him to help her sort out these weird appearances, or visions, or visitations—she really should decide what to call them. As she had told Ned, they had not recurred in the last week, although she didn't believe that they were over. After all, she'd spent the week cooped up at the museum or in this newish house—no ghosts in either. Maybe her ghosts were just giving her a little breathing room, but for some reason she was sure they'd be back. They weren't finished with her, or did she mean she wasn't finished with them?

She shook herself and stood up. This was no way to spend a sunny Saturday, and she had errands to run.

When she came back she took a leisurely shower and then contemplated her wardrobe. She couldn't remember the last time she had been to a real restaurant, rather than the ethnic bistro-type places and casual pubs that Brad favored. Not that she didn't enjoy that kind of place, but they weren't the same as places that had tablecloths and linen napkins and candles. Or maybe she was jumping to conclusions, and this Wayside Inn place was just a fast-food joint with a fancy name. She sighed and pulled on a turtleneck and wool pants—her everyday outfit. She was brushing her hair when the doorbell rang. She found her way to the front door, which she hadn't used, and hoped that the alarm system was disarmed. She peered through the peephole to make sure it was Ned, and luckily when she opened the door, no alarms went off.

Ned, standing on her doorstep, looked reassuringly normal. He smiled. "This must be the right place. You ready?"

"Unless you want the grand tour."

"That can wait. We've got a little drive ahead of us."

"Let me get a jacket." Abby collected her purse and a wool blazer, then stood in front of the alarm panel by the door, pressing what she hoped were the right buttons. "All right, we now have one minute to exit the premises before sirens go off. I think. I'd rather not find out."

Ned laughed. "Then let's go."

If Abby had worried about what to say about Brad and her current situation, Ned carefully skirted the issue, talking about the places they were passing through, the restaurant they were going to—all and any safe subjects. Abby found herself relaxing and talking easily. The restaurant, when they arrived, looked for all the world like a warm and welcoming colonial home—although she discovered inside that it rambled back quite a ways, the better to accommodate the dinner crowd, which was large. They were shown to a table—with tablecloth and candles—and presented with large menus.

"The food tries hard to be Yankee colonial, but it's not bad," Ned commented.

"It smells good, anyway. I never got around to lunch today," Abby countered.

After they had ordered, their conversation faltered for a moment. Abby decided that she might as well get over the next hurdle. "You know, you've been very discreet. Aren't you even curious about why I'm suddenly camping out in Concord?"

"I figured you'd tell me if you wanted to. You don't have to, you know. It's really none of my business. Unless you'd rather talk about it?"

So he had left it up to her. It seemed a little weird to think of dumping her personal problems on someone she didn't know very well. On the other hand, there really wasn't anyone else to tell. Did she want to talk about it at all? She wasn't sure. But Ned already knew the bare bones, so she figured she owed him something.

"I found out by accident that Brad was involved with this woman in Boston—her name's Shanna. I don't know when it started, but I've met her, so I can see why—she's tall, blonde, *and* smart." *Everything I'm not.* "She was supposed to be the girlfriend of one of Brad's coworkers—I talked to her at a party a few weeks ago, and she even offered to help me find a job. Well, anyway, Brad's been out on weekends a lot lately, playing golf or catching up on something at work or watching football with the guys. At least, that's what he told me." *Poor silly trusting me.* "I wonder now how much of that was true.

"So last Saturday, I was at the library in Concord, and I gather you called and left a message. And I got home and Brad jumped all over me, asking me who you were and why you were calling me. That caught me by surprise—I'd told him about you, and he'd even met you, right? And then he stormed out and didn't come back 'til late."

Their salads appeared, and Abby poked around at the colorful lettuce. "Then on Sunday, he said he was going to watch football with the guys again. But Bill—the one who was supposed to have this terrific gigantic television—called up looking for him, to ask him if he wanted to come over and watch the game. And I called Brad on his cell, and I could hear a woman in the background, and I sort of put two and two together."

"What did you do?"

"When he finally got back, I asked if he'd been with Shanna. He didn't try to deny it. I just said I'd move out, as soon as I could find a place. Which I did the next day, thanks to Leslie."

Ned was studying her face, as if trying to assess her true feelings. "I'm sorry. You've got a lot on your plate at the moment—new job, new place, your boyfriend dumps you."

"Excuse me, *I* dumped *him*." A small point, but it was important to her. "And don't forget the ghosts."

Ned looked at her curiously. "Is that what you want to call them?"

"What should I be calling them?" Abby asked. "They were real people, and they're dead, and I'm seeing them. Not that the term feels quite right. In a way, I'm seeing events, not people."

"You'll find something that fits." Ned waited while the waitress removed their salad plates and distributed their entrees. "You want to go on exploring your visions, or do you want to put it on the shelf for now? I would certainly understand why you might want to do that."

Abby began cutting up the duck she'd ordered. She took a bite—it was delicious. She tried to remember the last time she'd eaten a real meal, or at least one without tension, and couldn't. "Mmm, this is great. No, I want to figure this out. In a strange way, I think there's some sort of cosmic connection—why I'm here at all, why we picked Waltham to live in, why you brought me to Concord. If there are unseen forces managing my life, I'd really like to know about them." She took another bite of meat and chewed slowly, swallowed. "I've never been a religious person, and I've never paid much attention to mysticism, but for the last month or two I've really had the feeling that there are things just below the surface, things I'm not seeing, but they're still very real. Does that make sense?"

Ned swallowed his mouthful, taking his time. "Yes, I think so. Look, I'm a scientist, and we scientists like proof—we like things we can demonstrate, quantify, replicate. Whatever you've been seeing, or feeling, doesn't fit any of those criteria. But I believe what you say, when you see them. So I'm curious. I can be the voice of reason that throws cold water on all your half-baked theories. If you want."

Abby smiled. "Yes, I do, and thanks. I hope that two heads are better than one. But I wish I had any theories—right now I don't. The only thing I've figured out so far is that I seem to be seeing my great-grandmother, and her grandparents. That doesn't explain the Reeds, or that house in Weston."

"Nothing else lately?"

"No, no new appearances, but as I said, I haven't been anywhere new. So, what now, coach?"

"Keep digging, I guess. How's the family tree going?"

And they were off, on nice safe matters of genealogy, which carried them through dinner and dessert and coffee. Abby found she was enjoying the meal—and enjoying the unfamiliar situation where someone was actually interested in what she had to say. It was nice, she decided.

While they were driving back to Concord, Ned ventured, "You know, you don't seem intimidated by any of this stuff. Does it scare you?"

"It doesn't," Abby responded cheerfully. "Don't ask me why. Usually I'm very cautious about trying new things. But this? I guess it's just that it doesn't feel threatening. I just seem to be stumbling onto people from another era, because for some unknown reason I happen to be on that wavelength."

"That's an interesting way to put it." He pulled into her long driveway and drove up close to the house, but made no move to get out of the car. "I'll wait until you're safe inside, okay?"

Abby gathered up her things. "Sure. And thanks again—dinner was great. I'll let you know if I find anything else interesting—or if somebody new shows up." Keys in hand, she got out of the car and made her way to the door. She managed to get in and disable the alarm quickly, and turned to wave as Ned backed out the drive. He returned her wave and pulled back out onto the road.

Chapter 22

Abby's life fell into a pleasant, predictable pattern, which was fine with her. She got up early, made breakfast and watched the deer, or turkeys, or pheasants; drove the short distance to the museum; worked hard entertaining diverse tour groups and filled the time between tours with crafting and polishing her talks, or just wandering the galleries, familiarizing herself with the collections. Then home to a simple dinner and a book or a couple of hours of television. She didn't hear from Brad. She didn't hear from Ned. She went out a couple of times with people from work, but most of them had busy family lives, which left her the odd person out. One weekend she explored—historic sites, malls, bookstores—whatever caught her fancy. She started knitting a sweater.

A few weeks after she'd left, Brad forwarded an envelope full of mail that had come for her, including a couple of overdue bills. Among the letters was a response from the town clerk in Ware: there was no marriage of William Flagg recorded there, even though Abby knew he had been living there before the Civil War in 1860, and again in 1870—with his wife. Where should she look, then? One day, while she was doing something entirely unrelated, she realized that she knew when Elizabeth had died—surely she could find a death record for 1929, which would include Elizabeth's parents' names and Elizabeth's place of birth. A Google search told her that the Massachusetts Department of Public Health kept records from 1906 onward, but they should also be available from the Waltham town clerk. The Waltham option was a whole lot cheaper, and might be faster—Abby wasn't sure—so she filled out another request and sent it off, and prepared to wait. As long as her ghosts stayed dormant, she wasn't about to obsess about them.

But as Halloween approached, it was hard *not* to think of ghosts. Abby remembered Halloween from her childhood as being a relatively simple affair: buy or slap together some flimsy costume, grab a pillowcase, go out and collect as much candy as possible—and then eat it as fast as possible. Now every storefront boasted elaborate displays and offered an endless array of kitschy items, including lights and things that talked or howled or moved. Abby wasn't sure what the point was, even while she admired the ingenuity and/or absurdity of some of them. Her primary concern was to avoid being at home on Halloween night—not that she wanted to shortchange any earnest young trick-or-treaters, but looking around her neighborhood, she doubted that there were many young children, and even if there were, they would probably be reluctant to venture down her long and unlit driveway merely for a candy bar. It would be easier just to douse the lights and be somewhere else until all the festivities were over. The problem was, where to go?

She was relieved when Ned called on the Friday before. "Hi, Abby. Do you want to go trick-or-treating this weekend?"

"I hope you're kidding," she said dubiously.

"Well, yes, actually. But I thought it might be a little spooky for you, sitting in that big empty house while there were spirits—or at least random teenagers—milling about. I know a place that makes a mean pumpkin pie, in honor of the season."

Abby wondered if he'd read her mind. "That sounds great! I was wondering what excuse I could come up with to vacate the premises. My alternative plan was to turn off all the lights, climb under the quilt with a flashlight and read. Lame, huh?"

"Not at all. But the Eve of All Hallows is a great time to discuss the general phenomenon of spirits and hauntings. If you can stomach it. Have things been quiet?"

"As a tomb." Abby almost giggled. "Sorry, bad joke. But, yes, I'd like to know more about specifics, if you've got any good resources. As long as we're in a nice, brightly lit place."

"Not a problem. Pick you up at five? It gets dark about then, and that's when the spirits begin to prowl."

"Sure. See you then."

• • •

Ned appeared promptly on Sunday as the sun was setting. Abby grabbed a jacket and joined him in the car. As they drove back toward Concord, Abby could see small groups of children shuffling through the piles of bright leaves along the side of the road—few near her house, but in increasing numbers as they approached the town. She didn't recognize many of the costumes—things had moved on since she had been in their shoes. How long had it been? Ten years, maybe? And in this increasingly motorized society, where parents feared for their children's safety even in broad daylight, how long would traditions like this survive? But she remembered well the unaccustomed feeling of freedom, being allowed to run around at night, and actually being rewarded for it with large quantities of chocolate and sugar.

"What're you thinking?" Ned asked in an offhand tone.

"I was just wondering how long Halloween is going to survive in this country. It seems like such an anachronism."

"Ah, but it has very deep roots . . ."

The restaurant he had chosen was small and unpretentious but filled with good smells. They ordered, and then Abby sat back and said, "All right—tell me about Halloween."

"Well, for starters, the custom goes back over two thousand years—well before Christianity. The Celtic Druids thought October thirty-first was the end of the year, so they celebrated a successful harvest, and somehow wrapped it in with honoring the dead. Once the Romans conquered the Celts, they figured it might help convert them to Christianity if they absorbed some of the elements of the old culture. So by the seventh century, the church moved All Saints' Day, which was when they honored dead martyrs, from May to November. Tricky, eh?"

"Well, the Romans were pragmatists, as I recall. Good at getting things done—look at all those roads and aqueducts and stuff."

"Good point. Strategic people, especially when they were conquering other people. Anyway, to get back to our Halloween, it made it to this country early, with Irish and Scottish immigrants. Somewhere in there it lost its mystery and became more of an occasion for fun."

"Where did the costumes come in?"

"Well, one theory is that way back, people believed that the disembodied spirits of the dead would come back looking to borrow a new body for the coming year. This was possible only on the one day—sort of like a free pass between the spirit world and the real world. But the living didn't want to be possessed, so they would dress up in weird costumes and wander around the villages, making noise and trying to discourage the spirits, drive them away."

"And trick-or-treating?"

"Yet another tradition—Halloween really is a catchall. That was European rather than Celtic. On All Souls' Day, November second, which is the day after All Saints' Day, early Christians would wander around begging for cakes, promising to pray for the dead relatives of the donors in return. The more cakes, the more prayers."

Abby found she was enjoying herself. "You, sir, are a font of trivial knowledge. One more question—the pumpkin carving?"

"Probably Irish again, although they carved turnips in Ireland. They found it easier to use pumpkins once they got over here. Although I can't quite imagine carving a turnip—if they're big enough to carve, they're pretty tough. Anything else you want to know?"

Their food arrived. They chatted amiably during the main course, and then Ned insisted on the much-touted pumpkin pie. While they were waiting, Abby tried to put into words something that had been troubling her.

"You said that the Celts or Druids or whoever believed that there was a link between the spirit world and the real world—or the one we're living in. And that the spirits can pass through, at least sometimes. Do you think that's what's happening to me? That I'm seeing spirits from some other parallel world?"

Ned took his time answering. "I suppose it depends on how you define spirits. It pains me as a scientist to say this, but you seem to be running into very specific individuals, not projections of your own belief system."

"Hmm," Abby said pensively. "That's an interesting way to put it. You're saying that if I subconsciously wanted to see ghosts, I could convince myself that I was seeing ghosts, but they'd be generic, rather than real people?"

"Kind of. As I keep saying, it's hard to be rational about what you're seeing." Ned stared down at his coffee cup. "Look, you can tell me if I'm out of line here, but . . . did you ever tell Brad about what's been going on?"

Abby sighed. "I started to, but he said exactly what I expected—just told me either I was barmy or I didn't have enough to keep me busy. He cut me off before I got to the details. If you're asking, that wasn't what split us up. Maybe it was a symptom—he wanted me to be what *he* wanted, not who I really was. I went along with it for a long time. But if this thing with Shanna is any indication, he got tired of trying to mold me to his specifications. Throw in one off-the-wall problem like seeing things, and the whole thing comes crashing down."

Ned nodded. "I'm sorry. It's never easy, whatever the cause. Or causes."

You've got that right, thought Abby. She wondered what had happened between him and Leslie, and she wondered if she'd ever ask. They certainly seemed like very different people, but then, so were she and Brad, and that hadn't worked out. Good intentions did not guarantee a good relationship. She looked at her watch. "Think the hordes have retreated yet?"

"Probably. You ready to go?"

"I think so. I've got work tomorrow."

"How's that going?"

"Really well. I'm enjoying it even more than I expected. And I love this area—there's so much to do, when I can find the time. I think you and Leslie are my guardian angels. So maybe I should get home."

They drove the few miles back in a companionable silence. Ned turned into the long driveway and pulled up in front of the house. "Let me see you to the door, make sure everything's all right."

Abby was relieved—she hated walking into a dark house, although she was getting more comfortable with the place. She dug out her keys as they walked to the door and had them ready. "Thanks—for dinner, and the lecture. I'll let you know if I find anything else new, but right now I'm mostly waiting for people to answer my queries." She unlocked the door and stepped in to disarm the alarm system.

"I know how that goes—slow and painful. Well, I enjoyed dinner. Any time you want to talk, I'm around."

For a moment they stood facing each other awkwardly. Abby wondered if he was going to try to kiss her good night, but instead he reached out a hand to clasp hers.

When he made contact, she jerked away as if she had been scalded and stepped back hastily, staring at Ned. She managed to mutter a strangled "Good night," then slipped inside and shut the door quickly. Then she leaned against it and waited for her heart to stop pounding.

She hadn't been worried about Ned making a move on her. In truth, she had to admit she had wondered if he would, and when, and what she would feel. And she was no blushing virgin. But when he had touched her, skin to skin—it had been like an electric shock. And for a fragmented moment, the air had been filled with sounds, voices, *something*—she couldn't even describe it. It was like when a car full of teens passed by on a city street, radio blaring, bass thumping—a few seconds of intense sound, bracketed by silence. What had happened? What must Ned be thinking? And what was she supposed to do about it?

She hadn't heard his car pull away, but when she looked, it was gone. She was left alone to sort out her chaotic emotions. She needed to talk to him; she didn't want him to think she was repulsed by him. But she needed to understand what had happened, which was like nothing she'd ever experienced with a man before this. She should call him—but what could she say? When she could finally move away from the door, she threw down her coat and purse and paced restlessly. How long would it take him to get home? Should she call him tonight? Should she wait until she was calmer, tomorrow?

And had he felt anything like this? Or did he just think she really was crazy?

And then it hit her: it was touch. That was what had triggered all her other experiences, when she touched part of the Flagg house, the tombstones, the chair. Nothing had happened until she had laid hands on them. She tried to remember if Ned had ever touched her before. Sure, of course: he'd helped her up, guided her around obstacles. But there had always been clothing between them. A barrier. Tonight was the first time that she could remember touching skin to skin, and it had been like a bolt of electricity. Like what she'd experienced all those other times, but ten times stronger, and more chaotic.

Like an automaton she went through the house turning off lights, getting ready for bed. She lay down and turned off the reading light, and then lay in the dark, staring at nothing.

What was going on? There was only one way to find out: she'd have to talk to Ned. And the idea terrified her.

Chapter 23

Abby decided to take the easy course and wait until the next day to call Ned. It was cowardly, she knew, but she wanted to try to digest what had happened when he touched her. Had he felt anything out of the ordinary? Was her response somehow related to the "visions," as she suspected? Or was she really going over the edge now? She didn't know, and she was afraid to find out. Maybe the visions had only been the beginning, and something more—bigger, worse—was developing, like a spreading fungus or a cancer. Maybe she was going to start getting "shocks" from everyone, or from everyday things like the washing machine. Was she supposed to avoid touching people, and everything else as well? Not that she'd ever been a touchy-feely person anyway, but that had been out of respect for other people's space, not fear.

But had she been frightened last night or just startled? She certainly hadn't been prepared for what she had felt. She hadn't been prepared for any of the strange things that had been happening lately, but she was coping. Sort of. Except somebody kept upping the stakes.

She felt lucky to have her work. Monday morning she could go back to her untidy little office and work on her tour spiels. At least that space and those people hadn't thrown any curveballs at her—yet. She fervently hoped that they wouldn't: she needed to have some safe haven where she wouldn't flinch at every odd noise and movement, see things out of the corner of her eye. And she didn't think Ned would call her at work, so she could chew over what she wanted to say for a few more hours.

But once she got home Monday evening, she knew she had to call him. Holding her cell phone in her hand, she jumped when it rang. She expected it to be Ned, but when she looked at it, she recognized her mother's number.

"Hi, Mom," she answered, and braced herself, sighing inwardly: she had been putting off saying anything about Brad, and the job, and all of that, and now she'd have to come clean.

"Abigail Kimball, where on earth have you been? I called your apartment and most of the time nobody answers, and then when I finally get Brad, he says you moved out! Why didn't you tell me?"

"Well, it all happened kind of fast, and I wasn't sure it was permanent . . ."

"Well, is it?"

"Yes. I think so."

"Oh, baby," her mother sighed. "And I thought you two were so happy together. Everything seemed fine when we were there. What happened?"

Abby turned over her options. If she made some nice safe statement about growing apart, different interests, et cetera, et cetera, her mother would probably nurse the hope that it would all work out and that she and Brad would get back together. Better to bite the bullet now. "He was cheating on me."

"No! That weasel! Oh, sweetie, I am sorry. But . . . there's no way you can patch things up?"

"Mom, I really don't want to. That wasn't the only problem, just the worst one. But I'm really fine with it."

"But where are you now? What are you doing? Do you want to come home?"

"No, Mom," Abby said patiently. "I have a new job, at a museum in Concord, and I really like it—it's more like teaching again. And I found this great house-sit for the next few months, so I can stay here until I figure out what I want to do. I'm fine, really."

"If you're sure . . ." Her mother did not sound convinced. Then she went on in a brighter tone, "Will you be coming up for Thanksgiving?"

Abby hadn't even thought that far ahead. "I don't know yet—I don't know what kind of time off I'll have, with a new job and all. Let me check at work and I'll tell you later, okay?"

"Well, you know we'd love to have you. Oh . . . what do you want me to tell your father?"

Abby thought about that for a moment. She knew her father wouldn't judge her or try to change her mind, but she didn't want him to worry about her. "Just tell him I dumped Brad and I've got a great new job and a good place to live, and everything's fine. And if I can't make it for Thanksgiving, I'll see what I can work out for Christmas, okay?"

"Whatever works best for you, sweetheart. Now you take care, please. Maybe you think you're doing fine, but I know it's hard, and I don't want you getting all depressed. You'll call me if you feel blue, right?"

"Of course, Mom. I love you, and don't worry."

"Oh, one more thing. Ever since you asked me to find the family records, I've been sorting out the stuff in the attic, and I found something else that I think you should see. No, I won't tell you what it is—let it be a surprise. Give me your address and I'll send it off in the morning."

Abby reeled off her new address. She and her mother exchanged more good-byes, and then she hung up, but she didn't put the phone down. Before she lost her nerve, she punched in Ned's number and walked over to the window overlooking the meadow behind. Not that she could see anything, other than her reflection in the window. *Please answer, Ned. I need to understand this.*

"Abby." When he answered his tone was neutral, wary.

Abby felt a stab of panic and lurched into her speech. "Ned, I just wanted to explain about last night."

"Abby, you don't have to explain anything. I'm sorry if I made you uncomfortable."

"No! That's not what I mean. I mean, I didn't mind that you touched me, but it's what happened when you did." *So he hadn't felt anything odd?*

"Ah."

The silence lengthened. Abby could hear the faint crackle of static on the line. She wasn't sure what to say next if he hadn't noticed anything odd. Finally he spoke.

"Abby, I think we need to talk. Unfortunately I've got business out of town, and I won't be back for a couple of days. Can we get together over the weekend?"

She felt a brief flare of resentment that he was going to leave her to stew about this. "Sure, fine, whatever works for you. I just didn't want you to think . . ." What? She wasn't sure.

"Don't worry, I understand. I'll call you when I get back to town, all right? And keep working on your family tree."

With that cryptic comment, he hung up. Abby was left staring at the phone. That hadn't cleared much up, although at least he was still talking to her. Why did her family tree matter to him? Puzzled, she went slowly toward the kitchen to put together something for dinner.

• • •

Her exchange with Ned had left her dissatisfied, Abby decided, as she drove to work the next day. She wasn't sure how to interpret his response—what he had said, and what he hadn't. She really didn't know him all that well—even though, she had to admit, she had come to depend on him, at least to tell her she wasn't loopy. Heck, maybe he was crazy too and he was just egging her on. And why did he care about her family history? Well, she now knew—and he knew—that Elizabeth and William, and her great-grandmother's chair, were all connected to her, but that didn't explain the Reeds. And it didn't explain why some things brought on the "seeings" and a lot of others didn't. She still couldn't guess where the next "appearance" or "experience" or "event" would come from. She wasn't sure she was looking forward to it anyway—she had enough on her plate to keep her busy, psychologically, without spirits butting in.

After her morning tour at the museum she started to go through the stack of mail she'd grabbed on the way out the door. At least Brad had been forwarding things more consistently—not that there was very much anyway, and most creditors and vendors she had managed to notify of her new address by now. Sorting through the stack, she pounced on an official envelope from the Bridgeport town clerk. Sitting in her chair, she took a deep breath before she slit the envelope and pulled out the single sheet of paper inside. It was a death certificate for Samuel Ellinwood, son of Samuel Ellinwood and Ruth Pendleton Ellinwood, who had died in 1933 at the age of one. The second child, the one who had died in the arms of his mother, her great-grandmother, in the swan chair. Whose death had somehow driven his father away in despair, leaving her great-grandmother Ruth alone, with three-year-old Patience, in the midst of the Depression, to manage as best she could. And she had managed, in spite of Samuel. She had moved on, raised her daughter well, and all but blotted out her worthless husband, taking back her own name and never mentioning him again.

And Abby had known about this child and his death before this piece of paper. She had seen the child, had figured it out. Now she had official confirmation in her hand. Poor baby, poor Ruth. *And poor me,* she added. All this was in the past, so what did it mean to her? Except that she'd grown up in a family of strong independent females, starting with Ruth, and then her daughter Patience, and even her mother Rebecca, who was definitely the captain of her own ship, with her sweet husband the tugboat, providing a helpful nudge now and then to guide her. Abby wondered if maybe the gene pool had withered by the time it reached her, since she was having trouble living up to her matriarchal role models. She'd let Brad walk all over her and practically thanked him for it.

"You look like you're in a funk." Leslie's voice brought Abby back to the present. "Want to go grab some lunch?"

"Sounds good to me. I can use some fresh air. Can we walk?"

"Let me get a coat. Meet you downstairs."

Abby joined Leslie in the lobby a minute later and they headed toward town at a brisk clip.

"So, how're you settling in?" Leslie was clearly used to walking. Abby was having trouble keeping up.

"Fine. It's a nice house. You know, I can't imagine owning two entire houses."

"Yeah, Mary's done well for herself. She married Rob right out of college, and he got in on the ground floor in some computer company. Nothing like being in the right place at the right time."

"It's funny living in the middle of all their things. There are pictures of them around the house—it's like they're watching me."

"Ned knows them. Seen anything of him lately?"

Abby concentrated on putting one foot in front of the other as she tried to decide how to respond. Was Leslie curious? Was she keeping tabs on him? Did she harbor any lingering feelings for him? Abby realized she really didn't know very much about Leslie's life away from work. "Um, yes, a couple of times. He's been showing me around the area."

They had reached the main commercial street and Leslie led the way to a small restaurant. She waited until they were settled at a table before she picked up the thread.

"Yeah, Ned's really into local history. I think he's a real romantic—keeps seeing patriots on every corner, fending off the evil British Empire. It's not hard to do around here—you might even say it's a business."

"Oh, I like it. It certainly makes history a lot more alive, living in the middle of it."

"Hey, I'm not complaining—it pays my bills. But I don't get all misty-eyed about it, the way Ned does."

Abby was torn between wanting to ask Leslie about her life and wanting to find out more about Ned. Finally she ventured cautiously, "You said you two almost got married?"

Leslie snorted. "A million years ago. It never would have worked—he would have driven me nuts, and I would have tried to remodel him, which really wouldn't have been fair. But somehow we stayed friends. He's a good guy. And unattached, if that's what you're asking."

Abby was embarrassed. "Well, not exactly. But I did wonder why he had so much free time to drag me around." Why had nobody else snatched him up by now? Did he have some fatal flaw that she hadn't discovered yet?

"I told you, history is his hobby, and he enjoys showing it off."

"Well, I appreciate it. You know, I don't even know where you live, or much of anything else about you."

Leslie was happy to fill Abby in on her home in Littleton, where she kept two horses and a goat; on her husband George, who was a building contractor ("He wants me to say renovator and conservator, but that just means he likes to work on old buildings"); and on her two children, one in preschool, the other in first grade.

"So, what about you, now that you've dumped what's-his-name? How long were you together?"

"About two years. We met at a party in Philadelphia, and about a year later I moved into his place. He was a lot of fun. You know, a life-of-the-party kind of guy."

"Funny—I can't see you with that type." Leslie eyed her curiously.

"Well, I used to think we were complements, somehow—we sort of balanced each other. In the end I think I just bored him, and he went looking for a little more excitement. He didn't have to look very far."

"Hey, tell me if it's none of my business. I know it sucks. But either you're real good at hiding things or you're handling it really well."

Abby flashed her a smile. "Thanks. Probably some of each. I think, way down, I never really thought it would last—that he'd get to know me and find out just how boring I really was. But it was fun while it lasted. And my mother loved him."

"I know how that goes. And don't beat yourself up. Maybe you discovered just how shallow *he* really was."

Abby smiled. "You know, I think you're right."

Leslie launched into a tale about her mother and then another one about her mother-in-law. Abby listened with one ear and thought about what she'd just heard herself say. When it came right down to it, she really wasn't surprised that she and Brad had split up. She'd gotten swept up by his energy and his enthusiasm, she'd been flattered by his attention, and everyone liked him, so how could she resist? But at the same time, she was never sure that he'd really "seen" her. And she had always been afraid that if he did see her, he wouldn't like what he saw, so she hadn't pushed it. And here they were—apart. She'd been right. And Leslie had grasped Brad immediately, without even meeting him. Plainly Abby still had some work to do on reading people.

"Oh, God, look at the time—we'd better get back," Leslie exclaimed.

"This was fun—let's do it again!" She threw down some bills on the check and stood up, wrapping her coat around her. "Ready?"

Abby added her share to the check and followed. "Let's go."

Chapter 24

F riday morning Abby spied another official-looking envelope in among her mail. It was from the Waltham town clerk's office—they had certainly responded quickly, she marveled. Seated at her desk, she slit the envelope and pulled out the single page inside. She read it once. She read it again. And then she laid it on her desk and stared blindly at the wall in front of her.

Elizabeth Flagg's maiden name had been Reed.

Of course. She should have seen this coming. Sure, there were plenty of Reeds around, but Abby had no doubt that Elizabeth was somehow connected to the Reeds in the Concord cemetery. And the ones in the Wellesley cemetery. And the house in Weston? Probably. That could be verified.

All the people she had been seeing were her relatives; she was their descendant.

And was that why Ned had prodded her to keep working on her family history? Had he known, or suspected? Was he playing some sort of game with her, testing her, or was he sincerely interested in what had been happening to her and why? She shook her head: too many questions. But she knew she could find some answers on the Internet. Going backward from the mid-nineteenth century was easy, and she should be able to plot out the whole Reed line, going back to . . . what?

And why? Why did she need to know? Because she wanted—no, *needed*— to know why they were dragging her around Massachusetts and popping up at every turn. Either she came to terms with this phenomenon, whatever it was, or she'd have to move to California just to avoid the dead Reeds. She wasn't about to cut and run, so she'd just have to follow through.

For the first time since she'd started working at the museum, Abby couldn't wait for the day to end so she could get home and start working through the maze of online records. It took an extraordinary amount of self-discipline not to start before she left work, but Abby managed. She had the whole weekend in front of her. She smiled: she was going to spend two days putting together two or three hundred years of her family history.

Back at her house, she quickly scrambled some eggs and wolfed them down. She made a pot of tea and poured herself a cup, carefully adding sugar and milk, before turning to the computer. She felt as though she was entering a battle, but she was ready.

It seemed as though no time had passed, but the next time she checked it was two o'clock. After seven hours of steady work, three more cups of tea, and a half inch of printouts, Abby had managed to trace the Reeds back to 1623. The immigrant Phineas Reed had missed the *Mayflower* by a couple of years, but he had managed to marry a *Mayflower* daughter. Abby had nearly laughed out loud as the import of that fact sank in: she was a *Mayflower* descendant. Wow. That and four dollars would get you a latte at Starbucks. And then she could trace the sons of Phineas through six generations—Aaron, Henry, Lemuel, Paul, Ephraim, and William—before she arrived at Elizabeth, who had married William Flagg. Henry, Lemuel, Paul, and Ephraim had all lived in Weston at one time or another, and Abby was willing to bet that the house she had seen had belonged to one of them.

She stood up and stretched. She should really go to bed. Her brain was short-circuited and she was having trouble keeping names and dates straight. Tomorrow it would be better, and she could sort out all this information and put it into her genealogy program. And then what? She really didn't know. She had figured out the "who" but she still had no idea about the "why." All right, she was descended from all these people, and she had now "met"—she stopped to count on her fingers—at least three of them face-to-face, and probably a lot more if she could sort out her tangled impressions from some of the cemeteries. But *why* was she seeing them?

Bed, Abigail. Clear your mind and get back to it in the morning. As she was brushing her teeth, she realized that she hadn't heard from Ned. Wasn't he supposed to be back? She couldn't remember which day he had said—or even if he'd mentioned a day. Wait a minute—had she turned off her phone? After rinsing out her mouth, she found her purse and retrieved her phone, which was indeed off. But when she turned it on, there were no messages. She felt a small stab of disappointment: she was looking forward to telling Ned about what she'd found. What if he didn't call back? Would she call him? Abby was still embarrassed by her strange outburst the past weekend, and she doubted that she'd made herself very clear when she'd last talked to Ned. And he had seemed oddly distant on the phone. But he had said he would call, and he had always followed through before. Maybe he'd been held up. *Or maybe he's had enough of you and your hallucinations, Abby.*

No. She was not going to believe that. If he didn't call tomorrow, she would call him. He needed to know about what she'd found. With that resolve, she went to bed. She slept without dreams: apparently no ancestors were particularly dismayed about having been outed and they didn't trouble her.

Abby awoke slowly the next morning. The sun was bright in her eyes but her brain was stuck in first gear. Bits and pieces of her research from the night before filtered into her consciousness, until the picture was complete. The Reeds were haunting her. Fine. She needed coffee. She hauled herself out of bed and stumbled to the shower.

Half an hour later, clean and marginally rejuvenated, Abby contemplated the to-do list before her. She had the usual errands to run, if she wanted to eat for the next week. And there were a couple of things she wanted to check at the Concord library. Then there was the list of places she'd like to check—property records for Weston, for example—but she had no idea when she would find the time or opportunity for that, now that she was working. So much to do, so little time . . . Well, if she didn't start, she'd never finish.

It was close to four and getting dark when Abby returned to the house from her errands. As she approached, she realized that there was a car parked in the driveway. A car she recognized: Brad's. *Damn.* As she pulled up in front of the garage, she saw him sitting on the front steps. He looked impatient. Abby recalled all too clearly that he didn't like waiting.

She climbed out of the car and gathered up her bags of groceries. "Brad. I didn't know you knew where I was living."

"Well, you gave me the address, for the mail."

"Oh." Abby hadn't thought about that, not that she was hiding from anyone. Not Brad, certainly. But she wasn't pleased to see him here; this was her own territory and she was reluctant to invite him into it. She fished for her keys and opened the door. Once inside, she dropped her groceries and shut off the alarm system. Brad had followed her in and was admiring the house.

"Nice place you've got here. Not what I would have expected from you, but not too shabby."

"I'm just house-sitting, not remodeling it," she said, with some asperity. She gathered up her scattered bags again and headed for the kitchen. Brad followed and stood leaning against a counter as Abby put away her supplies. When she was done, she turned to face him. "What are you doing here?"

"What, no 'Hi, Brad, I've missed you'?"

She hadn't. She waited silently.

Seeing that his light tone had fallen flat, Brad put on a more sober expression. "Seriously, Abby . . . you left in such a big hurry. I thought we'd have time to talk about all this."

"Does that 'we' include Shanna?" Abby wasn't about to give him an inch.

"That's over. It didn't mean anything. I mean, she was fun, but it wasn't serious or anything. It wasn't worth you getting bent out of shape and moving out like you did."

So Brad was the injured party here? *I don't think so,* Abby thought. "Brad, Shanna was just the last straw. There was a lot wrong with our relationship before I found out about her."

He stared at her blankly. "What do you mean? We were fine. I thought you were happy—or at least you would be, once you found a job to keep you busy. And then you did, and you moved right out. I don't get it."

Abby sighed. "Brad, you were sleeping with another woman. And you accused me of seeing another man. Does that sound like a good relationship to you?"

He had the grace to look ashamed. "Well, every couple hits a few speed bumps along the way. But why can't we work things out? I miss you, babe."

I'll bet you do. You miss me making you dinner every night, and picking up after you, and making sure you have clean underwear. Abby looked critically at Brad: a nice-looking guy, tall, good hair and teeth, trendy clothes, promising future. And she felt totally unmoved.

"Brad, I'm sorry things didn't work out. But I just don't see us getting back together." *And I really don't want to try.* Abby was surprised to find that she meant it. She could look at him and feel no regret. Mostly now she wondered just what she had seen in him, apart from the obvious—and she wondered how she could have been willing to accept that as enough. Or what had changed in the last year or two—or more recently.

Her cell phone rang. She debated about ignoring it, until Brad said, "Aren't you going to answer that?"

She didn't say anything but retrieved her phone from her bag. Ned. Of course. "Hi. Look, could you call me back in a little while? This isn't a good time."

"Sure. Half an hour?"

"Yes, great. Talk to you then." She signed off.

Brad was watching her with something like anger. "Your new boyfriend?"

"Brad, I don't answer to you. It's none of your business whether or not I have a boyfriend. I told you, we're over. There's nothing more to say."

"You really mean it." Brad looked crestfallen. "Abby, I'm sorry, really I am. I messed up, and I can see why you're pissed at me. What more can I say?"

"Nothing, Brad. Look, I'm not angry at you. I just don't think we're a good fit, that's all. You're a great guy, and I'm sure you'll find somebody else." There, she'd stroked his wounded ego. Maybe he'd go now?

He crossed the room toward her, and then he bent down and kissed her. She didn't move. He pressed himself against her, wrapped his arms around her, and turned up the heat on the kiss. It took him several seconds to realize that she wasn't responding at all. She didn't fight him, she just stood there, inert. Finally he backed away.

"Good-bye, Abby." He turned and headed for the door, and she heard it open and close behind him. His car started, then moved away, and he was gone.

Abby still didn't move, turning over in her mind what had just happened. It really was over. If she hadn't believed it before, she certainly did now. He'd come to her, begging forgiveness, and she'd felt—nothing. The best she could muster was some vague soft regret for what once was, what might have been—what clearly never would be. He'd kissed her, as he had so many other times, and she'd felt nothing. She was free of him.

Her phone rang again, and she picked it up. "Hello?"

"It's Ned. Is this a better time?"

"Yes. Brad was here, but he left."

"Oh." A few beats of silence. "I'm sorry I didn't call earlier, but my plane got held up—some electrical failure in Chicago or something. But we need to talk."

"Yes, we do," Abby replied.

"Is tomorrow good? We can meet somewhere."

A neutral place was probably a good idea. "Fine—what about Lexington? That place we had lunch, around noon?"

"Great." Was that relief she heard in his voice? "See you then."

She had a lot to tell him.

Chapter 25

Abby spent Sunday morning filling in her family tree and printed out a tidy box structure. She was very proud of it. Saturday night, she had resolutely refused to think about Brad, Ned, or her family ghosts. She had found a stash of classic tear-jerker DVDs in a cabinet and had nestled into a fuzzy blanket with a pint of ice cream and indulged herself. It had been very cathartic. Certainly, she decided, her problems paled compared to those of some of the heroines she had watched.

She arrived early for lunch and found a table, nervously shuffling her notes. She looked up to see Ned approaching and studied him. He looked uneasy—why? She wasn't, although she wasn't quite sure why she was so untroubled.

"Abby." He sat down. "Sorry I'm late."

"You aren't—I was early."

Their glances met, and Abby found herself thinking, *he knows*. Wait a minute—knows what? What she was about to tell him, about her connection to the Reeds? And then she smiled. *Yes, he knows.*

"I've got something to show you." She turned her family chart toward him. "But I think you've already guessed. Haven't you?"

Ned gave the chart a cursory glance, and then he looked up at her. "Yes. You're related to the Reeds. That's what I assumed. It makes sense, given what you've seen with your more recent family."

A waitress appeared, looking expectant. They gave a fast look at menus, ordered something randomly, shooed the waitress away.

Abby pointed at her chart. "The people—or things, or places—that I've seen, they're all in a straight line. My great-grandmother, and Elizabeth, and the people in Concord, and Weston, and Wellesley—they're all directly related." She sat back triumphantly.

Ned was examining his fork carefully, without looking at her. "And what do you think this means?"

Abby felt as though he had just stuck a pin in her balloon. She'd been so excited by making the connection, by setting down the links on paper, that she hadn't given much thought to why she was seeing these people. "I don't know," she said, suddenly depressed.

Ned was quick to catch the change in her tone. "I'm sorry, I didn't mean to rain on your parade. You've made amazing progress, considering you started with nothing just a few weeks ago. Some people take years to get this far. I can't argue with your conclusion. And, yes, I did suspect there was a connection like this." A smile flashed across his face, then disappeared quickly. "But . . . No, let me ask you a question. Do you *want* to take this any further?"

The waitress appeared, her arms laden with food, which she began to set down. Abby was glad for the interruption and sat back and gathered her thoughts. When the waitress had withdrawn again, she ventured, "I'm not sure what you mean by 'further.' But if you're asking do I want to know why I'm being haunted by my family, the answer is yes, definitely."

"Good." Ned picked up his sandwich, took a bite, and chewed slowly. Abby wondered if he was stalling for time. When he had swallowed, he began again.

"Abby, there's something I have to tell you."

Abby felt a clutch of fear.

"I haven't been completely honest with you, first because I didn't think it was relevant, and then later because I didn't want to put any ideas in your head. I wanted you to work this out on your own, without preconceptions." He stopped, as if unsure how to go on.

"All right," Abby said cautiously. "But . . ."

He handed her a sheaf of papers. "I think this will help explain things."

She looked down at a family tree much like the one she had assembled, its orderly boxes marching backward, branching. And then a name caught her eye: Reed. Paul Reed. Startled, she looked up at Ned. "You mean we're related?"

Ned nodded. "Yes, about eight generations back. But that's not rare. Most old Massachusetts families cross somewhere. You've probably got hundreds of relatives as close or closer than I am. But . . ."

And suddenly Abby understood where he was headed. "You see them too. That story about Johnnie—was he a Reed?"

He sat back in his chair and let out his breath. "Yes. His mother was our Paul's sister." The smile flashed again.

Abby sat stunned, sorting back through the times they'd spent together. "When did you first guess what was happening with me?" she said slowly.

"I'm not sure. Probably in the cemetery in Wellesley, when you were drawn to the stones."

Abby digested that. "What do you see?"

"Fragments. Flashes of something. You know, I have to give you credit—

159

you were much more open to this whole thing. Me—I'm a scientist, right? I look for order, logic, reason—and this business just doesn't fit. After Johnnie . . . well, as I got older I fought it for a long time."

"Did you go into science because of or in spite of this—what are we going to call it?"

"I don't know—'seeing'? Visions seems pompous. Visitations is worse—besides, that implies action on the part of the visitor, and from what you've said, you're more of an observer. But, to answer your question, I'm not sure. Maybe I hoped that I could figure out what was happening and why. Or maybe I thought science would just drive it out of me. I don't know."

They both fell silent. Abby was overwhelmed by conflicting emotions. She was thrilled to find that she was not alone. And then she decided that she was angry that Ned hadn't explained things sooner, although she understood his scientist's desire not to influence the experiment. She was reluctantly intrigued by what this all might mean.

"You can't tell me you haven't done research on this," she said at last.

"Of course I have. But this is the sort of thing that gets filed under 'cranks and crazies.' Careful scientific research is conspicuously lacking."

"Didn't there used to be some sort of research center at Duke?"

"Still is—the Rhine Research Center. They've been around for quite a while, and they're fairly well respected. But they tend to focus on parapsychological phenomena, mostly ESP and psychokinesis. Stuff in the here and now, not the past. Once you start sniffing around ghost hunters, things get weirder. Don't get me wrong—I'm not saying they're all quacks. But they're not exactly scientific, either."

Abby realized she hadn't touched her food, so she picked up her sandwich and started in on it. She finished several healthy bites before she was ready to speak again.

"Well, cousin, where do we go from here?"

"I've been thinking about that. There are probably still some facts that we can fill in. But I'd like to try some experiments, if you're willing."

"What, drive aimlessly around Massachusetts hoping that six times great-grandpa calls out to me from beyond the grave?" Abby decided she was feeling better than she had for days.

"Not exactly. But there are other sites, particularly cemeteries, where we can prove your—our—ancestors have been. I'd like to know how you respond to them."

"What about you? Haven't you tried that yourself?"

"Of course. But I'd love to have corroboration from your experience."

"What, a data set of two people? This isn't going to turn into some sort of sexist thing, is it? You know, women are intuitive, sensitive—so I'm much more likely to be a good receiver?" Abby demanded.

Ned held up both hands in protest. "No way. But based purely on empirical observation, I'd say you're seeing more, and more strongly, than I have—at least since my friend Johnnie disappeared."

"Maybe we're just more open to it when we're young—everything is newer then, and we don't just write it off as crazy. Although I never used to see anything when I was a child, and I lived with odds and ends from my great-grandmother and grandmother until I left for college. Why didn't they affect me then?"

"Abby, I can't tell you. Maybe you just weren't tuned in to them. Maybe it took extraordinary circumstances—moving up here where you had no friends, trying to find a job, having problems with your relationship—to make you receptive, to break down your own resistance. Maybe you simply weren't ready before."

"I guess that makes sense." Abby shook herself and sat up straighter. "Okay, where? When?"

Ned looked ridiculously pleased. "Well, for the cemeteries, sooner rather than later—it's already getting cold. Somehow I'd guess that if you're freezing your tail off, you're going to be less likely to pick up messages from the beyond. I won't even mention snow."

"Makes sense. Okay, you've got more details on the family history— where should we go?"

Ned turned her chart so they could both see it. "You've already picked up something from William back through Ephraim, here."

"Wait," Abby interrupted. "Ephraim owned the Weston house?"

"Yes. Actually it was his father Paul who built it. Ephraim was forced to sell it when his father died broke. It sounds as though you saw both of them there."

"And they were sad or angry." And then another piece of the puzzle fell into place.

Once again, Ned noticed. "What?"

"Everything I've seen, or everyone—it's been at times of strong emotions. Deaths, funerals. Even joy, from my great-grandmother when she held my grandmother as a baby. I'm not seeing ordinary daily activities, I'm connecting with them when they're really stressed out, just as I am. So I'm not likely to run into any of them quietly reading a book in the parlor." She sat back triumphantly.

Ned stared at her. "I think you're right," he said wonderingly. "They leave a trace only under extreme conditions—that makes a strange kind of sense."

"If any of this does," Abby said cheerfully.

Ned looked up at her and smiled again. "If you want to test this further, then cemeteries are definitely the place to go. Funerals and burials are always sad events for the family and draw lots of relatives. Here's what I suggest." He traced a branch of his family tree with his index finger. "I say we go back, to Aaron. He's buried in Cohasset."

"Where's that? Don't forget, I haven't been around here very long. And apparently I didn't inherit any mental road maps."

"Cohasset's south of Boston, on the water. Nice place. You up for it?"

"You mean now?"

"Sure. It's a nice day, and we've probably got another three hours of light."

"Can I finish my sandwich first?" she asked plaintively. And as she chewed, she realized that Ned had said nothing about what had happened last weekend. Did she want to bring it up? No, she decided. *Let's take care of the ghosts first.*

Chapter 26

The drive from Lexington to Cohasset took just over an hour. Abby was relieved that Ned was driving. Apparently her intuition, if that was what it was, worked only within a short range: she had no intuitive compass. Navigating any large distances in the Boston area still dismayed her. Ned drove carefully, just over the speed limit.

It was nearly three when they left the main highway for local roads toward Cohasset. But before they reached anything that looked like a town, Ned turned and pulled over beside a fairly large cemetery. Looking across it, Abby could see that it was bounded by water on at least two sides.

He turned off the car. "This is it."

She turned toward him. "So, what am I supposed to do now?"

"Find Aaron Reed. He's there."

"What am I, a hunting dog?" Abby grumbled. "You've been here before."

"Yes, I have. Look, Abby, this isn't a test, and there's no pass or fail. I just wondered if you could find Aaron here, and if you did, how you would react. I don't expect you to behave like a trained seal. Believe me, I don't think of this as some sort of cute party trick. Just give it a shot, all right? If you get cold, we can go."

Abby gave him one more doubtful look, then climbed out of the car. Whatever else she might think, this cemetery was a beautiful place, for the living or the dead. In fact, she was willing to bet that if there weren't a cemetery sitting here, building lots would be going for an easy six figures. She walked toward the gate and surveyed the layout. Was it cheating to head for what she could tell were the oldest stones? *No, Abby, give this a chance.* She shut her eyes.

At first she could hear the sound of the few cars that passed on the road, the wind in the trees, a chain saw somewhere in the distance. She tried to empty her mind. And then, without conscious thought, she opened her eyes and started walking. The cemetery was well spread out, with plenty of space between the stones, and she caught glimpses of water as she moved through them. Who had called cemeteries "gardens of stone"? It seemed apt. She walked by a curious row of mausoleums, carved into a hill, and kept going, toward a small rise in the center of the cemetery. And then she stopped in front of a close-set row of old slate stones. The Reeds, father, son, grandson, and their wives, all lined up, facing the sun sinking behind her.

I'm getting better at this. Abby wasn't ready to touch the stones. Instead, she sank down and sat in front of the eldest, Aaron. Her ninth great-grandfather, if she remembered the chart correctly. He had died in 1736, and had been born in the middle of the century before—over two hundred and fifty years ago. And his family had had his name carved in stone, and here she sat in front of him, drawn here by something she couldn't explain. Feeling slightly foolish, she asked silently, *Aaron?* There was no answer. Well, what had she expected? That he was going to sit up and chat with her? It didn't work like that.

Abby got to her knees, casting a shadow over the face of the stone, and reached out a hand to touch it. The world dissolved.

It was the Wellesley cemetery all over again. Many voices; no single voice. Men, women, children. The space she saw around her was more open, few stones interrupting the long grass. She tried to keep the connection yet analyze what was happening at the same time. She could not decipher words, or maybe they all blended together. But, she realized, what she sensed was emotion, a sort of distillation, layers accumulated over time, of the sorrow that had emanated from the mourners of the past. These dead were not trying to reach out to her, to communicate with her, somewhere in their distant future; no, they were very much in their own moment, and they were sad, angry, frightened, lost. This was a place of farewells.

Abby lost all track of time. She had no idea how long she had been sitting there, eyes shut, when Ned laid a hand on her shoulder; she had not even heard him approach.

"Abby? Are you all right?" His voice was gentle.

She opened her eyes. The sun had sunk lower, and her shadow lay across the stone. "Yes, I'm fine." She looked for one last long moment at Aaron's marker, then scrambled to her feet. She realized she was cold, and her knees were stiff. "Let's get back in the car and I'll tell you about it."

Silently, they made their way back out of the cemetery. Ned opened the door for her and she climbed in. He got in the other side, started the motor, and turned the heat on high. He still hadn't spoken. Abby sat back in her seat and sorted through her impressions.

"I think that I've confirmed it, what we talked about."

"What do you mean?"

"Well, what I'm seeing are not exactly ghosts. They are from the past, but they're not traveling into the present. It's more like I'm picking up traces they've left behind. And since this is where they buried the people they loved, mostly it's sad. Sometimes angry. And it's all mixed together over time, like a soup, because people have been coming here, burying their family here, for a very long time."

Ned chuckled. "That's an interesting way of putting it. But I see what you mean."

Abby went on slowly. "The thing about the swan chair was . . . well, first, it was a lot more recent, so what I got from it was less muddled. Maybe these aftereffects fade over time, or after a certain number of downloads, kind of. But what was so confusing about sitting in the chair the first time was that it was a mix—both joy and grief, all muddled together. But looking back at it now, I think that was because it was two different experiences, overlapping somehow. You know, joy at the birth of the baby that lived and sorrow for the baby who died. But I couldn't disentangle those two experiences then. What do you think?"

"I think the idea makes sense," he began slowly. "I guess I'm more comfortable with the idea of some sort of residuum, something left behind, than with thinking that there are souls, or some other kind of integral being, wandering around through time and space."

They both fell silent. Abby felt tired, but not unhappy. This was beginning to make sense, in its own way. After several minutes, she ventured, "Well, what now?"

"We've got one more generation to check out. Not today—it'll be dark by the time we get back to Lexington, and we've got to work tomorrow, right? And I don't suppose you can get any time off yet. Which brings us to next weekend."

Abby was getting impatient. "Where do you want to go?"

"Charlestown. Back to the beginning."

"Ah. You mean Phineas Reed."

"Exactly. You found Aaron and his descendants here. I suppose we could wander around Cohasset and see if you find anything else, but that's a pretty long shot—I have no idea if anything the Reeds built or lived in is still standing, or where to look. But we know Phineas was buried in Charlestown. You game to try it? He's the earliest Reed we can prove in the area—heck, in the country."

"Why not? I think I'm beginning to see how this works. I wish there were more heirlooms—you know, things that I could be sure these people touched, held, owned. It might be an interesting test to see what else carries this . . . whatever."

"I'll have to ask my folks—maybe they've got something in the attic. Or, of course, there's their house. You might get something there."

"Your 'friend' never came back, did he?"

"No, not after that first year."

"I wonder . . . Going back to the swan chair, the first time I sat in it, it was overwhelming. And I told you, when I went back to it and sat in it again, it was sort of muted. Maybe that's just because I was expecting it, or I was more ready to handle it. Or maybe because whatever I was picking up is gone now. I've handled it since—I had to, when I moved—and I didn't pick up anything. Maybe these things wear off, or maybe we can only absorb them once. So, anyway, yes—it would be interesting to see your family house, see if there's anything there."

"Are you free on Thanksgiving? I'm sure Mom and Dad would be happy to have you. Unless you've got other plans?"

"Well, my folks are in Maine, and I don't have the time to make that trip for just a couple of days. No—I don't have any plans, and I'd love to come, if you're sure it's okay. I don't want to intrude on your family."

"Abby, you *are* our family, even if we have to go back eight generations. And Thanksgiving is an event that should be shared. Please come."

She gave him a real smile. "I'd be happy to."

It was after seven when Abby got back to the Concord house, after Ned had dropped her at her car in Lexington. It had been a day full of strange and unexpected revelations, and Abby wanted nothing more than to sit quietly and chew over them. Her ringing cell phone interrupted her: it was her mother.

"Hi, sweetie—I won't keep you. I just wanted to check in with you about Thanksgiving?"

Abby sighed inwardly. She hated to say no to her mother, but it was just too complicated at the moment. "I'm sorry, Mom—I just can't take the time off right now." No way was she going to mention Ned's invitation. After all, she'd made her decision before he asked, hadn't she?

"I'm sorry too. I wish we could see you. And I know it's hard to be alone during the holidays. Have you talked with Brad?"

Subtle her mother wasn't. "Yes, Mom. He came by to see me yesterday."

"And?"

"And it's over, Mom. It is not happening. I think he finally understands that."

Her mother sighed audibly. "Well, it's your life, sweetheart. But he is a good guy."

"Mom, I'm not saying he isn't. He just isn't the guy for me." She couldn't believe that such a cliché had come out of her mouth, but she meant it.

"So, what will you do on Thanksgiving Day? I hate to think about you sitting all alone, wherever it is you are."

"No, Mom. I'm going to have dinner with a friend and their family."

"Oh, that's nice! Someone you met at work?"

"No—someone I met in Waltham a while ago." *In a different lifetime.*

"Oh. Well, that's good. I'm glad you have friends, anyway. It's important to see people, get out."

"Mom, I do," Abby said patiently. "I've got lots to keep me busy. Look, please don't worry about me, okay? I'm happy. I've got a good job and a nice place to live and new friends, and everything's fine. All right?" *Unless you count the dead people.* She still hadn't made up her mind about them.

"Whatever you say, dear. So, can we count on you for Christmas?"

"Of course. I'll see what I can work out."

"Well, I'll let you go now, dear." Having won a small victory, Abby's mother had decided she could be magnanimous. "I'm sure you have things to do. Talk to me soon. Oh, I sent that package I mentioned the other day, so look for it in your mail. Bye!"

Abby turned off her phone with a sigh of relief. She loved her mother dearly but she found her energy exhausting. It was interesting that the Reed propensity for psychic connection had skipped her mother entirely: Rebecca Kimball was largely oblivious to other people's feelings.

So she was off the hook for Thanksgiving and could go to Ned's family's celebration with a clear conscience. It was only after the fact that she realized she had not told her mother that the friend with whom she was spending Thanksgiving was a man. Why was that? she wondered. Probably because her mother would start asking all sorts of embarrassing questions, most of which she didn't want to answer, or even think about. Ned was a friend, period. He was helping her understand something odd that was happening to her, that she really didn't even want to try to explain to her pragmatic mother. And he was kind enough to take in a stray for Thanksgiving.

Except that she and Ned hadn't talked about what had happened when he touched her.

Chapter 27

More than once during the week that followed, Abby thanked her lucky stars, or maybe her guardian angels, that she had her current job. She was busy from the time she arrived until the time she left, usually late.

Ned did not intrude upon her week. She wasn't sure how she felt about that. He had been so careful to let her find her own way, to come to terms with what was happening. Part of her remained angry that he hadn't told her earlier that he shared her strange ability, which might have given her some comfort, but another part of her understood why he hadn't. She needed to process this for herself, not accept someone else's explanations. This odd link with the past was a fragile thing and needed to be nurtured. Or so she thought on some days.

One day during the week, Leslie had popped her head in Abby's door. "Hey, listen, are you doing anything for Thanksgiving? Because you'd be welcome at our house—if you can stand two rambunctious kids."

"Oh, thanks, Leslie. But I told Ned I'd have dinner with his family."

"Ah, the plot thickens." Leslie eyed her speculatively. "His folks are interesting, his mom in particular. Sorry—that sounds like I'm putting her down, which I'm not, because I really like her. She's a fascinating woman, very talented, but you might not sit down to eat until ten o'clock—she had a tendency to lose sight of the pesky details of the real world, like how long it takes to cook a turkey."

"I'd forgotten that you used to know them. Ned asked if I was going to my family's, but they're in Maine and I really don't want to drive up there right now, so when I said no, he invited me. That's all."

"Uh-huh." Leslie looked unconvinced. "Well, I'm sure you'll have fun. And their house is great—1750-something, if I remember right. So, how's the schedule for the school holidays shaping up?" And then talk drifted to job-related things.

Ned called Friday night. "Abby? Are we still on for Charlestown tomorrow?"

"Sure. I'm looking forward to it."

"No, uh, other events this past week?"

"You mean have I 'seen' anyone else? No, it's been quiet. But then, I haven't been anywhere new."

"Right. Well, I'll come by around ten tomorrow, if that's all right."

"Sure. See you then."

Crisp, businesslike. No nonsense. She was looking forward to tomorrow, looking forward to seeing a new place, one she'd heard a lot about. *And,* a niggling little voice inside added, *looking forward to spending time with Ned? Ridiculous,* Abby told herself firmly. She had just extricated herself from one relationship and she was definitely not looking for another one.

The next morning, Ned once again appeared promptly. Abby was waiting at the door.

"How far are we going this time?" she asked as she set the house alarm, locked the door and walked toward Ned's car.

"Probably an hour, depending on traffic. Charlestown is just the other side of Boston. Where Bunker Hill is."

Abby settled herself into her seat. "One more place I haven't seen. I wonder where else these ancestors of mine wandered to?"

Ned pulled out of the driveway and onto the road. "You'd be surprised. We think we're a mobile society, but in the seventeenth and eighteenth century, people traveled around quite a bit. Take Phineas, for example. He landed in Weymouth, held property in Plymouth, where he got married, and then packed up and headed for Charlestown. He and his wife Mary had eight kids, and the kids ended up in—let me see if I can get this right— Long Island, Cambridge, Charlestown, Cohasset, Rhode Island, and Connecticut, all before 1700."

"Wow," Abby responded. "And you keep all this in your head?"

"Hey, I've been doing this for a while. You get to know these people, in a way. And I find it interesting, how and why people moved around."

"Does this, uh, ability of ours only work with lineal ancestors?" Abby asked.

"I think so, but we can keep looking for others if you want. I could have it wrong and you'll see a lot more people. I just know I haven't."

The drive passed quickly and pleasantly, their conversation firmly rooted in their shared family history. Abby marveled at the breadth of Ned's knowledge, which made her feel pathetically ignorant. She was surprised how quickly they passed Boston; they crossed a large bridge and took the exit for Charlestown. After traveling over surface roads, Ned pulled into a restaurant parking lot. Abby looked at him. "What are we doing here?"

"Look." He pointed across the parking lot and Abby saw a cemetery enclosed by a high iron fence atop a stone wall.

"That's it?"

"Yup. That's the oldest cemetery in Charlestown."

"Looks like people around here don't care much about it." From what Abby could see, it was surrounded by clearly modern buildings, with a busy four-lane street on one side. It was far from idyllic. It also appeared to be inaccessible. "How do we get in?"

"Follow me." Ned led the way past a senior-citizens center and down a dead-end street. They came to a gate, which sported a heavy-duty chain and a sturdy padlock.

"Great. Now what?"

"We climb."

"What?"

"See, there, where the wall and the fence meet? We can climb through there."

"You sure this is legal?"

"Well, I haven't investigated the law too closely. But I'd say we weren't the only ones to figure that out, if the wear on the fence is any indication. And I'm willing to bet that our motives are purer than those of most visitors here, based on what they leave behind. Come on."

He clambered up on the brick wall and squeezed through the gap between the fence and the gate, dropping down inside. Abby followed more slowly but found that it wasn't difficult to slip through. Once on the ground, she turned to face the cemetery, centered on a low, nearly round hill, and studied the tombstones. They were old, that was clear. They had been here for a long time—although possibly not in their current arrangement, which resembled nothing she had ever seen in a cemetery.

She looked at Ned, beside her. "You've been here before? And you know what we're looking for?"

"Yes, I've been here. You'll find him." He strolled off along the perimeter of the hill.

She gave his retreating back one last look, then set off slowly toward the center. Why did she think Phineas would be near the top? There was no apparent order to the stones. But she didn't question her path as she walked up the hill. And it was easy: there was Phineas. Or his stone, its inscription as clear as the day it had been cut, the death's head grinning with square teeth, its wing feathers still sporting the marks of the chisel. Phineas had died in 1680, a long, long time ago. Abby knelt in front of the low stone and smiled. *Hi, Phineas.* She reached out a hand, traced the letters of the inscription with a slow finger. She shut her eyes, but caught only wisps. Had his son Aaron, her ancestor, come here to bury him? Or to pay tribute to his grave? Probably. What about Phineas's wife? Or had she died before him? In any case, the residue here was faint: not many Reeds had come to mourn Phineas, or at least none who had cared about him and grieved for him. Abby listened for a moment. This place was surrounded by a busy city; the nearby highway carried a steady stream of traffic. If she turned her head, she would see the top of the Bunker Hill monument, marking a battle that took place nearly a century after Phineas's death. Had she had relatives at that battle? Descendants of Phineas?

She opened her eyes again. Ned was following the erratic paths between the tombstones, stopping now and then and bending low to read an inscription. She watched him while he was unaware of her scrutiny. Why was she here? How had they come together, and why? As if sensing her eyes on him, Ned chose that moment to look at her, and smiled. It was a singularly open, happy smile, and Abby's heart turned over. This unexpected sensation was followed quickly by a spurt of panic: what was she thinking? He came closer and stopped on the other side of the tombstone, facing her.

"You found him."

"Yes. You said I would."

"I *knew* you would. Seen enough?"

"For now." *I can always come back, if I want to.* But she had learned what she needed. She followed Ned back down the hill to the point where they had climbed in. He went over the fence first. As he climbed, Abby turned around for one last look at the cemetery, with the sun setting behind it. She sighed and turned to climb back over the wall.

From this side, it was a longer jump down. Ned was taller than she was, and had had no trouble. Standing below her, he extended a hand to help her down, and she took it.

The shock was even stronger this time than the last. Their hands linked, she felt as though she had plugged into an electrical circuit as the jolt passed through her entire body. For a moment, there was a cacophony of voices, a flashing jumble of images in bright color, shutting out the world; and then the chaos coalesced into a single entity: Ned.

He released her hand and she came back to the real world, on her feet but still reeling. Her breath came in short gasps, and her knees wobbled. With one hand, she grabbed the fence railing for support. Ned had not moved, and Abby raised her eyes to his face.

"You felt that," she said, in a near whisper. It was not a question. He nodded, watching her intently. She had no idea what to say. There was no way she could dismiss what had just happened with a flippant remark. She couldn't ignore it. And he had felt it too, whatever it was.

She drew a shaky breath. The sun was sinking, and she was getting cold. She felt as though she had been struck by lightning, but they couldn't just stand there staring at each other like idiots forever. He wasn't helping at all.

"Ned, I . . . ," she began.

"No," he said gently. "Not now. Let's go someplace quiet and warm and safe and talk about this like two rational humans, if we can. All right?"

She could only nod.

Chapter 28

They went back to the car and drove. Ned concentrated on navigating through detours and construction, back to the main highway, the bridge, Boston. Abby was grateful for his silence, because she was trying hard to impose some sort of order on her chaotic thoughts. Or maybe it was feelings? Whatever it was, she had never felt like this before, and she wasn't sure she liked it. After a while, she realized that they had cleared Boston and were headed west.

"Where are we going?"

Ned glanced briefly at her. "I'll take you home, if that's what you want."

"I . . . we need to talk about this. At least, I do." She wasn't even sure what "this" was—Phineas and all his descendants? Or what had just happened between them at the cemetery? And how were they connected in the here and now, if they were?

"Your place?" His eyes were on the road, his tone carefully neutral.

"Fine." Abby was acutely aware that, at that moment, nowhere felt like home. She was unmoored, unattached. The Concord house was the only place she was remotely familiar with, and it seemed better than a public place like a restaurant. Or than Ned's home, which she hadn't even seen. She needed a sanctuary, someplace where she could think things through. But she couldn't do this alone, because the problem wasn't only hers. If it was a problem. Hell, she had no idea what it was.

By the time they reached Concord, Abby felt calmer. Ned had not intruded on her thoughts, for which she was thankful. They pulled into her driveway in half dusk. He turned off the engine and looked at her mutely. Abby smiled tentatively and said, "Come on." She got out of the car, heading for the front door, and he followed. Carefully she unlocked the door, shut off the alarm system; he followed her in and closed the door behind them. The house was quiet, cool, impersonal. And they were alone.

Ned handed her a stack of mail he had retrieved while she was wrestling the door open. Abby recognized her mother's sprawling handwriting on a mid-sized padded envelope. She grabbed it quickly, grateful for some kind of diversion. When he raised an eyebrow at it, she said, "It's from my mother—she said it was another family thing." She wrestled with laying it aside or opening it immediately. She really wanted to know what was in it but she didn't want Ned to think she was stalling. Even though she was.

"Go ahead, open it," he said with a slight smile. "You know you want to."

"Thank you." She peeled the tape back from the envelope and pulled out a small box and a note from her mother.

I found this in with your grandmother's things—I'm pretty sure it came from her father. I thought you might be interested.

That was all it said. Standing in the hallway, Abby turned the box over in her hands. Small, rectangular, a little heavy for its size. The box was wrapped with bubble wrap, and when Abby pulled that off, there was a piece of rough string holding the top on the box. She untied that and opened the box to find an old-fashioned silver-plated pocket watch. She reached for it and . . .

This time the explosion was real. Her fingers closed convulsively around it, almost tight enough to bend the thin metal. She saw . . . smoky half darkness, men clustered around, holding beer steins. Looking down at something . . . someone on the floor. In her—his?—hand was a gun, smoke rising from it. The man on the floor was bleeding and looked . . . dead? And all the other men turned to stare at her . . .

She didn't know she had screamed; she knew she was fighting, but who was she fighting? The men in the dark room? *I have to get away. I didn't mean to do it. I have to get out of here.* She was trapped; someone was holding her down. Someone pried the watch from her hand and wrapped her in a bear hug. Ned.

She was sobbing, tears running down her face. Tears running onto his shirt. She couldn't seem to stop, and she kept fighting, until he laid a hand on her chin and turned her face to his. "Abby." His voice seemed to come from somewhere far away. "Abby, what is it?"

She tore herself away from him, turned her back, trying to regain some control. Her body still shook with sobs, now turning into hiccups. But now she knew . . .

"What did you see, Abby?" Ned asked softly, keeping his distance.

Without turning, she said, "I know why my great-grandfather left." She took a few deep breaths. Good, the sobs were slowing. "He killed a man. In a bar. He shot him. He didn't mean for it to happen. He must have told my great-grandmother, and that's why I could hear him. And then he went away."

"I'm sorry, Abby. I didn't want anything like this to happen to you."

"This isn't your fault," Abby said. "This happened to *me*."

"But all this didn't happen until we met. Maybe this thing is contagious, or maybe I somehow boosted your ability."

Now she could turn to face him. "No! I'm not going to make excuses. My great-grandfather was a murderer, and his wife knew, because when he left, she refused to speak of him. She was angry and ashamed. It wasn't the death of her son, or the Depression—it was the idea of being married to a killer that she couldn't accept. Oh, God, why did I ever come here? I could have gone through my whole life without ever running into another damn relative, and instead, Brad drags me here and dumps me in the middle of them all. What am I supposed to do now?"

He came a step closer, and another one, until he was nearly touching her. Then he took her face in both hands and kissed her.

The intensity of the contact shook her, and she nearly pulled away. But she didn't, she held on. She had to do this, had to find out, had to know. And then things steadied and she began to be able to focus, despite the whirling chaos in her head. She was here, she was real, and so was Ned, but there was so much more. For a terrifying moment, she felt as though she was inside him, looking out, at herself, and then in a strange seesaw, she felt him inside her head. The feelings were completely inarticulate, purely sensate—and overwhelming. She clutched at the shards of her identity and tried to look at him. See him. Not just as nice Ned, the mild-mannered geek who helped her with her research, but as the unique conscious identity that was linked to her in ways she couldn't even begin to explain, more intimately than she had ever thought possible.

He broke off the kiss and pulled back slightly, and Abby suddenly felt adrift in a cold and empty sea. "Ned?" she whispered, plaintively.

He looked as shaken as she felt. "That's what I was afraid of. Think you can handle this?"

She could only nod. This time, he reached out and pulled her close, and kissed her again, and she kissed him back and any sort of rational thought fled.

Several eternities later, he pulled back again, without letting her go. "Abby?"

"Yes," she gasped. "Downstairs." Reluctantly she put an inch, then two, between them. She felt an almost physical pain at the separation.

"Abby? We can slow this down." His human voice came from a great distance.

"Why would we do that?" She couldn't seem to get her breath.

"Because . . . because . . . hell, I don't know. I don't want you to get hurt."

"Believe me, this doesn't hurt." She pulled at him, but still he resisted. Abby made a huge effort to pull herself together and faced him squarely. "Ned, whatever it is we've got here, we've been building up to this since we first met, and I don't want to stop. Are you telling me you do?"

He shook his head vehemently. "God, no. I just want you to be sure . . ."

"I have never been so sure of anything in my life." And she reached out her hand and led him downstairs.

She didn't turn on any lights. They didn't need light; Abby was guided by some inner vision she didn't know she had. They fumbled briefly with the mundane impediments of buttons and zippers, and then they were skin to skin, together. How silly it was to worry about nakedness, Abby thought, when they could see right through each other. It was her last conscious thought for some time.

If her responses were not conscious, they were nonetheless memorable. Later, when she had returned to some approximation of coherent thought, Abby would reflect that if what she had had up until now had been sex, then she and Ned needed to invent a whole new terminology. Before had been kindergarten, a happy physical romp; this was graduate school in astrophysics. This was cosmic harmony, the music of the spheres. This was beyond words, beyond time, beyond reason.

Sometime later Abby came back to herself, in stages. She was here in her bed in Concord. It was the same day. It was dark. And she was more at peace than she had been for a long time.

Chapter 29

S he rolled over to face Ned, hardly surprised to find he was awake and watching her.

"Do you want something to eat? Drink? Coffee, or something stronger?"

"Coffee's fine. I think I'd prefer to keep a clear head right now. Abby, we need to talk about . . . all of this, starting with what just happened."

Here we go. Abby took a deep breath. "I know. And it happened before, didn't it? On Halloween, when you brought me home, you took my hand, and I guess I got a flash of it, and it scared me. That's why I ducked inside so fast. And then I wondered if you thought I was afraid you were hitting on me and didn't know how to say no."

"I wasn't sure. I thought there was something, but it went so quickly."

"You've never had that happen with someone else? Someone living?"

"No. Never."

Abby smiled. "All right, then we'll talk. Upstairs." She crawled out of bed, pulled on a bathrobe, and headed for the kitchen, where she put a kettle on to boil. Ned followed more slowly and appeared wearing his shirt, with a towel wrapped around his waist.

"Sit down." She gestured at the table in the kitchen as she concentrated on measuring coffee beans, grinding them, transferring them to the filter in the carafe. Simple, ordinary tasks. Things she knew she could handle, as though the world hadn't suddenly turned upside down. She stared at the gas flames under the kettle, waiting. When the water finally boiled, she poured it carefully over the coffee, and while it dripped, she looked for mugs in the cabinet; she filled them and carried them over to the table, and then went back for sugar. "Do you want milk?"

"No, Abby. Just sit down." He sounded impatient.

Armed with the sugar bowl and spoons, she went back to the table and took the chair opposite Ned, so she could watch him. He looked the same, but different. Or was she seeing him differently now? She added sugar to her mug and then wrapped her hands around it. "All right. We'll talk."

"Let me work through this, if you don't mind," he said, looking down at his cup. "I've been living with this a lot longer than you have—most of my life. And I spent a lot of time ignoring some of the things I heard, or saw, or felt. They didn't make sense to me, and nobody else talked about anything like that, so I sort of shut them out. Then after a long time, I started thinking about them again. I don't want to sound New Agey or anything like that, but I do think our culture downplays a lot of intangible things, and that's our loss. So I decided to try to combine both worlds—apply a rational analytic process to something that was irrational and intangible. I started looking at my family history and matching that up with the odd things I saw or felt. And what I found was that there was one line that cropped up consistently, one chain of descent, that led from Phineas to me. So, to test this, I did what we've been doing lately: I started deliberately looking for my ancestors. Places they'd been, places they were buried."

"And what did you find?"

"The data confirmed the hypothesis. The only people I connected to were the ones from the Reed line."

"So what did you do?"

"Unfortunately, not much. I had satisfied my own curiosity, but I felt funny talking about it to other people, because they'd think I was a nut job. And it wasn't a major part of my life, just sort of a hobby. I mean, since my childhood buddy, I haven't had a lot of face-to-face encounters, just bits and pieces. It was kind of interesting, but it didn't seem very important. Until you came along."

She nodded. "At the Flagg house. But you didn't have any reason to think that was anything to do with that other business, did you?"

He laughed briefly. "No, I just thought you were a damsel in distress. A very attractive one at that."

She stared at him. "That's what you were thinking? When did it occur to you that I might be . . . have . . ."

"This psychic connection thing? Not for a while. I figured it couldn't hurt if you found out a bit more about the Flaggs. And then you confirmed that it was William Flagg that you saw in your . . . event. Well, I thought, that's interesting. But I didn't know that he had married a Reed—my line branched off long before that, and for all the time I've spent in that house, I never sensed anything there. But you're a direct descendant, and you did as soon as you walked in. And then you picked up something at the cemetery at the Flagg grave, so I figured it couldn't just be a coincidence."

"Wait a minute," Abby interrupted. "I saw Elizabeth at the cemetery. I was seeing what Olivia saw?"

"Most likely, since she was your lineal ancestor."

"All right. Go on."

Ned sat back in his chair, warming to his subject. "After that cemetery episode, you and I got together again. We went to Concord, and you stumbled on the Reed tombstone there."

Abby interrupted him again. "Back up a minute. We got together after my first trip to the library, when I found the stuff on William Flagg. Why?"

He looked down at his coffee and smiled. "Abby, you told me the first time we met that you had a boyfriend. Normally I would have kept my distance. But I admit it, I was interested—in you, and not just as a new addition to my psychic phenomena folder."

"Oh," Abby said in a small voice. "But you thought there was something about what happened to me in that house, something that you recognized?"

"Yes. I was fascinated by whatever it was you were channeling, and I wanted to follow through. Besides, I'd have to say you were sending kind of mixed signals."

"What do you mean?" Abby said indignantly.

"Well, you kept calling me, for one thing."

"But you met Brad! You came to our place. You knew we were . . . together."

"Abby," Ned said patiently, "forgive me for saying this, but I really didn't think you two were right for each other."

Abby didn't know whether to be mad or amused. "You decided that based on a three-minute conversation with him? What makes you an expert on relationships? Have you even been involved with anyone since Leslie?"

Her comment had found its mark, and he looked pained. "Abby, let's not get into this—at least, not yet. I'm sorry, I just didn't like Brad. I know his type. And I didn't like the way he treated you."

"You never even saw us together!" Abby sputtered.

"I got the feeling that he wasn't really paying any attention to you. I know, I didn't watch you two together, but he kept going off and doing his own thing a lot, from what you said. Abby, how long was it before you told him about these experiences you were having? From my viewpoint, it looked like you were pretty shook up about them, at least at first. Did you share any of that with Brad?"

He'd certainly gotten that right. "Not for a while, and then he wouldn't listen."

"That's what I figured. I didn't think you two had any real emotional connection. And if you couldn't open up with him about something that was important to you . . . Well, I didn't think it was going to last."

"So you just hung around, hoping?"

"Abby," he began, then stopped. "Listen, can we sort through this ancestor thing first? Then we can figure out what we feel about each other."

That brought Abby up short. The two seemed inextricably intertwined, but she supposed he had a point. Maybe understanding the psychic side would help her get a handle on the strange thing that was going on between them. *And just what are you upset about, Abigail? That he took one look at your lover of two years and decided that he wasn't the man for you? That he was right and you didn't even see it?* Abby struggled to calm her roiling emotions. "All right. Where were we?"

Ned resumed his exposition. "You figured out who the Flaggs were, but you didn't know why you were seeing them. Then you got that chair and you had another vision, but again you couldn't figure out why. And then we went to Sleepy Hollow and you found the Reeds, and then in Wellesley you got sucked into the cemetery and found more Reeds. Okay, that established a consistent Reed link."

"And that's when you knew we were related somehow?"

He nodded. "And then you dragged me into the house in Weston. Abby, I didn't tell you then, but I know that house, who built it, who lived there."

"And you already knew it was a Reed, right?"

He nodded again.

"Why didn't you say anything then?"

"Look, maybe you don't think I was being fair or honest, but the scientist in me wanted to carry on the experiment, see what you came up with, without my interference."

Abby stood up abruptly. "More coffee?" She took his mug and hers and went back to the stove to fill them. She wanted time to let the pieces settle into place—who had known what, when. She wanted to review what he had said to her in the past—and what he *hadn't* said. And she wanted to figure out how she felt about it, once she got over feeling like a lab rat he'd been experimenting with. Pouring two cups of coffee wasn't going to buy her nearly enough time, but it was a start.

She passed his mug to him and sat down again. "Okay, somewhere in there I got the job in Concord—thanks to you. Were you trying to keep an eye on me? And then Brad starts acting strange, picking fights with me, disappearing a lot on weekends. I finally figure out about Shanna, and we have this blowup and I walk out."

"Abby, if I may . . . don't you think you already knew there was something wrong between the two of you, if you could walk away that easily?"

She considered protesting, but what was the point? "All right, yes. I think I probably had had doubts for a while, but I didn't know what to do about them, so I just followed Brad's script for us. I thought maybe the move up here would help bring us closer, move us forward, but it just made things worse."

"Well, if you want a silver lining, maybe all the stresses—moving, breaking up—made you that much more receptive to these other things."

"My relationship goes to hell, I have no place to live, I'm in a strange place where I have no connections and no friends, and I'm supposed to be happy that I start seeing ghosts?"

He smiled wryly. "Well, your karma's not all bad. You've got a job you like, right? And you lucked into this place, which isn't too shabby—and it gives you time to sort things out and decide what you want to do next."

He was right—the pluses did kind of balance the minuses. "Do you have some sort of theory about what this channeling thing that we share actually is?"

"I have a working hypothesis. If I have to define it, right now, I'd say that you got it more or less right in Cohasset: some of the descendants of Phineas Reed share some sort of ability to both leave some psychic residue and to recognize it when they find it. It appears to be hereditary, because it's passed on from generation to generation. I think you came to the same conclusion—you just described it differently."

"Like a gene for paranormal sensitivity." Abby thought about it for a moment. "But what is it that people are leaving and finding?"

"I think you and I would agree that we aren't seeing people, we aren't being visited by ghosts, according to the traditional interpretation. Right?"

Abby nodded.

"I think—and this is pure speculation—that our people generate a particular kind of energy in moments of emotional intensity—births, deaths, maybe other events like what happened to your great-grandfather, even if he wasn't a Reed—that lingers, attached to tangible objects, like tombstones, or that watch."

"Or the Reed house, in Weston," Abby interrupted. "When I touched the wall, I saw . . . someone, or more than one person. Generations."

Ned went on. "And again, the people with the gene, or the trait, or whatever it is, are capable of picking up this energy, after the fact."

"Assuming that's true, is it a one-shot thing? Like a single download? Because, well, take the case of the chair. The first time I sat in it, I was overwhelmed. The next time the effect was a lot fainter."

"Maybe. Or maybe the second time you were expecting it, were ready for it, so it felt different. That's the sort of thing I was worried about if I told you what I thought was going on—that you'd close down and that would alter the experience. As for the larger picture, I'm not sure. For one thing, I don't know how many of us there are. Think about Phineas's tombstone, for example. You felt something, right?"

"Yes, but it was kind of faint. I was thinking it was probably Aaron or someone else in his family who was there, obviously not Phineas himself."

"Okay. Well, how many descendants do you think Phineas has had? And how many of them have made their way to that stone? And how many of those have felt anything, anything at all, in order to leave their trace?"

"How am I supposed to answer that? Did you feel anything?"

"Hard to say. I came to that spot after I'd been doing research for a while, so I suppose you could say I had expectations. That's why I wanted to see what you felt. But the point I wanted to make was, if there were more than a few descendants with the right gene, the charge would have been gone long ago if they were absorbing it, right?"

"I see what you mean. But—does this get recharged? Because at Sleepy Hollow I got a very confused impression of lots of people, overlapping. So would that mean that there were a series of carriers who left their imprint, and I'm picking up a lot of them? Is there a cumulative charge?" Abby was suddenly struck with another thought. "And am I leaving a trail behind me? Do you pick up 'me'?"

"Ah, that's the question." Ned stopped, and Abby felt panic. "And that brings us back around to what just happened here."

"Whatever it was, I thought it was pretty terrific," Abby said, smiling. "Do you think it will last? Or was it a one-time thing?"

Ned smiled back. "Want to find out?"

They must have slept, because Abby woke up to sunshine, and Ned in her bed. She stretched, mentally and physically. Her first fully formulated thought was that she definitely was not the same Abby she had been the day before, and there was no going back. Was this—whatever-it-was—something that had been there, hiding, all along? Or was it something Ned had somehow given her? She rolled over onto her side and found him looking at her.

"Hey."

"Hey."

She reached out to touch his face, then drew back. "Is that going to happen every time I touch you?"

"I don't know. Is that a problem?"

"Only if I want to eat, sleep, or do anything else halfway normal."

And she touched him and they were lost on the merry-go-round again, but this time it wasn't as overwhelming. *Ah well,* Abby reflected briefly, *there's only one first psychic orgasm, but I sure hope there are lots more . . .* And then her thoughts shattered once more.

An hour or so later, Abby crawled out of Ned's arms and propped herself up on her pillows. "If I can inject a note of rationality here, I think I've figured out something."

He pulled himself up beside her, watching her face. "I'm listening."

"I've been wondering why all this 'seeing' stuff started, why it's been happening to me. I never asked for anything like this, and I certainly wasn't looking for it."

He nodded his encouragement. "Go on."

"But I've learned something. You were saying yesterday"—*how many lifetimes ago was that?*—"that you thought it was only the moments of extreme emotion that generated enough energy to linger, or to carry through, or whatever?"

"Yes. The peaks, like birth, and death—that's the easiest one to follow, thanks to cemeteries."

"Well, if that's true, then maybe I had just never reached that level before, and that was why it was such a shock to me. I've led a pretty calm life, no major tragedies. Maybe that's what you sensed with me and Brad— the emotional pitch wasn't high enough. I thought I loved him, but looking back, it all seems pretty tame. I thought I *should* love him, but I didn't really *feel* it, deep down. And maybe that's why it was so easy to leave him—there just wasn't that much there to lose."

"And now?" Ned's eyes were on her face.

"I've never been anyplace like where we were last night. That's a whole other universe. And it wasn't just good sex." Abby grinned at him. "Although I don't have any complaints in that department." Then she sobered again. "But there's a lot more there, between us. Isn't there?"

"No question. I could say, I love you, Abby, and I do. I think I did from that first day, even if I couldn't put it into words, even to myself. But people tend to use the 'love' word a lot, and there's something going on here that goes way beyond that, and I can't even begin to put words to it. But I don't have to, do I?"

"No, you don't. But don't stop trying."

Chapter 30

S omehow Abby managed to pull together the pieces of her life to get to work on Monday morning. Ned had spent the rest of the day at her house in Concord. Not all of their time had been spent in edifying discussion. Abby had to smile at certain memories, and kept smiling. She really wasn't sure what she felt at the moment, beyond the fact that she was wildly, unquestionably in love with Edward Newhall, her eighth cousin. Or first cousin eight times removed. Whatever. And she knew that he felt the same way. And that whatever they shared went beyond anything she had ever known, and made her relationship with Brad look shallow and colorless. Ned had finally left after dinner the evening before, arguing reluctantly that they both needed to get some sleep before they flamed out entirely. For the first time in her life, Abby could actually visualize such an event. But what a wonderful way to go!

Still, there were realities to deal with, like earning a living. She liked her job, liked what she was doing—or at least the Abby of last week had. This week's Abby was somebody else altogether, but she trusted that New Abby wouldn't jettison her sense of responsibility to the commitments of Old Abby's former life. When she had a lucid moment, she wondered what her new understanding of the electromagnetic principles of hereditary history would contribute to her talks to schoolchildren, but there were still a lot of details to be worked out on that front. Yet she knew she would never look at history in quite the same way.

She managed to arrive early and dumped her things in her office. Then she faced the issue she had tried to avoid thinking about: telling Leslie. She liked Leslie. She thought Leslie liked her. She liked her job, and Leslie was her boss. But she couldn't *not* tell Leslie about her relationship with Ned, since Ned had once been engaged to Leslie. Which apparently had ended by mutual agreement and without acrimony. It was complicated. Abby sighed and marched down the hall to Leslie's office. Luckily she was in.

"Hi, Leslie. Got a sec?"

Leslie looked up from the stack of mail that she had been winnowing. "Uh, yeah, sure. What's up?"

Might as well get it out fast. "I'm seeing Ned. Is that a problem for you?"

Leslie laughed heartily. "Of course not. He's a great guy, and I want him to be happy. Just because we couldn't work it out doesn't mean you two

185

shouldn't. Okay, give me the gory details. You've known him, what, since September?"

"Yes." The most astonishing two months of her life.

"Is that why you broke up with what's-his-name?"

"No, really. That was falling apart anyway, and then Brad started seeing someone else. If I'd had any brains, I would have broken up with him before we moved up here and saved us both a lot of trouble." *And never have met Ned, or any of my ancestors.*

"Ah. Well, I'm sure Ned didn't make a move until after—he's kind of old-fashioned that way. And?"

"And what?"

"Look, you don't have to give me all the dirt, but this whole thing between you came up pretty fast, so I'm curious. How'd you finally get together?"

"He's been helping me with my genealogy. It turns out we're related, about eight generations back."

"Figures. He seems to be related to everyone. And he's really into all that, as I'm sure you've noticed. So, I'm happy for you both. Seems like a good fit to me."

Leslie, you have no idea. "Thanks. I didn't want to sneak around."

• • •

"Ned, what have you told your parents?" Abby asked, as they drove from Concord to Lexington on Thanksgiving Day.

"Nothing."

Was that a smile he was hiding? "Really? Nothing?"

"Scout's honor."

"Oh, I get it, you're testing your parents. Or me. Is that it?"

"Maybe." He wasn't about to give up anything.

"Will they be happy, about us being together, I mean?"

"Are you worried about whether they'll like you? Not necessary—they'll love you. Of course, they love a lot of people, so that's not a great indicator. But they'll definitely love you."

"Hmm." Abby wasn't entirely convinced. She remembered meeting Brad's parents. His father was a hearty banker type, and his mother was flawlessly groomed and sharply dressed, making Abby feel like something the cat had dragged in. After the requisite polite small talk, they had ignored her, talking over and around her to their darling boy about his string of successes, going back to kindergarten. Abby had felt small and invisible. She didn't want today to be like that.

She and Ned had been together less than two weeks. "Together" really didn't seem to cover it. On the one hand, everything was still very new, and there was so much to learn about each other. On the other hand, Abby felt as though she had known Ned forever. She might not know the simple facts about him, like his favorite color or his taste in music, but she knew the core of him. Who he was. "Soul" wasn't right, nor was "spirit," but she was going to have to find a word for the essential being that was Ned. Still, however extraordinary their relationship was, enough of the old shy Abby persisted to keep her on edge about meeting his parents for the first time.

They were passing through neighborhoods that Abby had not yet explored. The monochrome November landscape was stark, but it was serene and dignified. She was surprised by how much open land existed this close to Boston, although she cringed to think what it must be worth.

They pulled into a driveway that led to a solid square house, painted a warm color somewhere between cream and sunshine. Even to Abby's untutored eye, it was plain that the building was an honest colonial, not a modern reproduction, and had settled into its landscape centuries ago. The front door was painted a dark red and was embellished with a bunch of Indian corn, marking the season. It was graceful and handsome, and spoke of "home."

Ned stopped the car and looked at her. "Ready?"

"I think so," Abby replied and climbed out of the car. Standing beside it, she looked up at the house. "It's lovely. You grew up here?"

Ned came around the car and took her arm. "Mostly. Let's go in." He opened the front door, which was unlocked, and they stepped into a central hallway, with a staircase rising in front of them. To the left Abby could see the formal parlor, which looked forlorn and unused. To the right was the dining room, with a large table already set for—Abby counted—ten places, and surrounded by mismatched chairs. And beyond that lay the kitchen, issuing good smells and much hubbub. With a gentle hand on the small of her back Ned guided her straight to the kitchen.

He stood in the doorway for a moment, grinning, waiting for someone to notice them. Abby tried to hang back, uncertain of her welcome, but Ned would have none of that and kept a firm hold on her. Finally a woman looked up and saw them, and broke into a huge smile. Dressed casually in faded jeans and an oversize sweater, she could have passed for twenty, until Abby noticed the gray in her long hair, pulled loosely back, and the gentle lines that showed when she smiled. She wiped her hands on a towel and approached them quickly.

"Ned! We were wondering where you were. And this is your guest. Abigail, is it?" The woman extended her hand, ringless, its nails clipped short, and Abby took it.

I really should be getting used to this, Abby reflected, as her polite social smile melted into a real one. At the woman's touch, she felt the same bond, the same spark, as with Ned, but softer somehow. The woman was studying her with something like joy in her eyes, and Abby found she could return the warm gaze honestly.

"Welcome to our home, Abigail. I guess we'll be seeing a lot more of you."

"Abby, please. And, yes, I think you're right."

"And I'm Sarah." Reluctantly she released Abby's hand, then turned to her son. "You! Why didn't you say something?"

Ned grinned at his mother and swept her into a hug. "Because I wanted to see what you'd do. But I can't fool you, can I?"

"Never, baby. But I'm happy for the two of you." She turned back to Abby. "Come on, we don't stand on ceremony around here. Everybody pitches in. Let me introduce you . . ." And she drew Abby into the crowd in the kitchen.

The meal took hours, but flowed seamlessly from the group efforts at cooking, through serving and eating, and even cleanup. If there were strangers at the table, they were drawn into conversation, kidded, consulted, and made to feel at home. Afterward, stupefied by food and wine and good talk, people drifted to different corners of the house, some to doze, some to continue discussions. A few went out back to toss a football around.

At some point, Abby found herself standing in the hallway, where she had begun, listening. Well, no, maybe listening wasn't the right word. Sensing? She still hadn't quite gotten the hang of it, but she was getting better at it. There were the wisps of generations of past Newhalls, or Reeds, or whatever, who had left their mark on the old wood and stone and glass of the building. Abby stood still and just let it flow over and around her. The spirits of the past and present skimmed by her, surrounding her.

Ned came up behind her and put an arm around her, and she leaned back against him. Without turning, she asked, "Does it always feel like this?"

"It's not usually quite this crowded. But, yes, it's always there."

"Show me the rest of the house?"

"The whole thing?"

"Sure. I love attics and basements. Do you still have a dirt floor in the basement?"

"I remember when there was one, but my folks had a concrete one poured . . ." He led her through the rooms, pointing out details both old and modern.

"Where was your room?"

"Upstairs."

"Show me."

His room was simple, spare. Abby liked the plainness of the colonial style, its honesty. The space was square and true. The walls were old plaster, showing a few cracks, the woodwork simple, polished to a warm honey color by time and many hands. The windows overlooked mown meadow and trees, much as they might have appeared two hundred years before.

Abby stood in the doorway, Ned's arms around her waist. Late in the day, the sun was sinking, and shadows filled the corners. She caught a flash of movement at the far side of the room and turned her head to see a young boy, who regarded her solemnly for a moment before dissolving. A boy with untidy hair, in a rumpled linen shirt and short breeches.

"Ned," she said quietly, "was that . . . ?"

His arms tightened around her. "Yes. I haven't seen him in a long time."

They stood without moving for another minute or two.

"Seen enough?" Ned finally asked.

"For now. Let's go join the others. The ones who are still breathing, that is."

About the Author

After collecting too many degrees and exploring careers ranging from art historian to investment banker to professional genealogist, Sheila Connolly began writing mysteries in 2001.

She wrote her first mystery series for Berkley Prime Crime under the name Sarah Atwell, and the first book, *Through a Glass, Deadly*, was nominated for an Agatha Award for Best First Novel.

Under her own name, her Orchard Mystery Series debuted with *One Bad Apple* and was followed by twelve more books in the series.

Her Museum Mysteries, set in the Philadelphia museum community, opened with *Fundraising the Dead* and continued with seven more books.

Her County Cork Mysteries debuted with *Buried in a Bog*, followed by seven more novels.

She has also published numerous original ebooks with Beyond the Page: *Sour Apples, Once She Knew, The Rising of the Moon, Reunion with Death, Under the Hill, Relatively Dead, Seeing the Dead, Defending the Dead, Watch for the Dead, Search for the Dead,* and *Revealing the Dead*.

Sheila was a member of Sisters in Crime, Mystery Writers of America, and Romance Writers of America. She was a former President of Sisters in Crime New England, and was cochair for the 2011 New England Crime Bake conference.

CPSIA information can be obtained
at www.ICGtesting.com
Printed in the USA
LVHW101033160722
723665LV00005B/358

9 781954 717831